Moon Over
Dark Water

Moon Over Dark Water

Iris Collier

PIATKUS

Copyright © 1988 by Iris Collier

This edition first published in
Great Britain in 1988 by
Judy Piatkus (Publishers) Ltd of
5 Windmill Street, London W1

British Library Cataloguing in Publication Data

Collier, Iris
  Moon over dark water.
  I. Title
  823'.914[F]   PR6053.04237

  ISBN 8-86188-705-0

Phototypeset in 11/12pt Linotron Times by
Phoenix Photosetting, Chatham
Printed and bound in Great Britain by
Billing's Ltd, Worcester

Moon Over Dark Water

Chapter 1

It was almost dark. The sun had dropped behind distant Cape
Stavros, and Nelson was ready to settle down for the night.
He'd anchored in six metres of water and, looking down over
the stern, he could see the anchor rope snaking away through
the clear water. Not a breath of wind disturbed the glassy
surface of the Bay of Chambra. He had the feeling of being
suspended in space, a strange disembodied feeling which he
found oddly disturbing.

He glanced again at the shore. The two men were still
there. Scuba divers, he supposed, packing up after a day's
sport. He could just make out the shape of the wooden jetty
which the fishermen used for tying up their boats. He could
still see the white sandy beach and, in the background, the
outline of the hills of Euboea. The air was incense heavy with
the scent of wild thyme and sage. He wondered whether
Ulysses had ever dropped anchor in this bay. He liked Ulysses
– a man after his own heart. He should have sailed single-
handed. He had been cursed with a reluctant crew. There was
nothing quite like sailing one's own boat, on one's own. He
would have got on with Ulysses, though. Together, they
could have resisted the Sirens.

It was time to go below. The lights were on and the whisky
bottle was ready on the table but he lingered for just a few
more minutes on deck. He loved these evenings in the
Eastern Mediterranean – the sky alight with stars. Soon the
sea would come to life with their reflections, and the shimmer
of phosphorus.

It was incredible, he thought, how suddenly the wind

dropped in the evenings. All day he'd been beating along the coast of Euboea in the teeth of a strong north-westerly. Now there was nothing. Not even a ripple of air to stir the United States flag in the stern. The Greek courtesy flag hung limply in the shrouds. Tomorrow, with any luck, the wind would back towards the west and he could run over to Skiathos. Then, after a few days, he would head south once again, for Andros and the Piraeus – and Bernie. It was a good life. He wanted nothing more.

He also liked his sundowners, and today's were later than usual. He turned his back on the night and went below. For a large man he was still very agile. Living on a yacht had kept him fit. He didn't look his fifty-five years but recently he'd put on a lot of weight, and he was conscious that he was short of breath when he exerted himself.

That day had been particularly exhausting. The wind had come up suddenly, as it frequently did in this part of the world, and he'd had to reef the mainsail by himself. It wasn't for nothing that the Greeks called the Sporades, the islands in the North Aegean, the 'Gates of the Wind'. Perhaps next year, he thought as he cleared a space at the navigation table and poured himself a drink, he would take on a crew to help with the heavy work. Or perhaps he could train Bernie. But even though she was a strong girl he doubted whether she would be able to heave up anchors. That's what really tired him. Perhaps he should think about buying a few more mechanical aids. But that year, he thought ruefully, he ought to give up his habit of sundowners. Sometimes he got through a half bottle of Scotch in an evening.

He'd also caught the sun that day – something he hated. He burned very easily. He had the red hair and freckled fair skin of his Irish ancestors, a skin which he only ever exposed in the late afternoon sun. Most of the time he covered himself completely in long khaki shorts, like an old-fashioned scout master, and a long-sleeved shirt. He even wore long socks up to his knees. But today the sun had caught him on the side of his neck, and the skin was hot and angry. He hated not feeling well. It made him a bit tense and irritable.

He drank the first whisky straight down, as he always did, and poured himself a second. But tonight he decided to make

2

the second one last. He glanced round the cabin at the heaps of crates, and thought, with some alarm, that there was no room for Bernie. She'd have to sleep on deck. But he could get to Piraeus in good time to clear the boat and put the crates in store. There was no hurry to ship them to Boston. They could wait for him in some warehouse, and Demetrios would keep an eye on them. Nelson made a practice of being on good terms with one or two customs officials in most of the major ports in the Mediterranean. He liked dealing directly with people rather than filling in lots of forms. He knew Demetrios was buying a new house, and was not above taking a few thousand drachmae instead of opening all the crates. Nelson was, after all, a businessman, and knew the ways of the world.

Nelson T. Donelly had three passions in life. He cared nothing about famines or plagues, wars or social injustice. He loved his god-daughter, Bernie, and his dark blue yacht, a thirty-five-foot Rival with the name *Nereus* painted in gold on its bows. Lastly, he liked collecting antiques. He was quite single-minded about all three passions. No-one but Bernie would inherit his fortune which he had build up from nothing over the last forty years. She would be the queen of his restaurant and hotel empire. He knew she would keep the Irish flavour of his business – the madonnas in the bedrooms, the supply of bottled Guinness in the bars. Not for nothing had she been christened Bernadette Fitzpatrick.

He always sailed single-handed. No-one but Bernie had ever been allowed to set foot on his boat. Certainly none of his business acquaintances had been allowed to sail with him. They'd never even been invited to have a drink with him. He hated company; had sailed across the Atlantic single-handed, in spite of his doctor's orders. He'd known it was a risk but then, he'd said to himself, what was life without risk? In the event, the crossing had been remarkably easy – the wind remaining in the south-west for the whole voyage, and never blowing above a force five. *Nereus* had behaved impeccably, and he'd spent a perfect year buying Greek amphorae which was this year's passion.

He'd furnished his Boston flat with Georgian antiques bought in London and Paris. Its walls were covered with

Turner water-colours, and paintings by the French Impressionists. Now he was turning to rarer objects from Greece and Rome. Recently, he had been seduced by Pharaohnic Egypt. He was a compulsive collector. Perhaps it was the legacy of a deprived childhood that made him want to copy the interiors of the houses of the European aristocracy, but he certainly had an unerring eye for the genuine article. He only ever bought originals and he always bought from legitimate dealers – Syrian Jews in Damascus, exiled Palestinians in Beirut, and Arabs in Morocco. He'd bought wonderful Minoan jars from a dealer in Tunisia: glazed amphorae with slender necks, used originally for storing oil and wine. He'd bought over a dozen of these jars, beautiful objects decorated with starfish and sea weed, silver-grey fish darting through the trailing fronds of water plants. One enormous jar, which filled a whole crate, had been wedged under the bunk in his cabin. It was over three feet high, bulbous and wide-necked. In ancient Crete it had probably been used for storing grain. He'd seen similar jars still in use in modern Crete but none of them had been as beautiful as this one. The yellow-cream glaze was flawless. A giant black octopus was its only decoration, except for water plants and bubbles. It was one of his prize pieces. It had taken him two days' hard bargaining and a lot of money to get it.

It was in Alexandria that he'd been introduced to the glories of pharaohnic art. He had stayed in Egypt for several weeks in May. He had bought amphorae in Alexandria: beautiful jars from classical Mycenae, decorated with processions of warriors and priests. He'd also bought twenty plates from the same period, each one decorated with warriors and hunters. Then, on a trip to Cairo, he'd visited the Ancient Egyptian Museum. He'd been mesmerized by the glories of the treasure of Tutankhamun, and had been deeply moved by the realism of the Old Kingdom figures. So when, in the hotel bar in Alexandria, someone had offered to sell him four canoptic jars, he had been overjoyed. Now they were stowed away in the bows cabin, along with the spare sails and the bottles of mineral water. Four perfect jars, used for preserving the entrails of dead Egyptians; each one with a stopper representing the four sons of Horus. He'd paid a lot for them.

4

He knew they'd probably been stolen from some tomb in the last century, and changed hands several times during the present one. He didn't know where he'd put them in his flat. If he ran out of room, then he'd have to buy another place.

In Alexandria he'd made his last two purchases. He still felt a twinge of unease when he thought about them. There had been something furtive about the man who'd sold him the things. He hadn't liked the squalid hut on the banks of the foul-smelling canal. Nor had he liked the flies, nor the dirty glass of water he'd been offered with his coffee. The man hadn't been the usual Arab or Greek. Nelson couldn't place his nationality. He might have been a Turk. But when the man had shown him the necklace, Nelson's indifference had turned to desire. And when the dealer showed him Selket, desire became lust. Nelson was a lost man. His night had been sleepless, and he'd gone back the next day.

The man had named his price and Nelson didn't bother to argue with him. It was all over and done with in an hour, and Nelson was back in his hotel by lunch time. In the afternoon he was back on his yacht with the precious bundle, and he had sailed for the Aegean straight away. He knew instinctively that he'd made a dishonest purchase, the first of his life.

But now the things were his, and had been stowed away underneath the floor of the cabin. They would have to stay there until he could think of a way of getting them back to the States. Bernie would be thirty-three on August 13th and now he could give her a birthday present beyond her wildest dreams. No-one, not even the Queen of England, would have been given a present quite like the one he would give Bernie.

He looked at the whisky bottle and decided to break his resolution and have the third drink whilst he prepared dinner. He always cooked his own meals, not trusting the local tavernas. Besides, it didn't look as if there was a taverna in this bay. There were no shops either so he'd have to open a tin. There was spaghetti and lots of onions. That would have to do.

Glass of whisky in hand, he looked down at the chart. Navigation fascinated him. He didn't read many books, fiction annoyed him, but he found his relaxation each evening in plotting the next day's course. If he wasn't going anywhere, then he'd plot imaginary courses. He liked the logic of it all.

There were no tides to worry about in the Mediterranean, so as long as the wind blew from the right direction he should get to the right place at the right time.

Tomorrow he'd sail the thirteen miles to Skiathos, the most westerly of the Sporades. He could re-fuel there, and stock up with fresh food. He might even stay there for a few days, or he could go and look at the other islands. Bernie wasn't expecting his call until the following week so he had plenty of time. He turned on the ship's radio to see whether he could catch the weather forecast put out from Athens in English. He was completely happy.

He didn't hear the two men climb on board. He felt the yacht rock slightly but thought it was either the wind getting up or the swell from a distant fishing boat. The two men were as silent as shadows. He was reaching for the pair of dividers when they attacked.

Too late he heard the noise. Too late he swung round to face the men. He tried to shout for help but no sound came out, then they were on him. He put up an arm instinctively to shield his face but one of the men caught his arms and dragged them behind his back. He saw their eyes staring at him indifferently – the impersonal look of people merely carrying out orders. Then he knew that this was the end. He thought of Bernie.

One man raised the knife. The other held back Nelson's head, and the first man slit Nelson's throat as it were a bullock in the slaughter house. Blood gushed from the main artery and Nelson slipped to the floor. He died immediately.

The two men looked round the cabin. They were both Greeks, of medium height and very fit. They wore wetsuits in spite of the temperature, and neither of them had bothered to wear a mask. The one who had used the knife wiped it on Nelson's shirt and put it back into the leather holder round his waist. The other pulled a couple of boxes towards them. He tore open the tops, only to find they were full of amphorae. He cursed and pushed them aside.

'We'll have to open everything,' he said.

For half an hour they ripped open wooden crates and cardboard boxes, then the knifeman, who seemed to be the leader, pointed to the cabin floor.

6

'Let's try there. There's nothing here.'

It didn't take them long to tear up the floorboards. Underneath, carefully wrapped in water proof sheeting, they saw the two objects. One was in an oblong box. The knifeman opened it and gave a nod of satisfaction.

'It's here,' he said.

'And the other?'

He pulled back the wrapping from the other object – larger than the first one, and about three feet long. Impatiently the Greek tore aside the linen covering underneath the waterproof sheet. The inscrutable face of Selket gazed up at him. Hastily, he covered it up.

'It's here.'

'Let's go then. Leave him until later.' The second man kicked the crumpled figure of Nelson, now lying in a pool of blood.

On deck it was now completely dark. There wasn't a light in sight, not even from the shore. The two men were at home on boats, and knew the waters locally. Both were natives of Volos, and had been brought up on boats until the bright lights of Athens had lured them away. They started the engine. It had been recently serviced and sprang to life without faltering. One of them pulled up the bows anchor, and the other cut the kedge line. They wouldn't need two anchors any more. The leader took the helm and turned the boat out into the Trikiri Channel, heading east.

Halfway across the channel, where the Admiralty chart registered a depth of seventy-two fathoms, the knifeman stopped the engine.

'We'll get rid of him here,' he said.

'Why don't we leave him where he is?' said his companion.

'And have him lurching around the boat, getting in our way later on? Don't be a fool.'

'There'll not be much left of him after the fish have had a go at him.'

'Unfortunately fish don't eat bone and teeth. There'll be one hell of a row if anyone should come aboard and bump into a skeleton in the hold. A wreck's a wreck, but a body means police.'

The younger man gave up the argument and shrugged his

shoulders. It wasn't his job to worry about a dead man. Leaving the boat to rock on the slight swell, the two men went below and dragged the heavy body of Nelson T. Donelly up the companion way, laying it down in the cockpit. It had been heavy work, and the younger of the two Greeks pulled out a packet of cigarettes. The elder impatiently dashed the packet from his hands.

'Christ!' he said. 'I told you: No lights.' Then he went to get the bows anchor, and together they tied it round Nelson's feet. They dragged him to the stern and heaved him on to the rail. It took all their strength. They then pushed him over the side. The anchor caught round the rudder and, for a second, Nelson's body hung in mid-air. The leader cursed, and knocked the anchor free. Then, with only a Greek curse as a funeral prayer, Nelson's body slipped over the side of his own yacht and sank to the bottom of the Aegean.

Just before dawn broke, the two men brought the yacht to the channel between the islands of Alonnisos and Peristera. There was two hundred feet of water beneath them, and not much time before the fishing boats came out of the tiny harbour of Steni Vala. Both men were impatient to finish the job.

One of them went below and smashed the hundred and fifty amphorae, as he had been instructed. He had no idea why he had to do this. He was merely obeying orders. Something he had to do before collecting the money waiting for him back in Volos.

Then he joined his colleague. Together they opened the sea-cocks and climbed over the side into the rubber dinghy which Nelson had used to row himself ashore. Without one glance at the sinking yacht, the two men made for the shore.

Just before the sun appeared over the distant hills of Iura, the dark blue Rival sank below the Aegean. It settled on its side on a shelf of rock off the island of Peristera. The smashed amphorae rolled out of the crates and piled up on the starboard side of the boat. No-one had seen the yacht go down. Everything had gone exactly to plan. The next night, the two men would come back with diving gear and wrap the yacht in its shroud of camouflage netting. Only then would it be difficult to spot from the air.

8

For two days a violent storm kept the two men shore-bound in the little harbour of Patiteri. It couldn't have happened at a better time. No boat could put to sea whilst the *Meltemi* raged. Even the hydrofoil had to stay in harbour. Now, if anyone should report a missing yacht, the reason for its disappearance would be perfectly clear. A small boat would sink without trace in that storm.

Four days after Nelson's death, the two Greeks arrived in their native Volos – a six-hour journey from Patiteri by hydrofoil. Their money was waiting for them, and the leader bought himself a new motor boat with a powerful Volvo engine. The whole family came to celebrate the launching.

Chapter 2

'I beseech you, in the bowels of Christ, think it possible you may be mistaken.'

It never failed. Audiences loved it. Their applause was spontaneous and prolonged. People stood on chairs to get a better view of him. Photographers moved forward to take pictures.

The lecture over, Nick Harding folded away his notes. Not that he needed them; he knew the lecture by heart. But he always brought them with him, and spread them out on the desk in front of him. He thought of them as his security blanket, because, although outwardly a confident and vigorous person, inwardly he was full of self-doubt. Even as the applause died down he was suffering from a moment's pang of uncertainty as to whether he ought to have used Cromwell's famous remark to cast doubt on the authenticity of a Minoan fertility goddess. But he knew it made his audience laugh. It was expected of him to be witty and amusing, and it was a good punctuation mark at the end of the lecture. Even so, he knew he was playing to the gallery. It was not what was usually expected of an academic.

And Nick Harding was certainly an academic. Arriving at the University of Sussex as the youngest Professor of Archaeology the university had ever known, he rapidly became one of its most popular and celebrated teachers. He'd been wooed away from his first subject, Natural Sciences, and King's College London in his early thirties, mainly through an enthusiasm for Celtic burial sites and admiration for Sir Mortimer Wheeler whom he had met through College circles, and for whom he had worked in summer vacations. Now, at forty-one, he could fill the main hall of the university with an evening lecture on the Minoan civilization. It was his most famous lecture, the one the BBC had been so impressed with. The subject was the truth behind the legend of the Minotaur, and the year before he had been asked by the BBC to make a television programme around it.

He had expanded the talk into a series exploring the Minoan civilization around the year 1000 BC, and his coverage of the Palace of Knossos had aroused a considerable amount of interest. His diffident witty delivery, coupled with his natural enthusiasm, had caught the popular imagination, and schools were soon reporting an upsurge in the numbers of students wanting to read Archaeology at university. The same thing had happened in the sixties with the Mortimer Wheeler series. The interest in the Minoans had been so great, and the sales of the BBC booklet on the subject so huge, that the series was to be repeated that autumn. The BBC made a lot of money out of Nick Harding, and he'd just heard that the programme was doing well in the United States and Canada. The BBC had made him wear jeans for the series, and he'd been astonished at the amount of fan mail he'd received after the programme had ended. People still asked him for signed photographs.

Basically a shy man, Nick had to admit that he liked talking to a live audience. He liked feeling the surge of adrenalin when the lights were dimmed and he called for the first slide. He was really a bit of an actor, only coming alive on stage. But afterwards, over the ritual cup of coffee, he went back into his shell. When the adrenalin subsided, depression took over, and he became shy and awkward. Then people admired his modesty, and called him a typical academic.

His appearance helped. Somehow he'd kept his youthful good looks, a legacy from his Celtic forefathers. Although his mother and father now lived in Newcastle, his grandfather had been a Gaelic speaker from the Outer Hebridean island of Barra. He'd inherited the dark curly hair, the blue eyes and fair skin of the typical Celt. These slightly melancholy good looks, coupled with his boyish enthusiasm for his subject, had endeared him to his female students. He was also much in

11

demand at the tea parties given by the wives of the older members of the teaching staff, although he was conscious that he never came up to expectations on these occasions.

He was comfortable in casual clothes, and had kept lean and youthful looking. In fact, he admitted to being a fitness freak. He played squash every day, and liked to walk over the Downs behind Rottingdean at weekends. His wife liked him to keep his hair long, and sometimes it curled down almost to his shoulders. She thought he looked Romantic – 'Byronic' she called it. But the more uncharitable members of the Senior Common Room often referred to him as 'That bloody George Best'. Nick Harding took both the praise and the insults with unwavering good humour.

He glanced at his watch. Half-past ten. He'd gone on a bit longer than usual this evening, and had started a bit late because the Dean had insisted on giving him dinner before the talk. Just a snack in his flat, he'd said, but it had turned out to be a four course meal with all the wines. It had been difficult to keep his head clear for the lecture, but as soon as he stood up on the platform he'd felt his accustomed surge of adrenalin. He'd done what was expected of him, but now he was very tired.

There were still a lot of people about. They were asking him to autograph copies of his book and there was no way out. He was not only a lecturer, but a television personality.

'That wasn't at all bad, Nick. I'm glad the Dean's claret didn't dim the old witticisms. But don't you ever get fed up with those bloody Minoans? Not much to them, really. All that poncing around with ringlets and ribbons.'

Nick looked up sharply. His colleague, Jim Evans, an overweight garrulous historian with a chip on his shoulder, had come up on the platform. He'd been at the Dean's dinner. Jim Evans resented the fact that history didn't have the glamour of archaeology – in spite of the fact that he'd spent a whole summer researching into Crusader castles in Syria. Also the BBC hadn't been at all impressed by his subject. They hadn't even bothered to answer his letter. Nick knew his colleague well. He knew how hard Evans tried to be popular and decided to ignore his barbed remarks; partly because he was tired, and partly because he was sympathetic

12

towards the lame ducks in his profession. Especially wine-sodden lame ducks.

'I keep going because I have to, that's all. Everyone likes the Minoans. All those ladies in bikinis, I suppose, gyrating along the walls of Knossos. You can't beat that with your Romans, can you? Who ever heard of Roman matrons wearing bikinis?'

'They did in Pompeii.'

Nick thought for a moment, and then burst out laughing. 'Well, there you are then! Get started. Give a talk on the Pompeii murals. You'll get them flocking in. It would go down well on Channel 4.'

'No, they'd only want you to do it. I don't look good in jeans, and I haven't your youthful charm. Anyway, I wouldn't lower myself to go commercial. Pompeii is more your subject. It's archaeology, not history.'

Nick ignored the first part of this remark and concentrated on the second.

'Depends which angle you look at it from. I'd go for the ruins; you'd go for the social context. But seriously, back to where we started, I'm more interested in the Cretan civilization. I still believe there are strong links with the Etruscans.'

'There you go. Can anyone stop this young, active brain? Subject for the next television series – Were the Etruscans really unsuccessful Minoans in disguise? Or better still: Tarquinia, the penal settlement of Knossos! Why don't you get your friends in the BBC to pay for your summer holidays in Tuscany?'

It was at this point that Nick realised how much Jim Evans detested him. But he felt too tired to take offence. Besides, what did it really matter? Everyone knew Jim Evans was a burnt out time server, living only for the next bottle of cheap Algerian wine.

'Not much hope of that, I'm afraid. Much more likely to stay at home and clean out the swimming pool. There were two dead rats in it yesterday.'

'Some of us would be only too pleased to own a swimming pool – with or without rats,' said Jim. 'But then we're not all paid high salaries by the BBC. Neither do we all have rich wives,' he said as a parting shot, turning to leave. Jim Evans' marriage had ended in divorce five years ago. Nick knew he now lived on his own.

Even so, he winced at this reference to his marriage. After ten years with Marian the going was becoming decidedly rough. His popularity at the university and on the television screen wasn't helping matters either, but he chose not to think about his wife too often. Too many problems, and no solutions.

He stayed on the platform chatting to his admirers, but refusing offers of drink. Always conscientious, the more tired he was, the more he felt obliged to push himself. So it wasn't until eleven o'clock, after the last person had left the hall, that he picked up his briefcase and went out to his car. He wanted to get home. It wasn't far to Rottingdean along the Lewes road and the Porsche never failed to give him a thrill of pleasure when he drove it, especially at that time of night.

Lavender Cottage was in darkness when he arrived. The garage doors were open, and there was no sign of Marian's car. He got out to open the gates, stopping for a second to savour the heady scent of the lavender hedge which gave the house its name. The white roses stood out like small ghosts in the flowerbed by the front door. It was a beautiful night.

They'd bought Lavender Cottage, an old thatched house, five years ago. A listed building, it had appealed to Marian and had the added advantage of being near the antique shop which she owned in the High Street. Now she'd bought the second one in Brighton, Nick had had to buy a second car. They had also had to extend the garage but the bank had been generous with its overdraft.

Nick was proud of his possessions. They gave him the self-confidence he needed. But tonight he felt, not for the first time, the stirrings of restlessness. What was he doing in a house like this? He had only just turned forty but this was the sort of house most people ended their days in. It was beyond the wildest dreams of his parents in Newcastle, where his father had worked until recently in the ship-yards and where they had just bought their own semi-detached house on an estate. A house which they owned with such pleasure. Why

14

then should Nick be so dissatisfied? What more could he possibly want?

He put the car away and shut the garage doors. His wife would have to open them herself when she came home. He couldn't afford to risk the Porsche. No doubt he would get told off in the morning for his thoughtlessness, especially if she'd been drinking. She was always bad-tempered the morning after.

Inside, the house was in order. It always was. Marian was a conscientious housewife. The parquet floor was polished to perfection. The antique furniture gleamed in the soft glow of the concealed wall lights that came on as he pressed a foot switch by the front door. A perfect house, he thought. Even the roses in the hall had been freshly picked that day. They filled the house with their scent. Marian always picked the fragrant varieties for the house.

He glanced at the hall table as usual. There was a letter for him with a London post-mark. It must have come by the second post, he thought, as it hadn't been there that morning. The address was type-written so he didn't think it important. He put it in his pocket, and took it upstairs with him when he went to bed.

Nick always read for a half an hour or so before going to sleep. It was a habit his wife deplored, and it was for that reason that they now slept in separate rooms. Marian always took two sleeping pills and went to sleep immediately. She complained that his reading light kept her awake.

Tonight, though, he was tired and a bit depressed. It was sad to think of people like Jim Evans teaching the young. Cynical, world weary, how could he raise any enthusiasm for civilizations past or present? That night, instead of picking up his book, Nick read his letter instead. It wasn't particularly interesting. He was really too tired to take it in. Someone who signed himself Arnold J. Ponsford, who seemed to be a trustee of the estate of the late James Rochester, a citizen of the United States, wanted to see him about a project in the Aegean.

Probably, he thought ruefully, they wanted him to do another commercial for American television where his series on Crete had been such a hit on the Public Broadcasting

15

Channel. It might be retsina this time. They would want him to stand on the shore of a Greek island, glass in hand, toasting a marble statue of a Greek goddess who would wink at the audience at just the right moment. Someone had asked him to make a commercial just like that, but for Metaxa, the Greek brandy, not retsina. They had offered him a lot of money, enough to pay off the Porsche, but he'd turned the offer down because he thought the Dean might not approve.

He pushed the letter aside and it fell to the floor. He'd telephone the man from college, tomorrow. Then he settled down to sleep, aware that his wife hadn't come home. It wasn't the first time she had stayed out all night.

It was July 3rd, and still he hadn't telephoned. Bernie felt a twinge of unease. It wasn't like Nelson to be late. Punctuality was one of his obsessions. Successful businessmen were all the same, she thought. A commitment to call at a certain time was as binding as an arrangement to meet. He had even confirmed the time in his last postcard which had had a Greek stamp on it and was dated three weeks ago. Still he was only a day late, and she knew yachts were unpredictable things, dependent on winds and currents. She was very comfortable where she was, and probably foolish to worry about him when he could be enjoying himself. He could be ill though, she thought, laid up in some Greek hospital. It was unlikely though, that he would be so ill as to forget to telephone her. And if he couldn't manage the call himself, then he would have asked one of the nurses to put it through for him.

It was past the hour when he had said he would call. Bernie was sitting on her balcony enjoying the scene below her, and thinking of the evening ahead. Her room was on the fourth floor of a small hotel overlooking the Piazza Navona. She had wanted a hotel in the centre of Rome, wanted to see people again, to hear the noise of radios and the roar of distant motor cycles. She'd had enough of solitude and quietness in that clinic. Now, silence only depressed her. She felt a strong urge to get back into the world despite its problems.

The three months in Europe had set her back upon her feet again. Paris, Venice, Florence, had almost exorcised the memory of Gerry. She could now look at the affair dispassionately. She ought to have known that a married man of fifty-five would never have deserted his wife and dependent son for a thirty-year-old girl. She wouldn't have wanted him to, either. It might have worked out better had she also been married and in her fifties, but she had wanted a home and children, and Gerry had panicked. She'd never seen David, Gerry's son, who had become ill during his first year at university and was now a hopeless schizophrenic. Somehow Gerry had blamed himself for the tragedy. Perhaps he should have let David go on the stage instead of trying to turn him into a real estate lawyer like himself. Gerry would carry a double burden of guilt with him until he died. He had pressurized his son and cheated his wife. It was strange, though, thought Bernie ruefully, that he had never once felt guilty towards her. Even when she told him she thought she was expecting his child, he had telephoned to call things off. After a two year love affair he had wanted never to see her again. He had offered money, and made the usual excuses.

Bernie had had a complete nervous and physical breakdown. She'd tried to drive away the memories through working long hours, but she had only succeeded in exhausting herself. A few weeks of almost continuous sleep in a clinic had restored her balance, and the office had suggested she should take a long break – away from New York and the office which only perpetuated the memories.

Nelson had been very concerned about her. She couldn't remember a time when Nelson hadn't been concerned. She knew it had been his money which had sent her away to the exclusive girls' school which her grandparents could never have afforded. It had been Nelson's money which had paid for her university course. She was a clever girl, and had left with a first class honours degree in Law. He had found her the job in the real estate office in New York. He had watched the affair with Gerry develop. He knew it was her first love affair, and he had warned her what to expect. Then he had waited for the collapse.

Now they were both in the same part of the world, and he would complete Bernie's cure by taking her cruising in the Aegean. He was more to her than her own parents who had both been killed when their small aircraft had crashed in a field in Maine. She had only been four at the time. Her father had just got his pilot's licence and had taken her mother up for her first flight. He had saved for so long to do just that. The 'plane had never come out of that dizzy spin, and both bodies had been burned beyond recognition.

She had often wondered why Nelson had never married. But, like her, he said that he had always been too busy for marriage. Bernie understood. She was nearly thirty-three now, with only one love affair behind her. It would, she had decided, be her first and last.

Reluctantly she stirred herself at half-past six to get ready to go out. She was letting a 'safe', kindly expatriate member of the British community in Rome take her out to dinner. She had met him in the hotel lounge on her first evening in Rome. He was in his seventies, but he was amusing and a witty conversationalist. They had explored the city together.

She brushed out her thick brown hair that hung straight to her shoulders. It used to hang down to her waist but she had cut it off during her illness in a fit of rage, she had so hated herself. She put on a blue linen dress and noted that she was putting on weight. It suited her. She had lost over two stone in that clinic. She was tall, about five feet eight inches, and Italians smiled when they saw her. Sometimes they shouted remarks after her which she didn't understand but the tone was always good-humoured.

Bernie was clever enough not to worry too much about her appearance. She was healthy and intelligent and made the most of her assets. She just wasn't interested in attracting men. That was all in the past. Now she wanted company, a good meal, followed by a film in Italian with English sub-titles.

She wondered for a moment whether Nelson might telephone whilst she was out, but she had waited in for his call last night and she knew he wouldn't want her to waste another evening waiting for him. She left instructions with the hotel operator that if Mr. Donelly called he was to leave a message, and she would call him back when she got in.

Still, she thought as she picked up her handbag and made her way to the lift, it was odd he hadn't 'phoned yesterday. He had been so emphatic about the time in his last postcard. It was all very strange.

For a moment she hesitated, as if to turn back. 'No,' she decided finally. 'I'll give him another week. He knows I'm here. Then I'll go to Greece.'

Chapter 3

'Ten thousand? In sterling?'

Nick Harding stared across at Arnold J. Ponsford in disbelief. Ten thousand pounds to spend the summer in the Aegean. It would pay off his bank loan very nicely.

'As you wish. The equivalent in U.S. dollars, if you'd prefer. It makes no difference.'

'I have to be back here by September when term starts.'

'That's all right. You'll be finished by then.'

They were sitting in Nick's study in the main university building. It was a small room, white-walled, with bright modern furniture. It was the end of June, and examinations were nearly over. Already the students were beginning to drift away from the campus. It was a hot, humid day. Through the open windows came the very English sound of a game of cricket. It was an all-day game against Exeter.

Nick got up and went over to the sideboard. He took out a decanter of sherry and absentmindedly poured out two glassfuls. He offered one to Arnold.

'When do I get paid?'

'You'll get half after you arrive, and the other half when you finish. You can have an advance if you like.' Arnold accepted the glass of sherry and sipped it fastidiously. Nick drank his in one gulp.

He couldn't quite weigh Arnold up. He had seemed charming enough on the telephone – almost ingratiating. He had also insisted on coming to meet Nick on his home ground which had made things a lot easier as it was difficult to get away from the university at the end of term. Also Nick

20

detested London, particularly in hot weather. It was one of the reasons why he had accepted the appointment in Brighton.

Arnold had obviously expected a short sharp interview with Nick as he had kept a taxi waiting for him outside. He must be either indifferent to money or so rich that it didn't matter. No-one in Nick's circle ever kept taxis waiting. Perhaps Arnold had banked on that, expecting a poverty stricken academic, desperate to seize any opportunity of earning a few thousand pounds. A quick proposition followed by an eager acceptance. But Nick wasn't so sure.

To start with, he didn't like Arnold J. Ponsford. He'd expected the typical brash American businessman – Christian names on the first meeting, followed by invitations to Baltimore. But Arnold didn't look American. Neither did he address Nick by his Christian name. Also, he didn't have an American accent. In fact his English was rather too perfect. He could have been a German originally, Nick thought. Certainly more European than trans-Atlantic.

The face opposite was close and guarded, the eyes blue and expressionless. Pale-framed glasses and hair that was almost white made him look like an albino. His skin was white and hairless. He looked like a creature who had been shut away in a cupboard for a long time, and now was frightened by the sunlight. His pale silver-grey suit matched his hair. Even his tie was colourless – pale grey silk, embroidered with a small monogram. His handshake was flaccid, his hands clammy.

Nick wasn't particularly worried that he didn't like Ponsford. He seldom liked people who paid him money. He'd actually detested the BBC director of his television series – a pipe-smoking Scot who knew nothing about ancient Crete.

Arnold now appeared to assume that everything was settled. He sat silently sipping his sherry. It was becoming embarrassing. Finally Nick, who hated long silences, decided to take the initiative.

'Just how many of these amphorae are there?'

'I understand about one hundred.'

Nick was startled. He put down his glass and looked at Arnold severely, as if talking to a particularly difficult student.

21

'You do realise that this is painstaking work? It's not quite like doing a jig-saw puzzle, you know. You can spend literally weeks just sorting the pieces. People spend a whole summer just assembling one storage jar.'

'That's why the divers will bring you the boxes one by one. Then all the pieces to a particular jar will be together.'

'But some of the boxes must have contained more than one pot.'

'Possibly. But it will still be easier to sort them out than if you were digging up pieces from a site, and didn't know how many more were still in the ground.'

Nick nodded. He was used to site work. 'Of course. But why not take them straight over to Athens, or wherever, and get a museum team to put them together? The Greeks are expert at this sort of work.'

'First of all, this is a private concern. The amphorae are the property of Mr. Rochester. The ex-Mr. Rochester, I mean. As one of the trustees of his estate, I must be quite sure that these valuable possessions are disposed of according to his wishes. He bought them for his own enjoyment, and I don't know whether he would have wanted them to go to a museum.'

Again Nick nodded. He was used to the selfishness of private collectors.

'Is there an heir to the estate?'

The pale face registered a flash of annoyance as if Nick had spoken out of turn.

'Of course. And he might well want them to go to a museum eventually. It depends how much he approves of your restoration.'

'Then why the hell doesn't he go the Greece and see them for himself now? He might well decide to shunt the whole lot into a museum immediately and save himself ten thousand pounds.'

Arnold fixed Nick with a steely look, like a butler in a country house faced with an obstreperous guest. 'Because he's a busy man, and can't afford the time. Also ten thousand pounds is just a trifle to him. You are a luxury – part of a whim. He has a desire to see his late uncle's collection intact, that's all. He has no particular interest in classical amphorae.'

22

Nick didn't like being classified as a luxury. He also thought that if money meant so little to his unseen employer then perhaps he should have asked for double the fee instead of being so obviously impressed with the original offer.

Arnold appeared to read his thoughts, 'Mr. Henry Rochester, the heir to the late Mr. Rochester's estate, has delegated the whole of this particular operation to me. He wants no more to do with it until I present him with the complete collection. And although he is a wealthy man, he will not pay more. He has named his price and he never changes his mind. What's more, if you're not interested then I shall go to someone in Southampton who is. He specialises mainly in Roman sites, but he should be able to stick a few pots together.'

Nick winced at this description of an archaeologist's work, and went over to the sideboard to get some more sherry. Arnold got up to join him and looked out of the window towards the waiting taxi. Nick's car was there in the car park, in the place reserved for the senior members of the university.

'Is that your car over there?' asked Arnold suddenly. Nick nodded. He was used to people admiring his Porsche.

'It must have cost a bit?'

'The bank was very understanding, and the BBC paid for most of it.'

'Banks have to be repaid.'

'True enough. They usually like some interest as well.'

'Then you'll accept?' Arnold looked at his watch as if tired of the interview.

'Where is this place again?'

'A small bay on the island of Alonnisos – one of the larger islands in the Sporades. The bay's called Agios Demetrios. You won't find it on the charts.'

'And where am I supposed to live?' He thought back briefly to the month he'd spent in Crete. Then Marian had come with him, and they had rented an idyllic white-washed villa.

'That's up to you. To start with there's a taverna in Steni Vala, just a few kilometres away from the bay. You'll need to hire a car or a moped to get down to the shore. The owner of the taverna is called Spiros. He knows me, and he'll make you comfortable. You won't need to pay him straight away either.'

23

'And how do I get to the taverna in the first place?'

Arnold was now openly impatient. He looked at the waiting taxi and adjusted his wrist watch. The taxi driver had lit a cigarette and was opening a can of lager.

'By plane, of course. I'll send you your air ticket. The airport's in Skiathos, and you'll have to make your own way to Alonnisos. There's a hydrofoil. So, I take it you'll accept?'

For a second Nick hesitated but the memory of Crete had prompted a new line of thought. The trip would not only rescue him from financial embarrassment, it might also give him the chance to save his marriage. Marian could join him out there. It was what they both needed. Time to talk, and time to plan the future.

So he glanced at Arnold, who stood tapping his foot impatiently, and crossed the Rubicon.

'Yes, I accept – providing I can bring my wife.'

Arnold shrugged his shoulders. 'As you wish. But at your own expense.'

'Of course. Now there are things I shall need. It isn't as simple as you think to "stick a few pots together".'

Arnold chose to ignore the irony. 'Of course. Just send me a list of your requirements. You've got my address?'

'Yes. It's over there, on the desk.'

Arnold picked up his briefcase and made for the door, obviously relieved to have ended the interview.

'One moment,' said Nick. 'How did this James Rochester die?'

Arnold turned and looked at him sharply. 'I told you; his yacht sank. He drowned.'

'But yachts don't sink. Not in the Aegean.'

'They do when the *Meltemi* strikes. Even an experienced sailor like Mr. Rochester couldn't control a boat in that wind.'

'When did it happen?'

'A fortnight ago, June 15th.'

'Isn't that a bit early for the *Meltemi*?'

Arnold was now very impatient. 'You ask a lot of questions. Just remember that your job is to mend pots, not to conduct a post mortem. The *Meltemi* was early this year, that's all. No-one tells it when it's July 1st.'

Nick thought briefly of Ulysses, and the storms and ship-

24

wrecks he'd endured. After all, it had taken him ten years to get back to Ithaca.

'No, of course not. Well, I'm sorry for James Rochester. I'll do my best to restore his collection for him. We can at least salvage something from this unfortunate accident.'

Arnold's face had settled back into its accustomed inscrutability. 'Yes, indeed. Mr. Rochester would have liked that. Incidentally, take care with the sun. We want the work completed as quickly as possible, and you'd only be a hindrance if you were laid up with sun burn. I personally destest the sun.'

It seemed an unnecessary remark. It was only too obvious that Arnold Ponsford was no sun worshipper.

'Don't worry. I'll see that you get your money's worth.'

They walked together to the front of the building. 'How far down is the yacht?' said Nick suddenly, his mind turning to technical matters.

'About two hundred feet.'

'Isn't that too far for scubas?'

'No, they come up in stages. Two hundred and eighty is the maximum depth.' They were now crossing the car park towards the waiting taxi.

'I look forward to seeing them. I might even join them sometimes – I know a bit about scuba diving. I've always been interested in marine archaeology.'

'Mr. Harding.' Arnold stood stock still and his voice was sharp with anger. The eyes that met Nick's were icy blue. He felt a ripple of fear, realising for the first time that this man could be dangerous. 'Your job is on shore,' Arnold declared. 'No-one – I repeat, no-one – is allowed near the yacht. It is private property. We do not permit trespassers. It's not like your *Mary Rose*. We are not providing Sunday afternoon outings for all and sundry. Only my men are allowed near the yacht. You must stay on the shore and do your work there.'

Nick shrugged his shoulders. It didn't really matter to him whether he saw the yacht or not but the man's rudeness has annoyed him.

'I suppose I'm allowed to have an evening swim with my wife, or perhaps we're only allowed to stroll along the shore?'

Arnold ignored the remark, and walked over to the taxi. He didn't say goodbye. Nick risked a final parting shot.

25

'Incidentally, why pick on me? Haven't you got archaeologists in America?'

Arnold paused as he was about to get into the taxi. 'Because you have a certain fame, or should I say notoriety? Henry Rochester thought you would add a certain glamour to his project. If he decided to display the collection in, say, New York, people would flock to see it because they have heard of you out there. You looked good on television. They think they know you.'

Nick watched the taxi drive away. He didn't know whether to laugh or be annoyed at the man's last remark. 'Notoriety' *was* the right word. Sometimes he felt like the proverbial empty vessel. The product of media hype. A vulgarized academic. He felt the old depression coming on. He was prostituting his skills for money. Pandering to a rich man's whim to pay off a car which was well beyond his means. A sensible man would have told Arnold J. Ponsford to get lost, sold the Porsche and bought a Ford Escort.

Still, he rationalized, it would be a good holiday for him and Marian. It was just what they both needed.

Marian had made an effort that evening. There was an exotic fish pie in a silver entrée dish, and two bottles of Rhine wine. She'd always been interested in cooking, and had spent the morning hunting around Brighton's fish shops for Mediterranean delicacies. She had picked four yellow rose buds from the garden, and put them in a cut glass vase in the centre of the table. She'd also lit the candles, although it was still quite early, and the sun was shining outside. But inside the house, they were locked in their own dark world. Two people wanting to hurt each other, wanting to go their own way, but fixed in space like two geostationary satellites, held there by physical forces outside their control. Until the batteries ran out.

Today she had also made an effort with her appearance. She'd put on some sort of Arab caftan which Nick couldn't remember seeing before. It was made of some thin green material, and had a low neck and long sleeves. She'd unpinned her hair and it hung down almost to her waist. Usually, she held it back with a girlish slide or ribbon, but tonight she'd washed it and brushed it out. Now it clung round her face, damp with perspiration as the night was warm. She seemed oblivious to the fact that she was almost five years older than Nick and her hair, once chestnut, was almost completely grey.

Nick also noticed that she had also put on a lot of weight recently; probably the result of her drinking too much. She was, he thought dispassionately, about two stone overweight and her body looked unhealthily bloated. Her abdomen, which he could see quite clearly through the thin material, hung down into her lap like the statute of a Chinese Buddha he'd noticed the other day in her antique shop.

The face that met his reproachfully was also swollen, eyes red from crying. Marian was usually particular about her make-up, but tonight her lipstick had smeared clown-like across her chin. Her lips were moist with spittle, and her eye make-up was disintegrating under an onslaught of tears.

She had been attractive when he married her ten years ago. Only five feet three in height, she had once been described as 'petite'. She had dressed fashionably and expensively, and had been fond of dramatic jewellery, which suited her. She had stood out from the crowd of other wives of his fellow academics, and he had admired her sophistication and glamour. She talked knowledgeably and wittily about things he knew nothing about. He'd been impressed and dazzled and flattered when she started to take notice of him.

Perhaps that was why he'd married her, he thought as he turned his attention back to the fish pie. Or was it because of her father's rolling acres near Cirencester? A bit of both, he decided. She certainly had an impressive knowledge of the Fine Arts, and an instinct for recognizing valuable furniture in the most unlikely settings.

She had been different from the girls he'd been brought up with in Newcastle. He'd only taken her once to visit his parents, and that had been a disaster. His mother had been overwhelmed and timid, and his father disapproving. So now he went home on his own. This year he'd already been back there three times. In his small back bedroom, overlooking the narrow strip of garden which his mother filled with vegetables, he'd felt a sense of relief. There, no one expected

27

anything of him. No one asked him any questions. No one demanded his attention, his approval, his love. That was always taken for granted, and his parents were never disappointed.

Tonight Marian had been drinking too much as usual. They were on to their second bottle of wine, but it was those three gins and tonic before the meal that caused the disintegration. When the guns were moved into place for the War of Attrition, thought Nick ruefully, there should be a ban on alcohol. It only hastened the end. It only increased the number of casualties.

There was no need, in their case, to prepare for battle. It was always imminent. But how could they stop this slow process of disintegration? Why must there always be this vindictiveness, why the hatred? And why did his mouth feel full of grit, making it difficult to swallow? Why was Marian looking at him like that – with contempt and loathing? Above all, what had he done? He had once loved her, and above everything else he still wanted to see her happy. Otherwise, he knew, he would have failed. He still couldn't bear the thought that he might possibly be the cause of her unhappiness. But how could he reach across the no man's land of the dining room table and tell her he still wanted her when she seemed set on battle?

'When did you hear about this damn stupid expedition?' she said, her voice shaking with anger.

'Only this afternoon, I told you. Ponsford came to see me in College.'

'But you must have had some inkling before. Why didn't you tell me? Why do you always have to be so secretive?'

Her voice grated on his nerves. Why did she suspect everything he did? Why these razor sharp misunderstandings? But he controlled his irritation.

'Because nothing was decided until today. He told me nothing in his letter. Look, it's only for the summer – for the end of July and the whole of August, that's all. We'll be back here by September. Think of it as a holiday, like that time in Crete. You enjoyed that.'

'You know damn well I can't leave the business in August. Besides, don't mention Crete to me! You were out all day –

28

photographs, site supervision, meetings . . . I might just as well have stayed at home. Left all day in a grotty villa, with no hot water and a one-eyed cat for company! *And* he had fleas.'

At first he thought she was joking, but looking at her resentful face, distorted with anger, he realised she was deadly serious. She had delivered her first broadside. The battle had started.

'You appeared to enjoy it when you were out there. You slept and drank enough.'

Her eyes blazed with hatred. 'Because that's all there was to do. And what about you? You were never at the villa. You were always out with those girls. What about Jane, and that Greek girl, Kalliope?'

The enormity of the accusation took Nick's breath away. 'Kalliope was the guide. Christ, she was a teacher in Athens! And Jane was one of my students. She's married now. Don't be so bloody unreasonable.'

He pushed away the plateful of cold food, and reached again for the wine bottle but it was almost empty. Cursing, he leapt to his feet and went into the kitchen to fetch another from the fridge. With a single movement he jerked the cork out of the bottle.

'Unreasonable! *You* can say that. You always were a randy so-and-so. Look at you now, surrounded by crowds of doting women. What is it you call them – your "handmaidens"? Go to your bloody island, if you want to. Go and fuck everything in sight, but count me out. I'm staying here. You'll soon run out of steam, then see if your "handmaidens" want you. But don't come crawling back to me when it all goes wrong. You're over forty, remember. Men run out of juice at that age. Don't think that I'll look after you in your old age.'

Nick felt the real world receding. Was this really his wife in front of him, this woman with the sad, bedraggled hair and sagging breasts? One half of him was involved in a nightmare battle in which there could be no victor, and no survivor. Just a desolation. Yet, one half of him stood back dispassionately from the scene, hating everything he witnessed yet taking notes and storing them away.

'You bitch!' Now he too was resorting to the language of the gutter. 'You're a fine one to talk. What about your fancy boy, Simon? Do we bring him with us to keep you amused in the Sporades?'

Marian leapt up from the table, and flew at him with her hands raised. But he was used to her displays of temperament, and caught hold of her hands.

'Well?' he demanded, delighted that his shot had found its mark. 'What will he do out there in between servicing you and fucking the local boys? Because that's the way he is, you know. Otherwise why should he be interested in you? Overweight, neurotic, and ten years his senior.'

'You bastard,' she screamed, trying to break free from his grip. 'Why do you always accuse me of being promiscuous? You know it's not true. Simon's my assistant, that's all.'

'Then why the all night sessions? Do you really expect me to believe that you're both sitting there doing the accounts at three o'clock in the morning?' He shook her roughly by the shoulders, his fingers bruising the soft white flesh.

'You know I went to Gloucester the other night! You know I stayed at High Beeches! I've got to go to auctions. It's my job, damn you. Besides, I like going home.'

'And Simon? Does he "go home" as well?'

'He comes with me, yes. Mother likes him. He fits in, unlike you. My family thinks you're a working-class lout on the make. Well, you haven't made me. Go and impress your little girls but leave me alone.'

So that was it, said his dispassionate half. First of all she calls you sexually inadequate, and now a social climber. Sex and class. The Englishman's hang-ups.

He tried to calm her, to take her in his arms, but it was no use. She was crying again now, working herself up into a state of hysteria.

'Get away from me! Get off to your damned island. Don't ever touch me again. You're just a bloody impostor. A little boy, trying to be a man. You couldn't fuck a real woman if you tried.'

Then he lost control. All those years of self-discipline, of acting the gentleman, were forgotten. He hated that woman in front of him, wanted to smash the face staring at him with such hatred. With a surge of rage, he raised his hand and struck her across the mouth. She cried out in pain, and raised her hands to protect her face. It was the first time he'd ever struck her, or anyone else for that matter. With a start of horror he realised that if he'd had a knife handy, he would have plunged it into her breast. The thought sobered him and he stood there bewildered, looking at the hysterical woman whom he had promised to love and cherish. Her face was distorted with pain and misery. Blood trickled from a small cut on her upper lip.

He moved towards her, deperately sorry and wanting to comfort her. She shrank away from him, and turned towards the fire-place.

'Marian,' he said, when he was able to speak. 'I'm sorry, so sorry – for everything. But you shouldn't have said that! No one has the right to say such things. Here, let me take you upstairs. Let me wash your face, and put you to bed. Things will be different in the morning. Darling, I'm so sorry.'

Putting his arms round her, he half carried her upstairs. She was still crying, but his violence seemed to have stemmed the hysteria. She felt heavy and almost relaxed in his arms. Gently, he removed the long dress, and laid her on the bed. Then he wrapped her in a sheet, as reaction was beginning to set in and she was shivering. There was a glass by the bed, and he went into the bathroom to fill it and fetch two sleeping tablets. He put them on the bedside table. She still wouldn't look at him, but he knew she would take the pills as soon as he left the room. As an afterthought, he went back into the bathroom and put the bottle of pills in his pocket. Then he tip-toed out of her room, knowing that she would soon be asleep.

He picked up his anorak from the hall, and walked out of the front door. It was still light. He walked for miles over the Downs until the failing light forced him to turn back. He saw the wind ripple over the fields of green wheat, like waves over the sea. He stopped to look at the new season's lambs, almost grown up now but still clinging to their mothers as if uncertain of their independence. They looked at him with innocent, curious eyes and he felt a wave of shame and self-loathing surge over him. His marriage was over and it was all his fault. He had never been the lover Marian had wanted. He had let her down both physically and emotionally – and he hated himself for it.

31

He couldn't meet even the eyes of a sheep. He reached out a hand to one of the lambs, needing contact with some living creature, but it shrank back in fear.

He turned and walked slowly home. Around him pale scabious, colourless in the evening light, swayed in the breeze like ballet dancers. It was almost too dark for him to make out the other flowers, just the ox-eye daisies standing to attention like soldiers.

He opened the front gate and the scent of roses and lavender greeted him. The moon had risen, and flooded the distant sea with a path of silver. An owl hooted from the oak tree opposite the house. All around him was the beauty of a perfect summer's night. Inside, an unhappy woman lay sobbing herself to sleep. And it was all his fault.

Chapter 4

The journey from Patiteri, in a car which seemed to have neither brakes nor gears, was a nightmare. Nick was glad when the taxi stopped at the edge of the road and the driver pointed down the side of the hill.

'Steni Vala,' he said. And then, as an afterthought, 'Spiros'.

Nick paid the man, and climbed out of the car. The driver made no effort to help as Nick dragged his holdall from the back seat, merely lit another cigarette, nodded, and reversed back along the road. Then, with nerve-racking speed, he accomplished a three point turn in the narrow road, his back wheels at one stage suspended over the edge of the cliff. With a roar of acceleration, and a cloud of blue smoke, he shot off towards Patiteri and his interrupted siesta.

Nick watched the car disappear, then looked at the track down the hill-side. There had to be another road to Steni Vala, he thought, that was suitable for cars. Ponsford had mentioned the possibility of hiring a car. But it was probably further on, and the driver had resented being asked to drive anywhere in the middle of the afternoon. There was nothing for it. Nick would have to climb down the hill-side on his own two feet. Next time he came to Alonnisos, he thought to himself ruefully, he'd catch the later hydrofoil from Skiathos and arrive in the evening.

It was very hot. The sun beat down from a cloudless sky. Nick's shirt was sticking to him, and his trousers, where they had been in contact with the car's upholstery, were soaking wet. Both the heat and the silence were almost tangible, the only noise the incessant chatter of the cicadas, the continuous ground bass to life in the Mediterranean.

Picking up his holdall, and thankful that he'd decided to travel light, he started to climb down the sandy track.

In the shade of the pine trees, he paused for a moment. It was deliciously cool there. He noticed the plastic bags tied round the trunk of each tree. Little bags to catch the resin that oozed from the cuts in the bark. Resin, he remembered, was the main ingredient in the local wine called, appropriately, retsina. So there were people living around here. Even if it felt like it, he wasn't the only person on the island.

Suddenly he heard the tinny sound of a bell. Just the faintest sound, but one that transported him instantly back to Crete. Looking round, he saw it – a largish, black, white-bearded goat, looking curiously like one of the local priests. It was staring at Nick with a pair of the wickedest eyes he'd ever seen. Then another appeared, and soon Nick was surrounded by a whole flock of the creatures, watching and appraising him. He walked on, the circle parting to let him through, and looked around for the goat-herd. There he was; a boy no more than ten years old, fast asleep under a rock. His black curly head was bowed over his drawn-up knees; his stick propped against the rock. He was wearing only a pair of torn and patched jeans, and his bare feet looked as if they'd never seen shoes. The goats continued to stare, curious but harmless. Nick suddenly felt a long way from home. He felt as if he'd strayed back into classical times, and looked again at the boy to see whether he had in fact cloven hooves instead of feet. But they looked healthily normal, and realistically dirty, and the black curls were certainly free of horns. Nor were there any pan pipes by his side. There was probably a transistor radio hidden in the shade.

The boy slept on and Nick walked quietly past him, anxious not to disturb him. The goats, their curiosity satisfied, didn't follow him.

Then he was through the trees, and the bay of Steni Vala was ahead of him. It looked to be a perfect natural harbour, a bite taken out of the coastline of Alonnisos. There were a few fishing boats tied up against the jetty. Heaps of nets piled up at intervals along the quay. A couple of yachts were moored at the far end of the jetty, their crews nowhere in sight. The whole place looked to be asleep. The sea stretched into the distance forming a perfect back-drop. A clear expanse of blue, surface undisturbed by a single ripple or a single fleck of foam. In the far distance lay the hazy outline of the other island he'd noticed marked on a chart he'd studied: Peristera, largely uninhabited. It looked heavenly. Marian would have loved it.

At the thought of his wife, he abruptly picked up his bag again and walked towards the olive grove ahead of him. The pine trees gave way to olives as the shore approached. He didn't want to think of her. He'd only seen her once again, briefly, after that dreadful evening. She had told him she was going to the Cotswolds to buy a Regency table and a set of dining-room chairs. He never saw her again. She had neither telephoned to wish him a good journey, nor to say when she would be back in Rottingdean. Wearily, he had set off for Gatwick, neither wanting to go nor wanting to stay behind to meet his wife's reproachful eyes. Perhaps, after an interval of two months, things would be different. With the onset of autumn, and the start of a new term, they might be able to work out some sort of compromise. He hoped so. What was the use of a successful career if his marriage had fallen apart?

Twenty minutes after leaving the taxi he found the taverna. He couldn't miss it. It was the only building in the place that looked remotely like a café. It was just a white-washed building with a wooden terrace built on the front. Vines provided the necessary shade, and scarlet geraniums in old petrol cans stood along the front wall. The tables were covered with clean blue and white checked cloths, and two scrawny cats were stretched out underneath one of the chairs. There was no other sign of life. Nick dumped his bag on the floor and sat down at one of the tables. Nothing happened. Just two sleeping cats and the chorus of cicadas. He began to relax, and found his eye-lids drooping. He stretched out his legs, rested his head on the back of the chair and almost fell asleep.

Suddenly he felt he was being watched. He opened his eyes and saw a girl looking at him. She was standing in front of the beaded curtain that divided the kitchen from the rest of the café. She was no more than eight years old, an enchanting child with a pale oval face and untidy hair that hadn't been brushed or combed for days. She wore a short purple dress. He smiled and pointed to his mouth. She nodded and disappeared behind the curtain. Seconds later she came out carrying a tray. There were two glasses on it, one filled with water and the other containing a clear liquid which Nick recognized as *ouzo*. There was also a dish of black olives.

The girl watched him mix the water with the *ouzo* and drink the mixture down in one gulp. Without a word, she fetched him another glass.

'Spiros?' he said when she came back.

'He sleeps,' she said, illustrating her remark by putting her head on her clasped hands.

Nick nodded. He knew about the long siestas. 'What time?' he said, pointing to his watch.

She shrugged her shoulders. 'As long as he pleases,' she said. Then, not wishing to appear inhospitable, she went inside and turned on the radio. A woman was singing in Greek. The reception was remarkably good. It was a plaintive song making use of the tonal scales of the Middle East. Nick had forgotten how near these islands were to Turkey. He shut his eyes again, his brain slightly clouded by the *ouzo*, and waited for Spiros.

Suddenly he was there, standing in the doorway scratching his stomach. A tall, wiry Greek with black hair and a thin moustache. He buttoned up his trousers, spat on the sand, and felt in his pocket for a comb. Then he saw Nick. Instantly his manner changed.

'My dear sir,' he said in perfect Home Counties English, 'I didn't know you were here. Why wasn't I informed?'

'Don't worry,' said Nick, pointing to his glass, 'The little girl looked after me.'

'Angie? That child is growing up.'

'Your daughter?' asked Nick politely.

Spiros thought for a second. 'No, the child of my eldest daughter. I have many children,' he added with pride.

He fetched a new bottle from the kitchen, and sat down beside Nick.

'Now', he said, 'you will stay here with me and my family.'

36

He emphasized the statement by pouring out another glass of *ouzo* for Nick then one for himself. 'We have a good room here, a new shower, and a toilet which flushes away the shit.'

He pronounced the word 'sheet'. It sounded incongruous coming from someone who spoke English so perfectly.

'That sounds fine. Can I eat here?'

'Of course, of course. Where else? There is nowhere you can eat as well as here. On this island, there is nothing.' He waved his hands as if to encompass the whole world.

That night, Nick drank a great deal of *ouzo* and ate fried squid and a huge red fish. He was dimly aware of faces looking at him – girls in bright dresses, boys of all ages who perched on the wooden rail of the terrace and watched his every move. Even the grandmother, an aged crone, toothless and dressed entirely in black, came over to inspect him. Then she retired to a corner of the terrace and watched the proceedings from a corner of the sofa, her feet tucked under her. He saw the children go over to her one by one before they went to bed. Each one received a blessing, and one small boy was sent back to wash his face again.

Then somehow he found his bed. It was in a comfortable room overlooking the harbour. He had a hazy idea that Spiros said something to him about a car, and that he was not to worry about anything. Then he was asleep and some-one must have covered him for he woke in the cool of the early morning to find himself cocooned in a rug.

He felt surprisingly refreshed when he woke up later that morning. The *ouzo* had done him no harm, he'd slept well and the sun was shining. He hadn't a trace of a hangover. The shower worked, it seemed almost a crime to use the sparklingly new lavatory, and breakfast was laid ready for him when he went downstairs. Spiros had disappeared, but Angie stood by his table and fetched him his coffee and fresh rolls. She seemed excited that morning, and stood impatiently by his side until he'd finished eating. When he stood up and pushed back his chair, she seized hold of his hand and led him towards the back of the taverna.

'The car,' she said. 'Come.'

A black Volkswagen was parked by the front door of

Spiros' house. One of the tyres looked suspiciously flat, and most of the body work had been eaten away by rust. He wondered how it had got there, and decided that there must be another way down to Steni Vala for motorists. Not for taxis, though. Passengers were expected to use the track. Especially during siesta time.

'It's yours,' she said. 'Spiros says. He's gone to Patiteri but will be back tonight.'

He asked her how to get to the next bay – Agios Demetrios. She nodded.

'I will show you later,' she said.

'And the road for the car?'

'I will take you.'

He pointed to the flat tyre, and pushed it with his fingers. 'This is not good,' he said. 'It will not get us there.'

She understood. Her black eyes were dancing with excitement, and she pushed the tangled mass of dark curls back out of her eyes. Then she dashed off towards the house. For a moment Nick half expected her to come back with a puncture outfit and a jack, but instead she re-appeared with a man walking several paces behind her. A true scion of the house of Spiros, Nick thought. Sure enough, she pointed imperiously to the flat tyre and the man nodded and set to work.

An hour later, with Angie beside him, Nick set off for Agios Demetrios which was to be his work place for the next few weeks. The car proceeded in a series of rapid jerks, and it was touch and go whether it would make the steep climb to the top of the cliff. The engine got very hot, and the gears were idiosyncratic. However, the brakes worked and at the top of the cliff he stopped. He could see the bay in the distance, and Angie got out.

'Down there,' she said. 'I have to go now. I have work to do.'

He was sorry to see her vanish back along the road. It seemed a pity to think that she would spend most of the day shut away in the kitchen making bread and cutting up vege-tables. The grandmother would be a slave driver, he knew. They always were.

It took him longer than he'd expected to get down to the

bay which was about five miles east of Steni Vala, and it was almost noon before he stopped the car under a clump of pine trees and walked down the path to the beach.

Nothing, he decided, could be better than Agios Demetrios as a place to work. Pine clad hills sloped gently down to the beach. It was greener here, and pleasanter than the part of the island around Patiteri. This bay had its own source of fresh water which trickled out of the sand-stone rock, down to the shore. Fig trees grew here in profusion, and olive groves fringed the bay. Already the fruit was forming on the trees but it was not quite ripe enough for picking.

He stopped and drew a deep breath. Never had he seen such a beautiful place, and what's more he seemed to be the only person there. There were no foot prints on the sand. Not even the sound of goat bells. Halfway up the cliff on the western side of the bay there was a white villa, half hidden by the pines. He thought how perfect it would be to live there – to buy the whole bay and live there alone. A Robinson Crusoe of the Aegean.

Still fantasising, he breathed in the scent of the thyme and rosemary and walked down to the sea. The turquoise water was irresistible. He'd forgotten how clear it was around these islands. He left his clothes in a pile on the sand and struck out for a group of rocks at the entrance to the bay.

Looking down, he could see fish as clearly as if they were in his own personal aquarium – exotic fish, with brightly striped backs. Thousands of them, drifting past him with expressions of supreme indifference.

There were squid in the crevices of the rocks, he knew. The locals came out at night with lights and harpoons, and speared them. Then they beat them on the rocks to make them tender, and hung them on washing lines outside their front doors to dry them. He'd seen them at the taverna last night.

The water was colder than he'd remembered it in Crete. He turned over on his back and looked up at the brilliant sky. He felt a surge of happiness, even contentment, to know he was going to stay in this place for two months. He felt like a wanderer in the desert who suddenly finds that the oasis-mirage is real. It was sad that it was a rich man's death which had brought him here. It was impossible to think of storms and drowning on such a day.

39

He turned to look at the island of Peristera, a hazy outline in the distance. Somewhere out there was a wreck. At this very moment divers could be bringing up amphorae. Any time now they might appear and his work would begin.

A workshop must have been provided for him, somewhere out of the sun with a door that closed at night. Nick swam reluctantly back to shore and then he saw it. A wooden shelter set back in the olive grove. That had to be the place. It was too new to be a fisherman's hut.

Not bothering to dry himself, he put on his trousers. The hut was a primitive structure – just a wooden framework, covered with tarpaulin. It was really no more than a substantial tent. Two flaps made up the front door. They could be tied together at night. He knew the islanders would respect his possessions.

He went inside. Someone, he suspected it was Spiros, had provided a wooden table and chair. It was rather an elaborate chair, upholstered in faded chinz like a cast-off from an unsuccessful English sea-side hotel. It was quite useless for work, of course. It was too low for the table but fine for a siesta. He sat down, feeling like a hotel guest waiting for the bar to open. It was warm in the 'tent' and the chair was comfortable. Nick soon fell into a sound sleep.

That evening he met Markos in the taverna. He had noticed the quiet dark man as soon as he sat down at 'his' table in the corner of the terrace. Markos was drinking *ouzo*. He sat by himself, apart from the company – mostly friends of Spiros – but obviously well-known to everybody there. Sometimes they shouted across to him, mainly for information about the weather or travel conditions, and he answered in monosyllables.

Markos was a handsome man in his early forties. He was powerfully built with strong hands, used to manual work, and broad shoulders. Yet he didn't look like a fisherman, nor a labourer in the fields. His clothes were practical and clean – a checked shirt and blue jeans. He could have been a successful garage owner or a property developer. Certainly a man who was his own boss. There was also an aura of melancholy about him which intrigued Nick. Obviously he had suffered in some way, and the experience had left him withdrawn and suspicious of people.

Spiros seemed to treat him with respect, urging the child Angie to fetch the man more olives and cheese. He himself brought the bottle and filled up Markos' glass. Nick noticed how his expression changed when Angie came up to him. His rather severe face broke into an attractive grin, and twice he offered her a piece of the cheese on a square of bread. Angie was quite at home with him, and used all the wiles of an eight-year-old to keep him amused. Nick watched the pair of them with amusement.

But his scrutiny was soon interrupted by a man whom he had seen that morning, sweeping the floor of the taverna and emptying the ash-trays. He was one of those people frequently seen in peasant communities but who have almost disappeared in England. A hundred years ago he would have been called the village idiot, but this man in spite of his awkward walk and distorted face, was no idiot. He understood everything that was said to him but he couldn't communicate. His tongue was too big for his mouth, and he had difficulty in controlling his saliva. Nick watched him trying to say something to Spiros' friends, but it was no good. He went through agonies of frustration trying to get out one word, but gave up and retreated with his broom amidst good-natured laughter.

In spite of the twisted feet that were bent in on themselves almost at right angles to his body, Nick could see the outline of the whole man who should have been there. Not for the first time he thought of God as a jester, who, when bored with his creation, made such a man. 'Look,' he seemed to say, 'I made this man, and he could have been you. Aren't you lucky?'

The man shuffled over to Nick and eyed him curiously. He knew a stranger when he saw one. He pointed to Nick, and then to himself.

'My name is Nick.'

The man's face twisted violently as he tried to imitate the sound. It was agonising to watch him but nothing came out of the thick mouth except grunts. So he lurched away to a clump of lilies which grew around the edge of the terrace. He picked

41

one, and presented it to Nick with a formal bow. The message was clear. Nick was being welcomed to the community. He took the lily and smiled his thanks, and it was at this point that Markos came over and joined him.

'Don't be scared,' he said in English. 'He belongs here. We don't hide our mentally afflicted in institutions. We think of them as blessed by God as they cannot see the evil in the world. They are not cursed by intelligence as we are. His name is Yannis. That would be 'John' in your country, I believe.'

Then he leant forward and stroked Yannis' hand – a gesture of affection which the man appreciated. He put the hand that Markos had touched against his face, as if pressing the affection into his brain. Nick felt strangely moved.

'Don't worry,' he said. 'I too sometimes think the handicapped are the lucky ones. They don't suffer like we do.'

'I'm not so sure. When they love, they love deeply and whole-heartedly. There is no compromise.'

'Perhaps that is the right way. So often we hide our real feelings, especially in my country. Englishmen have a reputation for being emotionally retarded.'

Markos looked thoughtfully at Nick for a moment then asked if he might sit with him for a while. Nick was delighted to talk to someone. He stood up, shook hands, and indicated the chair opposite. He beckoned over Angie but she had already anticipated the order and came over with a tray and two glasses.

Markos turned to Yannis who was still standing there looking at them.

'Now go and finish your work,' he said. 'Petra wants your help tomorrow. She wants you to sail with her, I think. Come up to the house in the morning and she will be expecting you.'

At the name Petra, Yannis' face broke into a broad smile. He nodded vigorously and walked away with a new vigour to his gait.

'He loves my sister,' said Markos, 'and he is useful and helps her with her boat.'

'Can he manage a boat?' said Nick in some disbelief.

'He's one of the best sailors in these waters. He understands the wind. Engines only confuse him. He can also swim like a fish, and dive like a seal. I am always happy when he goes out with Petra who can be rather over-daring. But come, let's drink to your stay on Alonnisos. My name is Markos, Markos Karakulas. I live further along the coast.'

He poured out two glasses of *ouzo* and handed one to Nick.

'Nick Harding.'

Markos nodded, as if he had already gathered the information, and together they drank and settled down in that timeless manner of the Eastern Mediterranean to discuss the world and find out about each other.

Markos was in fact the local builder. He was planning to build a complex of white stone-walled villas above the bay of Agios Demetrios. They were to be set amongst the pine trees, and each one would be self-sufficient. Already he had the necessary planning permission from Volos.

'But you, Mr. Harding, I understand your business is to do with the wreck. We are all curious to know more about it. It belonged to an American, so I gather?'

'Yes. He came to a sad end in a storm which I gather you had here in June.'

'Yes, it was untimely and disastrous. The American was not the only one to lose his life. Two fishing boats capsized, and if it wasn't for Yannis' extraordinary talent for survival, the men would have drowned. He kept both their heads out of water until help came. That's why we all respect him.'

So there had been a storm, Nick thought. Ponsford had been right.

'Do you have many storms around here?'

'Yes. The islands are surrounded by wrecks. There is an interesting one still there from Roman times in a bay in the island of Iura – the most northerly of these islands. On a clear day you can take a boat over the wreck and look down on all the jars. What do you call them now . . . amphorae, am I right? Petra told me. She's my half-sister, by the way. My father married twice. One marriage produced me, the other, Petra. He married a visitor to the island, a German lady who fell in love with him and gave up the Rhineland. You must come and meet us soon. My father's house overlooks the bay – Agios Demetrios. That's where you're going to work, I understand.'

43

Nick nodded. He remembered the beautiful house over-looking the bay which he'd seen that morning.

'Thank you. I should be delighted to meet your family. I saw your house this morning. It looked perfect. A spectacular view.'

Markos smiled.

'We think so. My mother, my step-mother really, keeps a small guest house there. Not many people come, but in August her relations come to stay, and sometimes they bring friends. But we have no-one at the moment. Should you need some peace and quiet after a few days in Spiros' noisy establishment, then you are welcome to come and stay with us. It's peaceful there and near your work. We should be honoured.'

It certainly was an interesting idea and Nick said he would give it some thought. He'd slept well in the taverna last night, but that was because he'd been exhausted from the journey and his conflicting emotions at leaving Marian.

Markos left around nine o'clock, and Nick ate a hearty supper. Spiros left the group by the kitchen door and came over to him.

'Mr. Harding, you have met Mr. Karakulas I see. An interesting man, and a sad one.' He filled Nick's glass.

'Sad? In what way?'

'His wife and child, a boy, were both drowned two summers ago. He has lost, how do you say, his joy of living. He has no heart now for anything. Just the *ouzo*. A man of ideas but no action. He will end like everyone else – a disillusioned romantic. His father will take care of him. Meanwhile he dreams of success and wealth. He ought to take another wife. There are plenty of lovely girls on this island and he's quite, how do you say, personable. And your wife, Mr. Harding, when will she come to join you?'

'Sometime, I expect. It might be too hot for her out here. And I start work tomorrow, so there won't be a lot for her to do. She doesn't like the sun.'

Spiros' face was inscrutable.

'The sun is not good for the Englishwomen. They burn very easily. But they have the most beautiful complexions in the world. Have you everything you need, Mr. Harding?' Nick had finished his meal, and had got up from the table to go to bed.

44

'Of course. I am very comfortable. But let me know how much I owe you for the car, and for all the food I've eaten, let alone the *ouzo*.'

Mr. Harding, you are my guest. Don't talk about money. I can provide you with anything you want – anything,' he stressed. 'Even a nice girl to keep you warm.' And then, in case Nick hadn't properly understood: 'A good girl. A nice fuck. No problems.'

Nick smiled his thanks but refused all the same. That night he slept well for the second time. Before he got into bed, he looked out of the window and saw the twisted silhouette of Yannis clearing away the debris from the tables.

He saw the white envelope immediately he opened his eyes the next morning. He was quite sure it hadn't been there the night before. He jumped out of bed and opened it. Inside there was a cheque for five thousand pounds, issued by Lloyds Bank in Victoria Street, London, and signed by Arnold J. Ponsford. The first half of the payment had come.

Chapter 5

It was noon before he heard the sound of a motorboat. He'd been there for two hours, and there had been no signs of life. He was beginning to give up hope, although he had been assured by Spiros that 'The men will come today.'

It was very hot, the temperature well into the eighties. Nick, dressed only in shorts, had spent the morning preparing for work. He'd borrowed two plastic buckets from the taverna, and filled them with fresh water from the stream. He'd laid out is own selection of brushes and scrapers and tubes of adhesives, and waited for the men to come. Already he was beginning to think that it was all some hoax. That there were no amphorae, and Ponsford had made a dreadful mistake. Someone had been persuaded to pay him five thousand pounds for sitting in this tent on a remote island. Here he was calmly anticipating spending the rest of the day washing pieces of pottery and coating them in polyvinyl acetate when in reality there were no pots; the men had shipped them off somewhere else before he arrived, and had told no-one. He knew from experience that things could go very wrong when dealing with local labour. Soon it would be siesta time when no-one did any work. So he had two swims, and composed himself to patience.

Nich had no talent for laziness. He slept when he was tired, otherwise he liked to be active and involved. He quickly became bored. He'd also brought no food with him. He was beginning to think about returning to Spiros's and ordering a plateful of *calamari* and a glass of cold beer when he heard the noise of the engine. It wasn't the sort of boat he'd expected.

In spite of his academic training, Nick was an incurable romantic. He'd imagined some sort of ancient Greek caique bringing the amphorae to shore. A wooden boat which could take all the diving equipment. It might even have a sail. But this boat was a fast modern speedboat; the sort of thing he'd seen in the South of France, usually owned by rich men who liked to race them.

This very modern, bright red boat now roared into the bay, stopping dramatically just off the shore. The water shelved deeply in Agios Demetrios, as it did in most bays in the Aegean. Boats could come very close to the shore without fear of running aground.

There were two men in the boat, both wearing wet-suits. One now dropped an anchor over the side, and then together they lifted out a large basket from the bottom of the boat. The basket at least was reassuringly romantic – the locally woven sort, often used by fishermen. Nick got up and went to meet the men. After his long wait, he was curious to see what they had brought.

The men waved aside his offer of help and between them carried the basket to the hut. They were both Greeks, and appeared not to speak English. It was a strange silent procession that walked up the beach. The two men in their diving gear looking like two sea creatures from ancient legends, the servants of some mighty Kraken bringing tribute to Nick the invader.

The men dumped the basket on the floor near the table and turned to go back to the boat.

'Wait,' said Nick, who felt he ought to establish some sort of raport with the people who were to be his colleagues. 'What are your names? Will you come every day?' He spoke first in English, and then in Greek. Both man stared at him as if reluctant to admit to understanding him. Then the taller of the two spoke – impatiently, as if he wanted to be off.

'I am called Giorgios. This man is Takis. Yes, we shall come every day, about the same time.'

'Do you live here in Steni Vala?'

'No, we come from Volos.'

Then, abruptly, they walked quickly away towards the boat. Nick watched them climb in, start the engine, and roar

47

out of the bay. At the entrance they turned east, and soon disappeared around the headland. Soon all was quiet once again except for the harsh chatter of the cicadas, who seemed to get noisier as the heat of the day intensified.

Whatever thoughts Nick might have about the strange taciturn men disappeared when he examined the contents of the basket. He was a professional through and through, and loved his job. He also knew a lot about the pottery of the Eastern Mediterranean in Classical times.

Carefully he took the pieces of pottery out of the basket and laid them on the table. There were clearly two amphorae, from different periods and different cultures. With growing wonder, Nick began to put the pieces together. Fortunately the jars had broken into large pieces, and it was easy to see the design. One he recognized immediately. He had seen something very similar in the Herakleion Museum in Crete.

It was a round Cretan jar which had probably been used for storing oil or grain. He guessed it had been made around 1000 BC. It stood about fourteen inches high, as far as he could judge, and was decorated with the graceful marine decoration which the Cretans loved, even though it had been broken into a dozen pieces. The great black octopus, with white suckers, was almost intact. He gazed at Nick out of a fringe of weeds. The rest of the pot was decorated with greeny-grey fronds of water plants. The whole pot was covered with a cream glaze.

Nick gazed at it in wonder. Where had this James Rochester found such a thing? It was priceless. How many more wonders was he going to see in the next few weeks? He felt a surge of anger that rich collectors were able to buy things like these, when they should be put into museums for everyone to see. He thought he might write straightaway to Arnold J. Ponsford suggesting that Rochester's heir ought to offer these amphorae to some museum. Any museum would be overjoyed to exhibit them. Both objects were so rare, and so beautiful, that for a moment he doubted whether he should be working on them. They really ought to have a team of museum staff to put them together.

He picked up a piece of the second pot – smaller than the first, but also astonishingly beautiful. It was of a later date, from Mainland Greece. It had been broken into slightly smaller pieces than the Cretan jar, but Nick could already see a bold frieze of dancing satyrs. There were musicians, playing flutes and beating drums. There were dancing girls, and small boys handing goblets of wine to those satyrs who were reclining on couches. The sea water hadn't damaged the black glaze, nor dimmed the bright red and white colours of the design. He thought it might be a wine cooler – a *psykter* the Greeks would call it. It might even have been painted by a man called Douris, one of the great artists of sixth century Greece. It, too, was priceless.

He worked on into the late afternoon, totally absorbed in his work. He didn't hear the boat come into the bay, or the flapping of the sails as they were lowered. But he did hear the voices. He carefully put down the piece of pottery he was working on, and walked to the door. He immediately recognized Yannis pulling up a small white sailing boat on to the beach. It was a local boat, the sort known as a 'caique'. This one was pointed at both ends, like the boats used by the Shetland Islanders. A girl was lowering the sails. Then she lifted out the mast and gave it to Yannis, followed by the sail then a basket from the bottom of the boat. Even so, Yannis put the things down on the beach to help her out of the boat, although she waved him impatiently away. He picked up the mast and the basket, leaving her to bring the sails, and together they walked up the beach.

Nick darted back into the darkness of the hut, suddenly reluctant to meet anyone. Besides, she looked absorbed in her companion. He heard her speaking in Greek, and Yannis' guttural replies. She seemed to understand what he was saying because the conversation proceeded perfectly naturally with questions and answers, even laughter.

They passed close to the hut, but didn't come in. Even so, Nick had seen enough to realise that she was very beautiful. Her long honey-coloured hair was tied back out of the way. Her skin was fair, tanned of course but not the olive skin of a Greek from these islands. She was strongly built with beautiful breasts and a slim waist. She was wearing a white bikini, and her legs were long and tanned. A girl, he thought, who likes the out-door life. She was young, no more than twenty-

49

four or five. He suspected that she was Markos' sister – or step-sister, he remembered. Hadn't his father married twice? The second time to a German tourist. That would explain the girl's blonde hair. She must have inherited her mother's looks. Her name, he remembered, was Petra.

After they had passed the hut, he went back to the door and looked out. Sure enough, they were walking up the path to the white house on the cliff. Soon they disappeared behind the pine trees. A strange couple, like two figures out of a fairy tale. Beauty in a white bikini, and a gentle beast who looked after her.

Back in the taverna, there were signs that a party was just about to start. In one corner of the terrace, a whole lamb was turning on a spit over the charcoal fire. Someone had put candles in bottles and stood them on all the tables. There were piles of bread on the improvised sideboard, and huge bowls of Greek salad, gleaming with onions, and a topping of feta cheese tomatoes and cucumbers. Already the music had started. A Greek singer, heavily amplified as befitted the occasion, wailed from the tape recorder.

Markos was sitting in the same place as the previous night. He raised his hand in recognition as Nick walked in.

'Hello. What's going on here? A celebration?' Nick dropped his bag on the floor, and took the bottle from the attentive Angie.

'Allow me,' he said, as he filled Markos' glass.

'I'm afraid so. We are always holding parties. It's a national vice. Tonight, though, it's really to celebrate Spiros' business ability. A party of Germans arrive in Skopelos, and stay in the best hotel. Spiros knows the manager so he persuades the man to ship the lot over here to his taverna, so that they can enjoy "traditional" Greek hospitality. In fact someone will pay the earth for it, and you can be sure it will not be the manager of the hotel. It's taken Spiros weeks to get this organised, but he got his way in the end. God knows, though, how they are going to ship this lot home tonight. They'll have to be carried back on board the boat, I reckon. But don't worry about your meal, Spiros will see to that. You'll get the best cut of the lamb even if you don't get any sleep.'

'It'll be as bad as that, then?'

'I'm afraid so. But you know what they say? If you can't beat them, join them.'

It was the last thing on earth Nick wanted at that moment. A boisterous party involving twenty or so Germans, hell bent on enjoyment.

'It's not my scene, I'm afraid. Does Spiros go in for many of these celebrations?'

'As the season wears on, yes. It brings him a lot of money. It's as quiet as the grave here in winter. We have to build up our fat now, to provide for the lean months. But tell me, how did your first day go? Interesting, I hope.'

'Fascinating. The most beautiful things, each one worth a king's ransom. This Rochester chap certainly knew what he was buying.'

Markos's face darkened with anger.

'It makes my blood boil to think that these things are to be shipped out of my country! How would you like it if someone came over to yours and bought up the crown jewels and took them off to some strange place? You wouldn't like it, eh? neither do we. And we've had to put up with this for centuries.'

He clenched his fists passionately and hit the table violently. He could be dangerous when roused, thought Nick. But he was a natural peace-maker and was prepared to like Markos. So he filled their glasses, and turned to look at the other people who were beginning to filter into the café. Most of them were Greeks, and obviously friends of Spiros. They sat around the edge of the terrace, leaving the centre for the German visitors.

'I do sympathize,' Nick said calmly. 'As a matter of fact, I intend to write to the chap who hired me to see if we can't get the lot put into a museum. I think the heir to Rochester's estate might be persuaded. He knows nothing about classical amphorae and, by the sound of it, cares even less. But at least these beautifuly things are being salvaged. Look at that Roman wreck off Iura. It's been there ever since the first century, and who's seen the amphorae so far? A few fishermen, and a handful of tourists who peer down at the pots from a small boat. what use is that? Who wants to gaze at ancient

51

jars through half a ton of seaweed? I'll try to get these into a museum. It will have to be on the mainland, though.'

It was almost impossible to carry on a conversation against the music and the excited chatter. Markos seemed to be mollified, though, by Nick's speech. At least he stopped frowning and for a few more minutes they drank together, watching the taverna fill up.

But when the party of middle-aged German tourists filed in, dressed in their best clothes and in high spirits, Markos got up to leave.

'Enjoy yourself, Nick. By the way if things get too hot for you here, don't forget we have a spare room at our house. There's only four of us living there at the moment.'

'That sounds a marvellous idea.' He thought of the white house overlooking the bay. It had looked idyllic.

'Good. Come and have dinner with us tomorrow evening, about seven. Then you can meet the family.'

Nick accepted, and shook hands. Then he watched Markos walk to the back of the terrace and into the kitchen.

Angie appeared almost instantly with a tray of supper. He was indeed to eat the first cut of the lamb.

He left the terrace well before midnight. He had no taste for boisterous parties, and besides he wanted to make notes on the day's work. He stood for a while at his window, watching the gyrating couples and the circle of stout German ladies who were still attacking the lamb. It was a perfect Mediterranean night, and if it wasn't for the noise he would have enjoyed the scene below. But he'd never been one for loud music, and had been strict with the students over the use of their radios.

After a few moments, he saw two men leave the terrace and walk across the grass to a corner of the garden by the harbour. It was Spiros, deep in conversation with Markos. So he hadn't gone home. For a while they stood there, and appeared to be arguing. Finally, Markos shook his head in a gesture of finality and walked back towards the road. Spiros stood looking after him for a moment, then shrugged his shoulders and went back towards his guests.

It was then that Nick heard the phone ring. It was after midnight and for a second he wondered who would want to

52

contact the taverna at that time of night. But it was nothing to do with him, and he sat on the edge of the bed and wrote for an hour or two. Sleep was impossible, and it was too hot to close the window.

Downstairs, Spiros took the call in the small room at the back of the restaurant which was used as a store cupboard. He recognized the voice immediately. It was Magnus from Marseilles.

'Spiros? Is all well?' He spoke in French.

'Of course. Everything goes like clockwork.'

Reluctantly, Spiros spoke the same language. It was one of the things he disliked about Magnus that the man refused to speak in any other language, not even in the international English language.

'This Englishman – this Nick Harding. Is he with you?'

'Yes, of course. Where else would he be? Don't worry. He is sleeping now. He started work today in Agios Demetrios. Everything was in order.'

'Does he ask questions? Is he sociable? Does he talk to anyone in the taverna?'

'No. He's a quiet academic gentleman who likes his own company.'

Spiros didn't feel he wanted to complicate matters by mentioning Markos.

'And the letter?'

'He found it, no problems.'

'There must be no problems, you understand? This Englishman must stay with you. Don't let him out of your sight. He must be watched at all times. But don't let him get suspicious – or it will be the worst for you. He mustn't go near the yacht. That is most important. You understand?'

'Yes, yes.' Spiros was getting impatient. Magnus seemed to think he was stupid. Bloody arrogant Frenchman! They were all the same. Besides, he could hear singing on the terrace and wanted to get back to his friends. The Germans were due to leave at one o'clock, and then the party would really begin.

'Then watch him, Spiros. He's clever, I hear. Clever with books. Let's hope that, like most professors, he's stupid about other things. Now listen, there's to be a delivery on

53

Thursday night. The usual time. Get the buoy lit at midnight. Takis will deal with the stuff and see to the light when he leaves. That's all.'

'Thursday. I shall of course see that everything is in order.'

'And keep hold of Mr. Harding. No midnight swims in the bay.'

'Don't worry. Mr. Harding is very proper. Very English. He's always in bed early.'

'Keep him like that. I'll be in touch again on Friday – the same time.'

He rang off. Spiros shrugged his shoulders and went to join his friends. Bosses were all the same: suspicious and demanding. And when they were French – that was the worst of all. Still, as long as they paid up, they could be as arrogant as they pleased.

For a second, he wondered what would be in the next delivery. But he was frightened of Takis, and thought it would be a lot more peaceful if he asked no questions. Spiros was not the first man to choose ignorance – as long as he was paid on time.

Chapter 6

Bernie left Rome on July 10th. She wasn't so much worried about Nelson's safety as his health, picturing him in some remote hospital where he couldn't communicate with anyone. Like a lot of Americans, he spoke only his own language.

It was her English friend who gave her the commonsense advice.

'A middle-aged American on a yacht shouldn't be difficult to track down. Why not start in Athens? You know the hotel where he usually stays, start with that. The manager should know something about his movements. I'll take you to the airport.'

So that was that. A decision made and acted upon in the space of an hour.

Athens turned out to be a disappointment. The manager of the hotel was delighted to see her, but couldn't give her much help. Yes, Nelson had been there but not since February. He'd only stayed a few days then had gone off to North Africa as he wanted some sun. No, there hadn't been a message for Bernie recently. He was sorry.

So she sat around in Athens for two days, hoping for something to happen, someone to tell her what to do. Hoping also that Nelson would either miraculously walk into the hotel lounge one evening, or at least telephone. She didn't like Athens, especially in July when the heat was stifling and the air thick with industrial fumes.

One evening she sat by the Parthenon and mourned for Athens. The leprous faces of the gods and goddesses, eyes and noses eaten away by the chemicals belching out from the refineries across the Bay of Salamis, gazed down at her. Salamis, where Thermistocles had smashed the Persian fleet, was now a resting place for the rusting hulks of tankers. Its water was foul with chemical discharge; its air heavy with the ochreous smoke of cement and ironworks.

The manager of the hotel was worried by Bernie's obvious unhappiness. He found her reading a book one evening in the little garden at the back of the hotel. It was July 13th.

'Miss Fitzpatrick, if I was looking for a man on a yacht I wouldn't stay here. I would go down to Piraeus. You can go by bus, or hire a taxi. It's not far. If Mr. Donelly phones, then I'll take the message. You can phone me from Piraeus.'

It was then that Bernie pulled herself together. The search had become serious. What had started out as a vague feeling that all was not quite right with Nelson, now became a conviction.

Bernie was a practical girl. She knew what she had to do. She had to talk to people, using her rusty Greek, and follow every clue. Someone, somewhere, had to have seen Nelson. He wasn't an inconspicuous figure but he did like his own company. He didn't like eating in local restaurants but he would have to go ashore to buy fuel and provisions. Also, she knew that every Greek loves boats and, although she'd never seen Nelson's boat, she knew that it would be memorable. Nelson liked his comforts.

She knew she would have to travel light and use public transport so she left two suitcases of clothes with the manager and bought herself a yellow holdall. She packed a second pair of jeans, a change of underwear, some shorts and tee shirts, and one cotton dress. She changed some travellers' cheques, said goodbye to the manager, and caught the local bus to Piraeus.

She found a small guest house near the harbour which charged only two thousand drachmae a night. Then for a week she wandered around the busy port of Piraeus, dodging the attentions of sailors, asking at cafés and shops if anyone had seen Nelson. She became a well-known figure – a topic of conversation. But on the whole, the café owners liked her and wanted to help her. She was also a good customer. They

56

thought she was probably looking for a lover who had jilted her. Or perhaps Nelson was really her father who had run off and left his family to starve.

She talked to everyone she met, either in Greek or English. It was during the evening of her fifth day in the port that two men joined her at her table where she was sitting alone eating olives and feta cheese. They were two middle-aged men who worked in warehouses checking inventories, the type one sees everywhere in busy towns – tired after a long day's work in a hot dirty shed. They wore white shirts with greasy collars, stained trousers and crumpled jackets. They took no notice of Bernie, happy to relax for five minutes and drink Metaxa.

When she interrupted their conversation, they were immediately suspicious. They were used to itinerant hippies and thought Bernie might want money. But after she had ordered a whole bottle of Metaxa and pushed it over in their direction, they were prepared to listen to her.

'We're not port officials, you know,' said the older of the two when she'd finished her story. 'We're only clerks. But everyone coming into Piraeus would have to go through Customs. Everyone has to; it's the law.'

'My friend didn't stay here. He always stayed on his yacht.'

'Even so, if he tied up in the Marina the customs men would know. They would want to see what he'd bought.' He poured himself out a glass of Metaxa, and passed the bottle to his friend.

After a moment, he said, 'Give me the name of the boat, and your friend's name. I'll try to make some enquiries. I know quite a few of the customs people. I can ask around and if anyone has seen your friend, I'll tell him to meet you here. Be here tomorrow around seven, and the same time the next day if he doesn't come tomorrow. Someone will be bound to remember him. We don't get many people sailing on their own around here.'

He picked up the bottle of Metaxa, and stood up. 'Thanks for this. And good luck.'

Once again she was on her own.

Bernie didn't notice the young Greek standing in the doorway of the café. It was two evenings since she'd spoken to the

57

clerks. She wasn't expecting anything to happen now. She'd have supper, and go back to her hotel. But the man by the door continued to stare at her, and eventually she became aware of his scrutiny. She turned to look at him. He was standing by the tub of geraniums – a young man, pale and uncertain. Finally he made up his mind, and came across to her table.

'You are looking for a Mr. Donelly,' he said in English.

She tried not to look too excited. 'Yes. He's a friend of mine. Do you know him?'

The man was suspicious. He was looking at her uncertainly. 'How well do you know him?' he asked.

For a second Bernie wondered whether she should give him some money, as she had seen people do in films. But she was not used to bribing people. Tipping, yes, but not handing over money to get information.

She told him to sit down, and called over the waiter. The man asked for *ouzo*. He looked very young, very thin, and in a strange way, frightened. The world had not treated him very well, she thought. He was like a dog who has been kicked around by everyone. She asked him his name.

'Demetrios Papadopoulos,' he said, after a moment's hesitation.

'And you've met Mr. Donelly?' she said patiently.

'Maybe' But what is he to you?'

'I'm his god-daughter. I was to meet him here a couple of weeks ago, and we were to go cruising. But he hasn't turned up. That's all.'

'I don't know where he is.' But the man was relaxing a little. She called for more *ouzo*. 'He did mention a friend he would have to contact. But that was a long time ago. The end of May.'

'So you have seen him this summer?' said Bernie. 'He must have mentioned his plans.' She tried to keep the excitement out of her voice.

'Rich men don't tell me their plans,' said the man. 'But Mr. Donelly was a very good man. A very generous man. He liked me to see to everything for him. He was going to come back here in June and leave everything in store until I could arrange to get the cases shipped over to America. But he

58

never came back. He was a collector, you know. He liked beautiful things, and he paid a lot of money for them. He liked people to be happy. When I told him I was buying a new house, and my wife was expecting her fourth child, he was very generous. I wouldn't want to tell you anything that would hurt Mr. Donelly, or cause him embarrassment.'

It was a hint Bernie couldn't ignore. When the waiter had left the table, she quietly took out a roll of drachmae and without counting them, passed them over to the man. Wordlessly, he slipped them into his trouser pocket.

'I can't tell you exactly where he is. I only know his plans from the last time I saw him. He planned to go to Alexandria. Then, in June, he wanted to sail north to the Aegean. There he was going to cruise about a bit, then come here and telephone a friend in Rome. That person is you, I see now.'

Bernie filled his glass. 'He didn't telephone. It's now July 20th. He was supposed to contact me in Rome on the second.'

The man shrugged his shoulders. 'Then he's somewhere in the Aegean. He has a wonderful boat. He's probably found a good place to stay. That's all.'

Bernie shook her head. 'He would never forget an appointment. Now, what route would a yachtsman take if he wanted to go north from here?'

For a moment the man thought. 'He would have to go along the eastern coast of Euboea. The western side is blocked by the bridge at Chalcis. He would keep to the coast because the winds can be strong in these waters and he was on his own.

'Now, the eastern coast of Euboea hasn't many good anchorages. In fact, none suitable for a small boat. He would have to go on to the sheltered waters of the Trikiri Channel. There are plenty of bays along that coast. He could have anchored anywhere along there. That's where you should go. He would have to go ashore for water, so someone is bound to have seen him.'

Bernie had taken out her note-book, and had made notes. Then she drew a quick sketch map of the eastern coast of Greece, as she remembered it. She passed it over to the man.

'Is that something like the coastline?'

He drew in a few lines. Euboea was larger than she

thought. 'Yes. When you find Mr. Donelly, give him my best wishes. Tell him the baby died.'

He got up and left the café, looking very young, and very unhappy.

Bernie was now certain that something had happened to Nelson. She was sure he was ill somewhere in a Greek hospital, desperately ill with a stroke or a heart attack, probably in some out of the way place where the hospital staff had never heard of a Consul or the American Embassy in Athens.

She paid the bill and went back to her guest house. The next day she bought a good map, a strong pair of walking shoes, and caught the bus to Chalcis.

Spiros' voice was rising to a shrill crescendo.

'Mr. Harding, sir, what's wrong with my house? Why don't you want to stay here? How can I make you happy? Is there anything you want? Anything?'

Nick looked at the man in exasperation. Why was Spiros taking his departure so personally? As a taverna owner, surely he was used to people coming and going. And it was obvious that if Nick was to stay on the island for any length of time, he would want more comfortable lodgings. Now he'd found a quiet room near his place of work, and wanted to move there as soon as possible. That was all. But he liked Spiros, and he had certainly done his best to make Nick comfortable. Nothing, however, could disguise the fact that he was living in a taverna, and a popular one at that. There was a fair prospect that last night's party would be repeated as July drew into August. At four o'clock in the morning, Nick had decided to move into the Karakulas household, whatever he found there tonight.

But there was no doubt about it, Spiros was distressed by his decision. He was taking it very badly. Impulsively, Nick left his packing and went over to him. He put an arm around the Greek's shoulders.

'Look, Spiros, of course I like it here. But Markos has offered me more convenient accommodation, and it will be quieter. Now let me get on with my packing. Of course I'll see you again. I'll be here often to eat. Markos didn't mention board as well as lodging. Now why in God's name did I bring these shirts?'

Through force of habit, and in a fit of absent-mindedness, Nick had packed three good shirts. They were made of pure cotton, white with narrow stripes in pale blue, grey or red. He'd bought them in Austin Reed last spring. He wore them to conferences, and sometimes to lectures when senior academics were to be present. He had wanted to expunge the jeans image.

There were also three silk ties to match, which he'd bought in Simpson's of Piccadilly during a sale. Now he looked at them in blank astonishment. Whatever had given him the idea that he would need three shirts with matching ties on a Greek island in July and August?

'Anyone would think I came out her for a wedding, instead of archaeological restoration work.'

But Spiros had already picked one up, and was gazing at it in rapture – his former distress forgotten.

'What a beautiful shirt! It's perfect. Austin Reed! My word, I bought a jacket there when I went to London a few years ago. My cousin, you know, owns a restaurant in Wardour Street. Very expensive. He's a rich man. I should have stayed there. He wanted me to stay and give him a hand with the business, but I was too cautious. Now I'm finished. In a backwater. Even my English guests leave me. They leave me for a beautiful girl, I realise that. But I warn you, Miss Petra is not what she seems. She may be beautiful but she's difficult. She's not like a Greek girl. They are soft and loving and do as they're told. Miss Petra lives without love. Without a man, even. She's a clever girl. Too educated, I think. Daughters should stay at home not go off to university. It doesn't do to educate women. There's no knowing where it could lead to. But these shirts . . .'

He clasped them to him in ecstasy. Nick gave in.

'Take the shirts, Spiros. And the ties. I'm sure they'll fit you. We're almost the same size. And as for Miss Petra, let me put you right from the start. I only saw her briefly yesterday and she didn't stop and talk. However "soft and loving" she might be, it would be of no interest to me. I'm a married man, Spiros, and too old for girls like Petra so just forget that idea. I'm leaving because I've been offered more convenient accommodation, and to be honest with you, I like to get six or

61

seven hours sleep a night. I have a job to do here, and want to be finished by the end of August. Last night's party was wonderful. I enjoyed your guests. But, alas, parties and work don't mix. Now take the shirts, I won't need them, but let me get on.'

Spiros was still speechless with gratitude. He picked up the shirts one by one, and held them against him. Nick draped the ties round his neck and Spiros walked over to the mirror.

'There you are,' said Nick cheerfully. 'The perfect English gentleman. Think what they're going to do for business.'

'Mr. Harding,' said Spiros, suddenly serious, 'I could be Mayor in these. Mayor of Alonnisos. Everyone will envy me. The girls will love me,' he added as an afterthought.

Nick smiled at the man's vanity, and added two pairs of woollen socks to the pile.

'And these? For me? Look, they are hardly worn. You are a good man, Mr. Harding, and my friend. You will come often to my taverna and drink *ouzo*? No charge, you know that. And I wish you luck with Miss Petra. She's certainly beautiful, and made for love. But difficult.' He sighed, as if remembering some past experience.

'Let me have the bill for my stay here, and for the car. I shall hang on to that. I might get out and have a look at the rest of the island.'

Spiros was still gazing at himself in the mirror. 'No charge for your stay here. Perhaps something for the car. My friend will expect something. I will fix it. You give me what you think. He'll be happy with that.'

Nick closed the zip of his holdall and took a roll of notes from his pocket.

'Here, take this.' He didn't know how much was there, but thought about twenty pounds. 'Now I must get off but I'll be around at lunch-time. Let me know if there's any more to pay.'

Spiros followed him to the car, still over-whelming him with thanks. Nick flung his bag into the back and drove off to 'his' bay. Looking back at Spiros, draped in his ties, he thought irreverently that he looked not unlike a Minoan Snake goddess. Just replace the trousers with a skirt, and take off the shirt!

62

Chapter 7

The woman stood watching Nick as he climbed up the steep path from the beach to the house. She waited for him until he was near enough for her to take his bag. She had to be Petra's mother, he decided. Her hair was the same colour, but now dimmed by streaks of grey. She had tied it back into a loose knot, and here and there strands had escaped and curled round her face and on to her neck. She was a handsome blonde woman of around fifty with smooth fair skin, well protected from the sun, and capable strong hands. She had neat, unvarnished finger-nails. She wore a long, rust-coloured skirt down to the ground, and a white cotton blouse with a lace trimming round the low peasant neckline. She looked not unlike the senior professors' wives he knew in Brighton. Her feet, as he had suspected, were in leather sandals; her toe-nails unpainted.

She smiled warmly at him and shook his hand.

'I'm Elisavet,' she said. 'Elisavet Karakulos. Marcos told me you were coming.' Then she led him into the house. 'There is a road, you know,' she said, as they went into the long cool hall. 'It leads down from the top of the cliff. It's quite safe for cars. We use it all the time.'

'I thought there must be. But my car is quite all right for the time being down under the olive trees. I enjoyed the climb. This is a fantastic place.'

She smiled with pleasure at his enthusiasm.

'Thank you. We like it. My husband and Markos built it between them when we first came to live here in the seventies. Most of the other buildings on the island had been destroyed

63

by the earthquake in 1969, so we were able to take our pick of the sites. There was a small farm here before.

'Let me take you to your room now. We usually meet outside on the terrace around seven for a drink before dinner. There's no hurry. Markos isn't back yet.'

His room was on the first floor, at the end of a corridor. As he entered it he was aware of coolness and quiet. White-washed walls like a monk's cell, a small shuttered window and a single bed. He noticed a dressing table which would do double duty as a desk, and two chairs. She put his bag down on the bed, and went across to open the shutters. Immediately the room was flooded with warm scented air. In the distance, coming from somewhere down below the house, there was the sound of goat-bells.

He joined her at the window. Below, the cliff shelved gently down to the sea. Sure enough, he saw the goat herd bringing the flock back home for the night, the bells calling them to evening service.

This part of the cliff had been intensively cultivated. Olive trees and vines grew in orderly rows. To the right of the house was a vegetable patch full of tomatoes, and what looked to him like rows of potatoes. The last time he's seen those lush green tops was in his father's allotment in Newcastle. Someone in the household liked gardening. And he suspected it was Elisavet, Petra's mother.

'It's perfect. I feel I have come home. You'll never get rid of me, I warn you.'

She laughed, a full uninhibited sound, the laughter of someone who enjoys life to the full.

'In that case, I shall leave you to unpack and make yourself at home. The shower room is next door. To the right, as you go out.'

She still spoke with a strong German accent. Germans, he suspected, like the British, have difficulty in burying their nationality.

After she'd gone, he unpacked his few possessions and went back to the window. It was strange, he thought, how quickly he had settled in to this place. He had come to the island as a result of a tempting offer from a stranger, an opportunity to distance himself from an unbearable domestic

64

situation. He hadn't expected much. Just a chance to escape and lick his wounds, and think about the future. And now he was already beginning to feel as if he had always lived here. That his home was here. Rottingdean, his job, his sad-eyed wife, were all a part of some previous existence. Now they were behind him, beyond his control.

He looked round the room. It was the sort of place he dreamed about. An austere bed with a simple pine frame that could have been hand-made. A peacock blue bed-spread, made in some rough cotton material probably woven locally. A tiled floor with a rug by the side of the bed, brown and cream, with a Greek design. A bookcase, which he hadn't seen when he first came in. It was full of books, most of them in English. He picked out a volume of Shakespeare and thumbed the pages. Someone had been reading it seriously, and had underlined passages in pencil. There were a couple of local histories and a map of Alonnisos, a collected Milton and several paperbacks. Iris Murdoch and Graham Greene. It was an eclectic selection of books. Someone in the household liked English literature.

Over his bed hung an icon in a black and gold frame. He walked over to it and looked at it closely. It might be old. True the golden halos around the heads of the Madonna and Child were untarnished but that could have been due to the skill of the original painter.

He used the shower, and came back into his room to look for something suitable to wear for the evening. Now he'd given Spiros his respectable shirts, he was left with only one long-sleeved garment. Soon, he thought, he'd have to go to Skopelos and buy another. Not for the first time he cursed his impulsiveness. He combed his hair, noticed that his face had caught the sun, and then went down to join the others on the terrace.

Petra was already there, standing by a tall man who was obviously her father. There was no sign of Markos. Elisavet came in as if on cue, carrying a tray with five glasses on it. She came forward and introduced Nick to the other two. Petra had indeed inherited her mother's looks. Only her eyes were different, and her skin was tanned to the shade of a ripe apricot. Her eyes were not the bright blue he'd expected, but the deep brown of a Greek. That evening they glowed with interest, and he was moved by her beauty. She wore a simple bright blue cotton skirt, and a low-necked blouse like her mother's. It had the same trimming around the neck-line, and he suspected that they were both made by the same person. Either Elisavet, or someone locally. Petra reminded him straightaway of his own students. There was a detached thoughtfulness about her, as if she was studying him closely, trying to weigh him up. A clever girl, he thought. And beautiful, And, as Spiros had said, she might well be 'difficult'.

There was nothing difficult about Andrikos Karakulas, though. He was an unforgettable man, larger than life quite literally as he stood well over six feet tall, and was strongly built. He wore his thick mane of grey hair long, down to his shoulders, and his curling beard flecked with white reminded Nick of the sea-god, Poseidon. His clothes, too, were unconventional, the clothes of a man certain of himself and sure of his position in the community. He wore a loose linen jacket, belted at the waist, baggy trousers and sandals. He looked, Nick thought, a cross between a Judo instructor and one of his more liberal academic colleagues.

The welcome was like the man, warm and vigorous.

'Welcome to our house,' he said. And then, with a roar of laughter, 'That sounds very patriarchal, doesn't it? Forgive me for being pompous. It's a habit I'm acquiring with advancing years.'

'Nonsense, Father,' said Petra. 'It's a habit you've always had. It's just that tonight you look more like a Biblical prophet than usual. Mr. Harding will forgive you, I'm sure. He must be used to prophets amongst his academic colleagues.'

Nick looked at her sharply, detecting blue-stockinged waspishness. Her father, however, put an arm round her, and Nick realised that he was used to her teasing. Father and daughter, he saw, were very close.

So he entered into the spirit of the game, and said with a smile, 'Naturally. All academics like to be thought of as prophets, even if they don't look like them. But thank you for your welcome. I'm sure I shall be most happy here.'

Elisavet had come back with a collection of bottles. To

Nick's surprise the wine she poured out was not the resin-flavoured wine of the islands but a sophisticated and full-bodied wine from the Rhineland. Andrikos must have noticed his surprise because he said, 'Yes, my wife likes her German comforts. Most of them, needless to say, I regard as unnecessary. But I like to indulge her. She is the wife of my old age,' he said pedantically, 'and I spoil her. And my daughter, too.

'But I must admit I approve of this particular extravagance. I like German wine. You can grow tired of the Greek variety after a time, although we drink it most days. We keep this mainly for guests, and drink it ourselves on holidays. My wife orders it from her native Cologne, and her family arranges the transport.

'At least this wine is better than her potatoes,' he went on. 'She has a thoroughly Teutonic passion for the vegetable and tries to grow them here, in Alonnisos. But they're not the same as the ones she remembers back home. She would dearly love to import the seed potatoes from Germany, but that's not possible. So she forces them to grow in the sandy soil of Agios Demetrios, and you will eat them tonight. But don't worry, they're not too bad.

'Whatever made her marry an old Greek like me, I can't imagine. Just think of it: to leave her family in Cologne and come and live here with an ageing satyr twenty years her senior.'

Elisavet came across to her husband and put an arm round his shoulders.

'I married you because I fell in love with that ageing satyr, as you call yourself. And I have never regretted it, even if I do have to live without proper potatoes. But I shall never go back to Cologne. I'm here to stay now.'

Andrikos kissed her and stroked her hair. Nick was strangely touched by their evident love for each other. He looked away for a moment and caught Petra watching him, her eyes alight with amusement.

'I've finished with ambition,' said Andrikos as he motioned Nick to sit down on one of the cane chairs. 'I leave all that to Markos now. I've got enough money to live on. Not much, but enough to do all the things I want to do. I've sent Petra

67

away to Athens, to the university there, to pick up some education. I'm over seventy now, and want no more from life than this. A good house, built by myself and my son. The love of a good wife and daughter, and a decent bottle of wine. And friends, of course.' He raised his glass to Nick at this point, who returned the compliment.

'Soon I shall be ready to say the Nunc Dimittis and depart in peace. I have no regrets and no guilt. So I am a happy man, am I not?

'But now there is only left this daughter of mine. All I want to see is Petra settled with a good man and then I can spoil my grand-children. But she's not like her Greek cousins, who were all married at her age. This one insists on working for her living, and rejects all the nice men I find her. That's what comes of educating your daughters, Nick.'

'But you wanted me educated, Father. You shouldn't have sent me away to Athens if you wanted a dutiful stay-at-home daughter for your old age.'

'I sent you away to learn philosophy. Wisdom, in other words. Not to teach sailing to a lot of decadent tourists.'

'Is that whay you do?' said Nick, accepting a second glass of wine from Elisaver and helping himself to olives.

'Yes, in the season. Most mornings I go to Patiteri. There's a sailing school there. It's a growth industry, water sports. If Markos can go ahead with his building project, I could probably set up in business here, in Agios Demetrios. Tourists who come out here always want to learn how to manage a boat, and how to look at fish underwater. Now the airport's opened up in Skiathos, tourism is steadily increasing. We need more local attractions. There are the flotilla companies, of course, but they're not home-grown, so to speak.'

'You didn't have to learn philosophy to teach what you've been able to do since you were a child,' grumbled Andrikos. 'She could always swim like a seal,' he added for Nick's benefit.

'Only because Yannis taught me. You've met him?' she said, turning to look at Nick, who nodded. 'He's the son of one of our local fishermen. His brain was damaged at birth but he understands everything.'

'And thank God he goes with you on your mad expeditions,' said a new voice behind them. It was Markos, very businesslike in a blue suit with white shirt and patterned tie.

'Forgive me,' he said to Nick, 'for not being here to welcome you. I was held up.'

He took a glass of wine from Elisavet, smiled his thanks, and sat down next to Nick.

'I'm glad you've come,' he said. 'We need new faces. But how's the work coming along? You've made a start, of course?'

They talked easily and naturally about Nick's work, and the importance of marine archaeology. It was a subject which interested everyone. Markos and Petra were both keen scuba divers, and had been down to the Roman wreck off the island of Iura.

'Then you must have been down to see the wreck in the bay? Rochester's wreck, the one I'm working on. Or rather the amphorae removed from the yacht. The water isn't too deep out there, I've been told. Otherwise my two divers wouldn't be able to manage.'

Petra looked thoughtfully at Nick. 'No, we haven't been down. We're not allowed to see it. It's a private yacht, I understand, and it's closely guarded. We wondered at first whether you would be sociable. We never see anyone connected with that wreck, and no-one knows anything about it. I suppose the things on it are very precious and the salvage people are alarmed in case anything should get stolen. But as you know, we are very honest in these islands. We would never touch anyone's possessions. Your things will be quite safe down in that hut on the shore. It's sad, really, as the things on the yacht are Greek, I understand, and yet we can't look at them. It seems terrible that they have been bought up by an American collector, and will be shipped back to the States, and we can never see them. It makes us angry.'

'But at least you can come and see what I'm doing,' said Nick impulsively, feeling deeply ashamed of the selfishness of his American employers. 'It's ridiculous that this yacht is "guarded", as you say. One day we'll all go there and have a look it. I can just about manage a scuba outfit. We'll go one evening, when the divers have gone home.'

69

'And Yannis can come with us, and save us if we get into difficulties,' said Markos.

Elisavet had been quietly bringing in platefuls of food and now the meal began. It was delicious, an esoteric mixture of Greek and German cooking. A plateful of *mézes* to start with: pieces of fried liver, olives, and Greek cheese. Then veal with potatoes, and a pudding made of honey and almonds. A Turkish recipe, Elisavet said.

It was when they reached the coffee stage that Markos told them that he'd failed to raise money locally for his business venture.

'Tomorrow,' he announced, 'I'm going to Athens for a few days.' He looked as gloomy as if he'd announced he was going to the moon.

'So far?' said Nick, who was also coming to regard Skiathos as the end of the world.

'For money it is necessary,' said Markos sadly. 'I've come to the end of my last loan, and I shall have to go further afield. It costs a great deal to transport and work with stone. When we built this house, labour was cheaper. It was just after the earthquake and people wanted work, and wanted to see the island rebuilt. Now it's difficult to get local labour. A good stone worker costs as much as a car worker in an English factory, and as for carpenters – they're like gold dust.

"But when the villas are built, the bank will get its money back. We can't lose. Meanwhile we need to pay our workers and the freight on materials brought over from the mainland. It's dispiriting to have to go to banks cap in hand but I might find someone in Athens prepared to back me. These islands are going to develop and it's important that they do so with a proper respect for the natural setting. Look what's happened to the Spanish coast. Get a load of foreign property developers here and it will be the end of the Sporades as we know them. It's a job for a local man with local knowledge.'

Darkness fell as the meal drew to a close. Petra lit the lamp, and they sat together in a companionable circle watching the moths roast their wings on the glass lamp shade. Petra was the first to leave. As she got up to go, Nick invited her to inspect his work on the following afternoon. She was obviously interested.

70

'We saw your hut yesterday, but didn't want to intrude. I'm very curious to see how you set about restoring the urns. I have to go to Patiteri in the morning but will come down to see you in the afternoon. After siesta time, Mr. Harding', she added with a smile.

'I will let you come and inspect my work only on one condition,' he said with mock seriousness.

'And what's that?' she said in some surprise.

'Only if you call me Nick.'

'Goodnight, Nick,' she said dutifully as she kissed her parents and Markos.

When Nick stood up to leave, Markos got up too.

'Come, Nick,' he said, 'Let's have a nightcap, as you say in England and then let's stretch our legs in the garden before we turn in.'

He filled two glasses with *ouzo*. Nick said goodnight to his host and hostess and followed Markos down the steps into the garden. For a few moments the two men stood there in silence, looking out to sea. Markos seemed at a loss for words and it was Nick who took the initiative, sensing that his companion wanted to say something of importance.

'You have an enviable house here, Markos,' he said. 'And a wonderful family. You must be very proud of them. I would wish for nothing better.'

'Except that this place belongs to my father. I am only a lodger here. I need my own place again. I can't live on my father's generosity forever.'

'What happened to your own place, Markos?'

He remained silent for a few moments, then turned to look at Nick. 'I had a wife once, and a small son. Both drowned out there one day, in the straits. It was a freak storm, like the one that capsized Rochester's yacht. They do happen from time to time, and that is why these waters are dangerous. It's for this reason that I like Yannis to go out with Petra. He might be inarticulate, but he knows everything one can know about the sea. He can actually smell bad weather approaching and we always take notice of him. He's the best weather forecaster we've got around here. Even the fishermen respect him.

'But back to my story. When the funeral was over I tried to live alone, but it was not possible. The house had too many

71

memories. I thought I might go mad with the loneliness. When my parents invited me to live with them, it seemed an obvious solution. So I sold my house, put the money into the business, and came to live here. The money laid the foundations, so to speak, of my present scheme. Only it wasn't enough.'

'But what about yourself, Nick? I understand your wife might be joining you out here. Forgive me for asking. It's not out of vulgar curiosity, just interest.'

'Yes, I have a wife,' said Nick lightly. 'At the moment she seems light years away. Maybe she'll join me but I doubt it. She has her own interests in England. There's not much for her to do out here and she hates sitting in the sun.'

In the nearby bush a night bird burst into song. Overhead the moon had risen, and flooded the garden with light. Somewhere under the same moon was Marian. Was she happy? Did she want him to return?

'Your wife, Nick. Is she beautiful?'

He thought for a while and then said, 'Once, a long while ago. Now, she's just – ' He hesitated. 'A little tired. She's older than me. She likes a quiet life.'

He turned to go back into the house. Suddenly the garden had lost its charm. He wanted to sleep. Things would look brighter in the morning.

Markos, however, lingered behind and Nick turned to him impatiently.

'Look, forgive me, but I must go to bed. I have a lot of work ahead of me. Let's talk tomorrow. One day I'll tell you all about Marian and me, but not now.'

'Nick, forgive me. Your private affairs are your own concern. But tomorrow I'm off to Athens for a few days. I have to go, but Petra – I love her very much. We all do. Please remember she is very young, and very impulsive. I couldn't bear to think that she might get hurt, and by someone we have invited into the house. Please, she is a child. She has known very few men. Maybe in Athens, I don't know. But in any case they would have been students, like she was. I can see she likes you, Nick, but she is not for you. You're not free, so please, I beg of you, don't encourage her.'

Nick stood there, speechless with astonishment. First

72

Spiros and now Markos. What did they think he was? A seducer of young girls? Did he look that depraved? He felt a surge of anger and rounded on Markos.

'Forget it, Markos. I'm here to do a job. The last thing I want is woman trouble. Yes, your sister is a beauty. But no, I'm not interested. And you've got a bloody cheek suggesting I might be so dishonourable! I know how you and your countrymen feel about their women, and I wouldn't for one minute want to hurt your sister. Tomorrow I shall show her my work, and then we will hardly meet again. Now, please, let me go to bed. You can go to your bloody Athens with a peaceful mind as far as I'm concerned. Good night.'

He turned and left the dark figure standing in the garden. In his room he walked to the window and looked out over the darkening sea. The wind was getting up, Not much, just enough to agitate the pine trees. Somewhere nearby a dog barked, then another. Then there was silence. He undressed quickly and got into bed. He was asleep before Markos blew out the light on the terrace.

Spiros always took an afternoon siesta. Every day between three and four he retired to his bedroom at the back of the taverna with his wife Alexia. But every Friday she went to Patiteri to look after her old mother and father. She was a local girl. All her family lived in Patiteri.

It was then that Spiros took Katerina to his bed. Katerina, the young, dark-skinned daughter of Lycurgos, who owned four fishing boats. Katerina, full-breasted and smooth-skinned, who loved him passionately. She already had two children whom Spiros supported. He felt certain that Alexia knew of the arrangement, but she tactfully asked no questions. Probably, when her parents died, she would find other members of her family to look after on Friday afternoons.

But on that Friday, two days after Nick had moved in with the Karakulas family, Katerina hadn't come to see him. She'd sent a message that old Lycurgos had been taken ill, and she had to wait for the doctor to come from Patiteri. So Spiros was alone in his room. It was hot; the window was open, and he was tired. He must be getting old, he thought as he dropped off to sleep. For once he didn't miss Katerina. He was glad to be on his own.

73

At half-past three he woke up suddenly. Someone was in the room. Someone was watching him. He sat up in alarm and looked towards the door. Takis was there, sitting on the chair watching him. Spiros felt a sudden stab of fear. He was frightened of Takis. There was something inhuman about the man. He hated his pale, inscrutable face, the purple-shadows under the eyes, the sleek black hair. But above all he hated the eyes which gave nothing away. Just expressionless pools.

He wasn't frightened of Giorgios who was sitting at the end of his bed. He was strong and therefore useful but Spiros knew that he was in fact a coward. He'd leave Takis to face the mob if he saw a way out for himself. But he had the muscle.

Spiros sat up in bed. This was not the usual visiting hour. In fact they had never come to see him together before.

'What is it?' he whispered. 'What do you want?'

'The Englishman,' said Giorgios. 'You were told to hold on to him. Where is he?'

'With the Karakulas family. I couldn't keep him here. He wanted to go.'

Spiros relaxed and lay back on his pillow. It was all right. There were no new plans.

'You disobeyed Magnus. He's very angry.'

'Tell him to go to hell. How can I keep a man here against his will.'

He turned over to go back to sleep.

Takis got up. He made some sign to Giorgios and they went over to Spiros who was naked under the thin sheet. Together, they dragged him over to the little wooden table where Alexia always put a vase of flowers. Almost tenderly, Giorgios lifted the vase and put in on the floor. The lilies were top heavy and fell over spilling the water over the rug.

Then Giorgios dragged Spiros forward and laid his hand on the table, palm downwards. Before Spiros could open his mouth to scream, Takis had drawn out a knife – a stiletto dagger – and stabbed him through the hand. There was a sickening crunch as the knife smashed through the bone and Spiros was crucified to the table. His metatarsal bone was shattered. The pain was excruciating. Spiros fainted.

Minutes later, he came to. Someone had laid him on his

74

bed. Blood was streaming down on to the floor. He couldn't move his hand.

'A warning, that's all,' said Takis, who was standing there looking at him. 'Next time it will be both hands, but cut off at the wrists. Now do as you're told and you'll not get hurt. Tomorrow there's to be another delivery. Be in your usual place. We left your right hand whole because you'll need that. Not a word to anyone, and watch that Englishman. Do you understand?'

The men left the way they'd come, through the window. Spiros wept tears of pain and humiliation. It would be several weeks before his hand healed.

He told everyone that he'd fallen over in the vineyard, and had put out a hand to save himself and impaled it on an old vine stalk. Everyone believed him. It was the obvious explanation.

Chapter 8

'When is your wife coming to join you, Nick?' said Petra suddenly. It was two weeks after he'd met her at that first dinner. She was in his workshed carefully washing a plate which had broken neatly into two pieces.

Nick looked at her in some surprise. She hadn't asked him about his personal affairs before. Sometimes she asked about the pieces of pottery she was washing, questions mainly of a technical nature as she knew a great deal about Classical civilization. She was a good worker, and Nick had grown used to her visits. It was like having a student working for him again. She didn't look at Nick when she asked about his wife. Her hair had fallen over her face, so he couldn't see her expression.

He went over to look at her work. The plate was one she had particularly admired. A perfect, black-glazed dish with red and white representations of athletes round the rim.

'She's got her own work to do. She runs a couple of antique shops, and can't really afford to take the time off. July and August are her busy times.'

'But she could sit here and watch you work. And there's always the sea when it gets too hot. Surely she'd love things like this plate, if she deals in antiques?'

Nick fought down a sudden vision of Marian sobbing in her bed, the pillow case smeared with her lipstick.

'Perhaps she didn't want to come. Perhaps we don't get on as well as we should. She's probably a lot happier on her own.'

He turned back to the job he was doing, slightly resenting Petra's inquisition. He didn't want to talk about Marian. He

76

was happy. Happier than he'd ever been before. The weather was perfect, the *Meltemi* had held off, and he had a delightful and intelligent helper.

The dark figure by the door of the hut stirred slightly, and pulled his hat down over his face. The sun was still strong.

'The watch dog's back,' said Nick. 'He'll not let you go far.'

Yannis came down to the hut each day, arriving just a few minutes after Petra. It was almost as if he'd spent the day waiting for her to come back from Patiteri and go down to the hut. At first Nick had resented his intrusion, but as Yannis never interfered with their work, and never came inside the hut unless invited, he had grown accustomed to him. He had his uses. He helped them clear up at the end of the day, and fetched clean water from the stream whenever Petra asked him. He took no notice of Nick, pretending he'd not heard an order until Petra gave it to him. All the same, Nick felt a prickle of annoyance when he arrived. It looked as if Yannis didn't trust him.

Yesterday, Yannis had been particularly obstreperous. It had given Nick a glimpse into the darker corners of the man's mind. The incident occurred at the end of the afternoon. Petra had picked up a piece of pottery that she had admired earlier in the afternoon. Nick had taken it away from her, merely to estimate the size of the break. For a second Petra, who was trying to identify one of the classical figures, resisted. To the astonishment of both of them, Yannis had leapt into the hut, pushed Nick violently in the chest, and seized hold of the plate. Then he had handed it back to Petra. It was only a small incident, and Petra had laughed it off, but suddenly Nick had felt uneasy. He felt sure that had Yannis possessed a knife he would have plunged it into Nick without a second thought. He had a glimpse of a streak of jealousy which alarmed him.

At Petra's reprimand, Yannis had slunk back to his place outside the door, and Nick had ignored the incident. They had packed up in silence, Petra coolly ordering Yannis to go up to the house ahead of them. Nick had half expected him not to come the next day but he was here as if nothing had happened.

Petra seemed to have forgiven Yannis. She smiled as she looked at the silent figure by the door.

'We mustn't be too hard on him. He loves me, that's all. And he doesn't know you, so how can he trust you?'

'How long have you known him?' said Nick, suddenly feeling desperately sorry for Yannis and regretting his irritation over yesterday's incident.

'Since I was a child. At first Elisavet was frightened of him. But she got used to him, and now the family encourage him. He's never hurt anyone in his life. He always kept watch over me when I was a child. The funny thing is, no-one knows how old he is. He's always looked the same to me. His father, Apostolis, thinks he must be about forty but he's not sure. Yannis was his third son. All the others were normal but Yannis was strange from the start. His mother had a troublesome pregnancy, and a difficult birth. He's one of nature's mistakes but he's always been very attached to me. He has a sort of sixth sense where I'm concerned and he worries when I'm away. We had a terrible job explaining to him that I wasn't leaving forever when I went to Athens.'

Then she picked up the plate she was working on, and called Yannis to fetch more water. Everything was back to normal.

Nick's life had settled down to an orderly routine. Each morning he started work early, as there was a lot to do. The pile of potsherds never seemed to diminish, and it was work that couldn't be hurried. Each piece of pottery had to be washed, catalogued, identified, and fitted together. Around twelve, Takis and Giorgios appeared, carrying a fresh basket of pottery which they dumped casually on the floor just inside the hut. Then they nodded to Nick and went back to the boat.

He had soon given up trying to be sociable but there was a lot he wanted to ask them, especially about diving. Once, he'd asked them if they had seen the Roman wreck in Iura, but all they'd said was: 'We know nothing.'

After that, he stopped asking questions.

Both Petra and Nick had been curious to see how the crates were collected in the evening. Nick would pack his day's work in straw in the empty crates, and he usually left before anyone came to pick them up. But one day, he and Petra waited to see what happened. They sent Yannis on up to the house. He had set off reluctantly, only to wait for them halfway up the hill.

78

They hadn't had long to wait. It had all been very straight-forward. A grey van had driven out of the olive grove and backed up to the hut. Then two men, not Takis and Giorgios, using a fork lift loader, lifted the crates into the van. Then they carried two empty crates into the hut to replace the ones they had taken away. They then drove off towards the main road that ran along the top of the cliff. Petra and Nick had been slightly puzzled at the fork lift loader, as the crates weren't very heavy and the two men could have lifted them easily between them. But, as Nick said, when one worked for rich men, money was no object, and someone was doing well out of Rochester's heir.

This afternoon they worked on later than usual. They were both engrossed in their work when Yannis stumbled into the hut. Nick looked up in surprise as no-one had asked him to come in. He walked over to Petra and admired the designs on the pots. Sometimes she put aside some of the more attractive pieces to show Yannis as she knew he liked to see them, but previously he had always waited for her to ask him. That afternoon he seemed restless and picked up one of the potsherds, trying to say something to Petra. Then, as she didn't understand him, he became very agitated, making the same sound over and over again.

'What's the fool trying to say?' said Nick, annoyed at the interruption and thinking Yannis was just trying to get Petra's attention as she hadn't spoken to him that afternoon.

'I don't know,' she said. 'But whatever it is, it must be important. He's not usually like this. Now calm down, Yannis. What is it? Slowly now. It's no good getting excited.'

The poor man continued to grope for words, and in spite of his resentment, Nick felt a wave of pity. He watched as Yannis walked round the hut, tearing his hair in frustration as he tried desperately to communicate. Then an idea came to him. He walked over to Petra, and pointed to the bracelet which she always wore on her left arm. It was a particularly beautiful gold bracelet, engraved with traditional Greek designs, which her father had given to her. Nick had admired it on the first afternoon she'd come down to join him. Now Yannis was pointing to the bracelet, and was saying the word over and over again. His face was wreathed in smiles. He

79

seized Petra's arm, and stroked the bracelet. Nick felt suddenly annoyed. Petra shouldn't let him touch her like that, he thought. Then dismissed the idea as unworthy of him. Poor Yannis had to touch and feel. It was the only was he could communicate.

By now Yannis was shaking with excitement. He took hold of Petra's hand, and led her over to the basket of potsherds which Takis had left that day. He stood there, pointing to the basket and then to Petra's bracelet, and repeating the word over and over again.

'Gold,' she said. 'Gold.' That's what he's trying to say. Where did you see the gold, Yannis?'

Instead of answering, Yannis continued to point at the basket. Nick and Petra stared at each other.

'Ask him if there was a boat,' said Nick. But Yannis shook his head. There was no boat. He took them outside, and pointed along the shore to the next bay. Not out to sea.

'Gold in a basket on the shore. How very odd.' For a second Nick thought hard, then he shrugged his shoulders. 'Come one, the mystery will solve itself. Yannis must have seen a fisherman wearing a gold watch. It's getting late. Time for our game of chess.'

Nick had started playing chess with Andrikos before supper. Andrikos always won, but Nick was determined to take at least one game before he left the island.

Petra tried to persuade Yannis to talk again but he had lost interest. He picked up the buckets to empty them, and waited as usual outside the hut.

'He's getting worse,' said Nick, as they climbed up to the house. 'Perhaps he ought to see a doctor. He's hallucinating.'

Petra said nothing but all her liveliness had gone. Nick put an arm round her shoulders. It seemed a perfectly natural thing to do. Fortunately, Yannis had gone on ahead and hadn't seen him.

'Don't worry,' he said. 'It's nothing.'

'Still, it's strange,' said Petra. 'Yannis is never wrong. He must have seen something. He never lies.'

A few days after Yannis's outburst, Petra came down to see Nick earlier than usual. She looked enchanting that day. She was wearing denim shorts, and a white shirt knotted at the front. She'd tied back her mane of tawny hair, and her feet were bare. Her eyes were bright with mischief.

'Nick, it's a perfect day. Let me take you out in the boat. Not for long, but you ought to see the coastline. There are some fantastic caves.'

He looked at the pile of potsherds he was sorting, then at Petra. The invitation was irresistible.

'OK. Work over for today. Lead on.'

Together they raced over the sand towards the little white boat. Mast and sail were already in place, and it was the work of moments to pull it down the beach into the water. Nick paused for a moment to look at the great blue eye painted on the bow. This was the *oculos* which Mediterranean fishermen have painted on the side of their boats from time immemorial. Nick knew it had originated in Egypt at the time of the Pharaohs. The eye, used by the Greeks to ward off evil spirits, was the Eye of the Sun-God, the all powerful symbol of the Pharaohs. Now it was a common good luck sign. Girls wore the 'eye' round their necks, on a gold chain, to ward off bad luck. You could buy the charm in countless shops and stalls around the Mediterranean shores.

'How long have you had the boat?' said Nick as he held the boat steady for Petra to climb in.

'Three years. Markos got it for me. It's a local boat but he stripped it down and put on a modern rig. We can go practically anywhere in it. Hold her steady, and I'll put the sail up.'

The wind was fresh, blowing as usual from the north-west. As soon as the sail was set, Nick turned the boat towards the next island and they were off. A shout from the shore made them both look round. A tall ungainly figure was running towards them over the sand. He was waving his arms frantically, like the sails of a windmill. Over the noise of the sail and the wind, they heard the one word, 'Stop.'

But Nick hauled in the main sheet, and the boat raced over the waves. 'You're too late,' he called back. 'We won't be long.'

As they watched, they saw Yannis stumble over his twisted feet and sprawl headlong in the sand.

'Stop, Nick,' shouted Petra. 'Wait for him. He always comes with me.'

But Nick was determined that this afternoon he would have Petra to himself. He was tired of the watch-dog, and tired of the implication that he was not to be trusted. So he urged the boat on, grinning at Petra who was looking back towards the beach.

'Nick, we should have stopped. He'll be so upset.'

'Not this afternoon,' shouted Nick. 'No watch-dogs. No jealousy. No responsibilities.'

He had learned to sail off the coast of Crete. He had also raced with his brother-in-law in the Solent. He loved the sport. He wasn't afraid of the wind, which to him meant power. Like all people who sail, he was an incurable romantic. Without a doubt an engine would have got them to the caves more quickly. It would certainly get them home again faster and with less effort. But an engine would have shattered the spell of that golden afternoon. The coastline would have looked ordinary, and the gods would have slept.

'Where's Markos' boat?' said Nick, as they rounded the headland.

'In Steni Vala, tied to the jetty. He likes to go fishing. He'll have more time to take it out now, since he hasn't got a loan. He might have to think of becoming a fisherman again. He's like a bear with a sore head when he's not got enough to do. His boat is a great ugly wooden thing with a powerful engine. Thirty horsepower, I think. He's no romantic. He likes to get to places as quickly as possible.'

The wind was freshening appreciably, and Petra kept close to the shore. She had learnt to be cautious. The straits between Peristera and Alonnisos were flecked with white horses.

'Where's Rochester's boat?' said Nick suddenly. 'Out there?'

'Yes. Sometimes at night you can see the light on the buoy which marks the spot. I suppose it must be a mile or so away. The water around here is very deep; but out there, the yacht came to rest on a shelf. Fortunately, really, otherwise the divers couldn't have got to it. The water can be very turbulent in that shallow part when the *Meltemi* blows. She must have foundered in those wild seas.'

82

'Let's go and have a look at the place.'

'Perhaps, but not today. The wind is too strong and we'll never get back. And as a matter of fact there's nothing to see, so Markos tells me. The water is too deep to see the yacht. You'd have to go down.'

'Can you dive?'

'Yes, of course, with the right equipment. But we would have to borrow Markos' boat and equipment. This one is too small for all the stuff. Another problem is that the diving team out there don't like visitors.'

'I can't imagine why.'

'Well, they're there every day like two sentries. Maybe when all the pots are off the boat, they'll try to lift it. Markos says it would be quite easy. The water's only about two hundred and fifty feet out there.'

They had reefed the sail before they set off, and as the wind freshened, as it often did in the late afternoon, they raced along the coast. But near the cliffs they were caught in mysterious currents that swirled them dangerously near the rocks. Once Nick caught a glimpse of a whirl-pool. It was then that Petra insisted on taking the helm. She knew these waters and didn't want to take any chances.

'Watch out for Charybdis,' he shouted.

'Don't worry. That rock over there is far more dangerous. Scylla sits there every Sunday afternoon, and plucks sailors out of their boats. She eats them for tea. You must never come here on a Sunday.'

It didn't seem too fanciful to believe in the ancient legends that afternoon. The coastline of Alonnisos ws riddled with dark caves – the homes of monsters and mythical beasts. Landslides had hurled great rocks into the sea, where they sat like brooding sea beasts. A series of volcanic eruptions had opened up huge rifts in the limestone cliffs, hurling boulders into the inlets. The soil in these rifts was a different colour from the rest of the coastline. It was red, like the soil of Devon. The sand in the bays was the colour of burnt ochre not the silver white sand of their own bay.

'Come and see the Kraken,' shouted Petra, her eyes dancing with excitement. 'We can just make it but it will be hard work on the way home.'

At the eastern end of the island, the headland had crumbled away into the sea. Some subterranean convulsion had hurled the rocks around to form the outline of a sleeping sea-beast, a mighty Loch Ness monster crouched on the surface of the sea, almost blocking the passage between Alonnisos and the island of Iura. At one end, a huge snout reared out of the water. Two small caves on either side of the head formed a pair of sightless eyes. The rest of the body uncurled across the sea to join the headland.

'The Kraken,' shouted Petra. 'Waiting for Poseidon to summon him. No wonder the ancients believed in the gods. Look, faces everywhere. Watching us.'

It was a tortured coastline, riddled with caves. Some opened directly into the sea – dark holes, like the eyes of sleeping giants. Some opened further up the cliffs. In some places wild thyme and rosemary had managed to find a foothold on the rocky protuberances between the caves which then looked even more like faces sprouting repulsive fungus.

The wind had dropped for a moment, and Petra used the oars to row up to one of the caves. It was larger than the others. A huge gaping mouth, its interior as smooth and glistening as the inside of a whale's throat. Into this hole the sea surged and retreated, as if the beast was constantly sucking in great mouthfuls of water.

'The cave of Cyclops,' whispered Petra. 'We could go inside, but I haven't brought a torch. It would also be a lot safer in Markos' boat. The cave narrows quite suddenly at the back, and it's possible to get stuck. The tunnel goes back a long way into the hills. Sometimes, when the wind blows from the south, the sea is forced right up the cave and bursts out of holes way up the hillside. It's a weird sight when you're not expecting it. Once, one of these water spouts burst up out of the ground directly in front of me. It could have been dangerous, as there's never any warning.'

Nick peered into the huge interior. He could just make out the faint sheen of stalagmites and stalactites, like broken teeth, along the inside of the mouth. The only sounds were the eerie sighing of the water as it was sucked into the cave, and another sound which at first he couldn't identify: a frantic high-pitched wine. Almost an electronic sound, as if made by a small generator.

'Bats,' whispered Petra. 'Millions of them. We've disturbed them.'

The wind had freshened again and it was with a feeling of relief that they edged away from those huge yawning jaws.

It took all their skill and strength to tack home, and by the time they rounded the headland and saw their own bay in front of them the wind was almost blowing a gale. They were both soaked to the skin, and very hungry. Petra ran the little boat as near to the shore as possible, and Nick lowered the sail. He than jumped out to pull the boat from the water.

But someone was there before him. Yannis was waiting for them. He roughly shouldered Nick out of the way and pulled the boat up on to the beach. Nick was about to protest, but then he saw the expression on Yannis' face. It was a look of undisguised hatred. For a second, he felt a ripple of fear. Wisely, he turned away. There was no doubt about it; Yannis would cheerfully murder him.

It was Yannis who helped Petra out of the boat, and Yannis who carried the oars up to the hut. Laughing, Petra grabbed hold of his arm and made him run with her up the beach. Nick followed slowly after them.

Chapter 9

Nick came to dread the arrival of Yannis. As soon as he heard him shuffle across the sand, and saw the daylight obscured from the doorway of the hut by the dark figure, he felt tension gather inside him. The gaiety vanished from Petra who became silent and withdrawn. Their peaceful intimacy was shattered. It was as if the snake had entered Paradise. Yet, in spite of his resentment, Nick still felt sorry for the man. He knew it was ridiculous to be jealous of someone so deformed and whose mind was that of a ten-year-old. He knew, too, that he had no business to feel jealous of anyone. Petra was no more to him than a gifted pupil whose company he enjoyed. But all the same, whatever reason told him to the contrary, he resented the silent sentinel by the door.

For days the weather kept them shore-bound. The *Meltemi*, the strong northerly wind, arrived during the third week in July. The calm waters of the straits were lashed into a seething maelstrom of wild, white-capped waves. Petra and her watch-dog stopped coming down to the beach, and Nick was left to his own devices. For a time he welcomed the respite.

Each day, before he went back to the house for his evening meal, he walked out to the far end of the headland. He would stand there, feeling the wind tearing at his hair, almost driving him to hurl himself down into the raging water at the base of the cliff. He felt the promontory tremble with the onslaught of each wave, and he thought of the caves and tunnels which honey-combed the cliff. He could almost feel the pressure of the sea as it forced its way up into the hill-side, to be released in gigantic water-spouts.

It was then, in the midst of the storm, that he was able to look at himself dispasionately. He didn't like what he saw. The cool academic, the unemotional dispenser of knowledge, involved with a fool and a beautiful girl. A wise man jealous of a fool, who hated him. And a girl, who admired the wise man but loved the fool, her childhood companion. So dark were his thoughts at these moments, and so extreme were his feelings, that he seriously considered taking the next plane back to England. Better the dull routine of Rottingdean than the emotional turmoil of Alonnisos.

For days the wind raged, and Nick missed his pupil. Then one morning he woke up to find that the sea had gone back to its innocent state, and the dolphins had arrived in the bay. Petra turned up at the hut around four, as usual, just as if nothing had happened. Her boat was still there on the beach, just as they'd left it, and she suggested that they took the opportunity of the lull, to sail again to the Cave of Cyclops.

Nick felt a surge of happiness as he threw down his brush and raced across the sand with her. She ran lightly and easily, her hair streaming out behind her like a flag. She was wearing the white bikini which she'd worn on that first afternoon he'd seen her landing on the beach with Yannis. She was bronzed by the sun, her legs long and slim, and suddenly Nick felt a surge of desire which took him by surprise. Instantly, he dismissed all thoughts of going home. This island was his prison. The girl, the fool, and Professor Nicholas Harding were three flies trapped in amber.

A shout from behind made him stop and turn round. It was Yannis, who had suddenly materialised out of the olive grove. He was shambling across the sand, his dark face contorted with despair.

Quickly Nick got into the boat and pushed off from the shore. That afternoon he had to have Petra to himself. Even for an hour. He hoisted the sail and seized the tiller.

'Quick, let's get going. Caliban can wait for once.' But Petra refused to leave. She was furious with Nick.

'Nick, no. Not again. Don't be so unkind. He doesn't understand. We'll have to take him. Turn back, quickly.'

But Nick refused to turn, and Petra, with one furious look at him, promptly stood up in the bows and jumped over the side of the boat. They were no distance from the shore, and she was a strong swimmer. To Nick's amazement, she walked up to Yannis and put her arms round him. She ignored Nick, who had to bring the boat back on his own.

For a moment, he felt beside himself with rage. Part of him, his rational dispassionate half, knew that Petra was right. They should have taken Yannis. But the other half felt nothing but rage and loathing.

He brought the boat back quietly to the shore, pulled it up on the beach, and walked back to the hut, ignoring the two of them. They were sitting together on the sand. Yannis had put his head in Petra's lap, and she was gently stroking it, as if he were a child. She didn't look at Nick as he stalked past.

For days afterwards, nothing happened. He saw no-one. Just the two silent figures of Giorgios and Takis who came every day as usual. Soon he began to loose interest in his work. The designs on the pots became monotonuous and unoriginal. The work became tedious, and he began to look forward to the time when it was finished and he could pack his bag and leave the accursed island.

He began to take his evening meal in his room, excusing himself from the family circle by pleading pressure of work. Even Markos no longer talked to him, but seemed to have withdrawn into a silent world of his own. Petra avoided him, and it was Elisavet who brought his tray of food up to his room each night and left behind a bottle of retsina. He longed to speak to Petra, to apologize for his churlishness, but she refused to look at him.

Then, one afternoon towards the end of the month, she turned up again as usual. She looked, he thought, tired and strained, and there were dark circles under her eyes. He sensed, too, a new shyness in her, but put it down to the natural embarrassment after a tiff. He felt a surge of elation when he saw her, but was afraid to show his pleasure. He looked down at the slender, long-necked vase he was mending and waited for her to speak.

'Nick, don't let's quarrel. Not over Yannis. Let me see what you're doing.'

She was pleased to examine the vase, and exclaimed with delight over the other pieces that he'd finished. They were almost back to normal but he found himself waiting for her guardian's appearance. She seemed to know what he was thinking because she stretched out her hand and touched his arm.

'Don't worry. We're on our own. Yannis has disappeared. He often does this. He goes off hunting for squid amongst the rocks and stays out all night. We're quite safe. Look, there's a strong wind. Let's run down to Steni Vala to have a look at Markos' boat. When the weather subsides, we could take it out one day. Across to the other island, or out to the wreck. Even to the Roman wreck off Iura. Come on, Nick. It's quite safe. I love the wind.'

For a moment, he hesitated. Then he thought of the excitement of sailing with Petra, and sure enough, Yannis was nowhere to be seen. He walked down with her to the beach and together they launched the boat.

The wind had been blowing a gale all night, and the sky was overcast and unsettled but they weren't going far. Petra allowed Nick to take the tiller, and went up into the bows. He watched her leaning over the side as the boat surged through the waves, talking to the dolphins that had come up to them. He caught sight of dozens of grey, gleaming backs, arching out of the water and pirouetting in the bright air. They followed the boat along the coast, racing alongside and leaping across the bows. Petra was laughing and calling out to them, and they seemed to understand her. Certainly, they shared her mood of jubilation, and danced with joy in front of her. It was a moment Nick would never forget. Whatever else happened to him, the sight of Petra shouting with delight to the strange intelligent seabeasts would remain with him for ever.

They soon reached the tiny harbour of Steni Vala, and Petra said goodbye to the dolphins. Nick lowered the sail, and rowed up to the wooden jetty. They were both dripping wet with spray, and thirsty from the salt water. They tied the boat to a post and went up to Spiros's taverna. They ordered beer from Angie, and asked where Spiros was.

'He sleeps,' she said, and Nick was reminded of that first afternoon when he had arrived at the taverna hot and tired from his journey from Patiteri.

89

'How is he?' he asked the child.

'His hand gets better,' she said. 'But he's sad. No more jokes. No more parties.'

They were both sorry for Spiros, whose accident had been the main topic of conversation at the taverna for days now.

They carried their drinks down to the jetty, and walked along to look at a large wooden fishing boat at the far end. It was the sort of boat which fishermen use all over the world. A strongly built motorboat made of wooden planks, arranged one over-lapping the other in a style known in England as clinker built, it was large enough to take six people and all the paraphernalia for an afternoon's scuba diving. The gunwales were leather bound to stop the wood from rubbing against the side of the jetty, and its name was painted in gold letters along the side, near the stern. *Centaur*. It was, thought Nick, a singularly appropriate name for such a boat.

'Marcos' boat' said Petra, somewhat unnecessarily. 'He's not a sailing man. Not since the wind and the waves killed his wife.'

Nick looked at her sharply. He would have liked to ask more about the incident, but Petra shook her head. 'Some other time. Not now. The wind's getting stronger, and we ought to be on our way home.'

The sail back to Agios Demetrios was hard work. By the time they reached the tiny beach, they were both exhausted and cold from the spray. The waves were high, and Nick was soaked through by the time he'd pulled the boat high enough out of the water. They stood together on the shore, laughing and exhilarated by the exercise.

It was at that moment, that they saw the procession making its way along the top of the beach. Four men, carrying a stretcher. A body upon it, covered by a grey blanket.

Nick instinctively put an arm out to restrain Petra but she tore herself away from him and raced across the beach. She reached the men before Nick was able to stop her. They called out a warning but she was too much for them. She ordered them to put down the stretcher and they obeyed. It was their nature to obey. Then she pulled back the blanket and looked down on the bruised and torn face of Yannis. His face was distorted as if in agony, and his tongue lolled out of the corner

90

of his misshapen mouth. His face had been repeatedly battered against the rocks, and was bloated by two days submersion in salt water.

She fell on her knees beside the stretcher and touched the part of his face that was still intact.

'Yannis,' she said. 'Yannis. What happened?' The men stood there awkwardly, not knowing what to do. Nick had arrived, and gently covered the face with the blanket.

'He must have been out there on the rocks,' said one of the men. 'Catching squid most likely. But the wind and the waves were too strong for him, and he must have fallen off the rocks. Out there off the headland, the waves can pound a man to death in a matter of minutes. I'm sorry, Miss Petra. There's nothing we can do. Let us take him back home.'

Nick gently helped her to her feet. She still looked dazed, as if she didn't understand.

'He can't have drowned,' she said. 'He was the strongest swimmer around here. Don't you remember when that French yacht capsized, he swam at least a mile to help the survivors? The sea was his element. Where did you find him?'

'In the next bay. Washed up on the rocks in that tiny inlet at the end of the headland.'

'On this side?'

'Yes. But let us take him home now to his family. Come and see him again when we've cleaned him up.'

The men quietly lifted the stretcher and headed off towards the road. Nick put an arm around Petra who was shivering with cold and shock. To his surprise, she pushed him roughly away.

'Don't you dare come near me,' she said, almost hysterical with shock and grief. 'You killed him. You always hated him.'

For a moment he thought she must have gone out of her mind.

'Petra, don't be foolish. How could I have killed him? I was sorry for him.'

'No, you weren't. You hated him. He couldn't take your dislike. He wasn't used to it. He was always surrounded by people who loved him. He was one of the blessed.

'He killed himself! He threw himself off the headland in despair – and you were the cause. You wanted him to die, and he knew you did.'

Then she raced off towards the house, leaving Nick to follow slowly behind her.

That night, the whole household mourned the death of Yannis. Nick ate his supper alone in his room. No one came near him. That night, the *Meltemi* raged, and Nick spent many restless hours thinking of the twisted body of Yannis hurled against the rocks by giant waves. Somehow the body faded into images of monsters dancing in glee on the beach. Monsters who went to sleep eventually as dawn broke, and turned into dolphins escorting a beautiful girl in a white boat into a safe harbour.

Chapter 10

At the eastern end of the island, near the headland which dissolved into the Kraken, stood a small white-washed monastery. From the road, nothing was visible except the grey-tiled dome with its white stone cross on top. The rest of the buildings were hidden by cypresses and stone pines.

Petra had brought Nick to this place three days after the death of Yannis. For the first day she had been inconsolable, and had shut herself away in her room, refusing to talk or eat. Nick had worked on alone in his hut, wanting now only to finish as quickly as possible and get back to England. He missed Petra more than he could have thought possible. It was, of course, inevitable that he should have fallen in love with her. She was everything his wife was not – beautiful, lithe, practical and intelligent. And she admired his work.

On the third morning, she had turned up as if nothing had happened. She was paler than usual, and there were dark circles under her eyes, but the rest of her was bright enough. She was wearing a simple cotton skirt – blue with a scattering of white flowers – and carrying an old-fashioned wicker basket covered with a white cloth on her arm. She'd tied her hair back out of the way.

For a moment she stood at the door of the hut shyly. Then she walked over to examine the urn he was working on. A beautiful specimen of Cretan art, like the others this one too was decorated with a huge octopus and other sea creatures which darted in and out of trailing water plants.

'It's lovely, Nick,' she said.

He nodded, without looking at her. 'One of the best, and

they've all been marvellous pieces. I only hope I shall be able to finish them before the end of August. July's almost over as it is and there's still a lot more to be salvaged. Takis was quite chatty for once today.'

She walked round the table, picking up pieces of potsherds in a desultory way. Suddenly she said, 'Nick, I must talk to you. I'm sorry about the other day. I shouldn't have said what I did but I was shocked. It was a terrible way for him to die.'

He went over to her, and on impulse put his arms round her. She didn't draw away.

'Don't talk about it,' he said. 'I understand. It was a perfectly natural reaction. Especially as I had been so arrogant about the sailing. But I wanted to be with you, just you, and he was always there. But you know I would never have harmed him.'

He was aware suddenly of her warm body pressed against him. He bent down and kissed her hair which smelt of fresh herbs. Then he drew away abruptly.

'Where are you taking me then?' he said, suddenly light-hearted. 'Why the basket? What's it to be this time? Caves, rocks, sea monsters? Remote light houses?'

'No, none of those things. Just a peaceful place. No-one goes there now, except Markos and me. We'll need your car, though.'

The day had brightened. He put on his shirt, and hand in hand, friends again, they walked to the car. It was cool under the olive trees, and the air felt refreshing after the stuffiness of the hut. Petra got in to the car beside Nick, the basket demurely on her lap.

'To the headland,' she said. 'The Kraken headland. I'll show you the way. There's only one road.'

Nick drove to the end of the island. He parked off the road, under some cypresses, and together they climbed the steep track to the main gate of the monastery. It was no longer necessary to ring for permission to go in. No one lived there. Petra pushed open the gate, and they walked in. It was quiet except for the cicadas. The air was heavy with the pungent scent of the pines. Below them lay the sea in an unbroken stretch of blue. Above them was a cloudless sky.

'The Cyclops' cave is just over there,' said Petra. 'We can see the Kraken from the garden.'

94

She led the way along the sandy path towards the church. They were completely alone. No-one seemed to have set foot in the place for centuries.

'The monastery of Saint Michael,' she said, as she pushed open the wooden door which looked as if it had been there ever since the church was built. 'There used to be fifty monks living here. But they closed it down three years ago because there were only two left, and both of them were over eighty. No-one ever comes here now – perhaps the occasional tourist – but the drinking trough is still there by the front gate for the pilgrims to use. The water is very pure. It comes from a spring higher up.'

The church was cool inside. They both talked in whispers, so as not to disturb the peace of centuries. Some small birds had nested above the altar, and they twittered frantically at the intrusion. Petra and Nick stood looking up at the inside of the dome, where the traditional painting of Christ Pantocrator looked down with out-stretched arms. The colours were still as fresh and vivid as when the artist had first used them over three hundred years ago, Christ's halo an untarnished gold.

Petra took him down some stairs into a tiny crypt with a low vaulted ceiling. Nick had to duck his head to get under the lintel of the door. Here, the walls had been decorated with pictures of Christ on the way to the cross. Again, the colours were as fresh as if they had been painted yesterday. Nick stared at them in amazement. The artist had depicted Christ's agony with astonishing realism. The dark eyes were filled with pain, and his face was twisted in agony. Nick thought of Yannis and turned away.

At the back of the crypt Petra showed him a small wooden trap door, just big enough for a man to squeeze through.

'A well?' asked Nick as he pulled up the lid and peered down into a dark pit.

'No. It leads down into the back of Cyclops' cave, so they say. I've never been down there. It was an escape route for the monks for when the Turks embarked upon one of their frequent bouts of persecution. These islands once belonged to Turkey along with the rest of Greece, as you know. Sometimes the monks had to leave here very quickly. There should be a ladder fixed to the wall somewhere. I don't expect it's all there now, but it might be. People built things to last in those days.'

She lay down flat on the stone floor and felt to one side of the opening.

'Yes, it's there. A ladder, and it seems to be made of metal of some sort.' She stood up.

'I wonder how often they used it,' said Nick.

'At certain times, frequently. It would certainly be better to escape down a hole than to face a horde of Turks on the rampage.'

'I suppose they also used this shaft for hauling up supplies when they were under siege, like they still do on Mount Athos. I've seen the monks there hauling up their provisions in a basket.'

They left the cool peace of the church and wandered out into the garden. The vines were heavy with ripening grapes, and the fig trees, standing like rows of old men, were laden with fruit. The air was heavy with the scent of herbs, and it was hot and languorous under the laurel trees. All around them thousands of insects hummed and twittered.

They sat down under one of the ancient trees. Below them they could see the sea.

'Look, there's the Kraken. He's still asleep. Nothing is going to happen this afternoon.'

'He's a sensible monster,' said Nick, stretching out on a blanket of pine needles which covered the sandy soil of the garden. 'I think I'm going to follow his example.'

'Not yet. Not before you've eaten,' said Petra, who had sat down cross-legged in front of him and was busy setting out the contents of the basket on fig leaves which she had picked from a tree.

She had brought fruit and retsina. There were cakes made with honey and almonds, and hard boiled eggs which they ate with black olives. To finish, there were huge slabs of *halva*, which Nick loved as it was made with grated nuts and honey. He'd eaten it before in Crete, and Elisavet, noticing how much he enjoyed it, left a plateful of it in his room each day.

'I used to come here and study,' said Petra, 'when I was on

96

holiday from Athens. What better place to study philosophy than in an ancient monastery?'

'Perfect. But didn't the gods disturb you? There are wood nymphs all around us. That isn't really a laurel tree over there you know. It's Daphne escaping the clutches of Apollo.'

'Of course they're here,' she said,' but they never disturbed me. They were here long before Christianity. But that Christ we've seen in the Church fits in here too. He's all part of the same scene. All the legends have the same message. There's nothing new. The Virgin Mary is only the Minoan earth goddess. She's also Isis, the mother of Horus. And so it goes on.'

It seemed quite natural to talk of gods in such a place. Petra, sitting cross-legged in front of him, her skirt tucked round her knees, looked like a teacher lecturing a pupil. A pupil who was succumbing to too much retsina. He leant over and filled her glass.

'Well, don't let us forget Bacchus. Otherwise he'll get annoyed. I feel a bit under his influence already.'

'Don't worry.' She laughed. 'Most people on these islands are under the influence of Bacchus. The police take no notice when you drive on the wrong side of the road.'

'Have you got any police here? Where do they all live? I haven't seen any since I arrived.'

'There's a small station in Patiteri. But if anything serious happens, then they come over from Volos on the mainland. They roar over in large motor boats, and make a great deal of noise.'

'When did they last come?'

'This time last year, when a woman murdered her husband and tried to hang herself in her own garden. Markos discovered her just in time.'

Nick rolled over on his stomach and looked up at Petra.

'You're fond of your brother, aren't you? Even though he's not your real brother.'

'Yes. We're very close. Especially now, since his wife died.'

'He never told me how it happened.'

'No, he wouldn't. He never talks about it. It happened a couple of years ago. Soula, that was his wife, was an expert sailor, and he'd bought her a small sailing boat. They had been married eight years, and had a son, Mitsos.

'One day, whilst Markos was away, she took Mitsos out in the boat, although the weather wasn't suitable. We don't know what happened but the boat was found later on the shore of Peristera. They never found the bodies.'

She was silent for a moment, and then began to pack up the remains of the meal.

'I hope one day he'll be happy. He needs a home of his own, and Andrikos and Elisavet won't live forever. He's still unhappy. He's also beginning to drink too much and that's bad. He drinks not because he likes it but because he wants to forget.'

'I'm sorry. I like Markos. He introduced me to your family.'

'Yes. He likes you. But you're both very different.'

He smiled. 'Yes, I suppose we are. He's Greek to start with, and I'm English mostly. There's quite a dash of Celt in me as well.'

'Yes, but Markos is emotional and ambitious. He exposes his feelings for everyone to see and then he withdraws into himself, and no-one can reach him. He loves passionately, and hates. He would kill if he thought it right. Very Greek.'

Petra looked intently at Nick. 'But you, you're different. You hide yourself. We never know what you're thinking or feeling. You English are the most difficult people on earth to understand.'

'It's the way we're programmed at birth. Were just the same as everyone else, but we have a different computer programmer. The same hardware; different soft-ware.'

'Somewhere there must be a book of instructions. "The Key to the Englishman's mind".'

'Yes, but I keep it hidden. I only give it to one or two special people.'

She had packed up the lunch things and now stood up to carry the basket into the shade. She stood there, watching the sun begin its descent behind Skiathos. Then she said softly: 'Would you let me read the instruction book? I promise to return it.'

He too had stood up, and came over to her.

'Maybe. But I warn you, it's not easy to understand.'

She turned to face him, holding the basket between them. 'Let me try, Nick,' she said pleadingly.

Then it seemed perfectly natural for Nick to take the basket away from her, and put it on the ground. She moved towards him and they were in each other's arms. He kissed her with all the pent up emotion of the last few days and felt her returning his kisses with mounting urgency. Yannis' death seemed to have removed all restraint between them. He realised then that he'd been wanting to do this for days.

He kissed her face and hair, and lifted up her white cotton blouse. She was naked underneath and her breasts were firm and rounded, her skin like silk. He bent down and kissed each breast. She pulled his head down to her.

The afternoon dissolved around him. He tried to pull her down on to the bed of pine needles but she drew back.

'No, Nick. Not now.'

He fell on his knees in front of her, and clasped his arms round her knees. He was trembling, and she stroked his head to calm him.

'Nick, I want you. And we shall be together, soon. But, listen. I brought you here not to make love but to tell you something about Yannis. Nick, listen.'

Slowly he got to his feet and took her hand. He saw that she was quite serious. Her face had gone very white, and the lines of tension had come back around her mouth.

'What is it, Petra? he said.

'Yannis. There's something not quite right about the way he died. It wasn't an accident, I'm sure of that.'

'But he was drowned. There's no doubt about that. Surely there's no mystery about falling off the edge of a cliff and drowning in a high sea.' He spoke to her patiently, as if she were a child; sensing that something was worrying her desperately.

'But no-one goes to that place to catch squid, Nick. The waves are too big. The usual places are the holes in the rocks, out there, in the entrance to the bay. There's always plenty there and they're always easy to catch. No fisherman makes unnecessary difficulties for himself. Yannis would never have gone out along that headland alone, not in that wind and certainly not at night. Not for squid when there were lots of easier places to get them.'

99

'Perhaps he went out there for the challenge. Not to catch squid.'

'But fishermen can't afford challenges. They like certainty. And there's another thing: that place where they said they found him, on this side of the headland. Had he fallen off the cliff, the wind would have brought him further along the shore, nearer us. The wind, if you remember, veered to the north-east, building up to the *Meltemi*. It couldn't have washed him up to our side of the cliff.

The other thing is the current. There is a strong one along the coast. Not a tide, just a movement of water. You saw the whirlpools the other day. This current never changes direction. It always runs from east to west. Had he fallen into the sea, the wind and the current would have brought him into our bay. He couldn't have been washed up into a bay on the lee side of a cliff. It's just not possible. He could have been trapped against a rock, but not brought into that inlet. He must have been killed by someone else, and his body dumped there. There were marks on his throat which didn't look like damage from being beaten against the rocks. But why? Why would someone kill him?'

Nick couldn't answer. All he could do was to hold her close to him and try to comfort her. 'But Yannis was harmless. Who'd want to get rid of him?'

'I know. But Markos says he was creating quite a stir in the taverna the other day, talking about gold he says he saw on the shore. People laughed at him, of course, but someone might have got worried. Maybe they wanted to shut him up. Do you remember he tried to tell us that day?'

He nodded. 'Yes, I remember. But he didn't tell us exactly what he saw. It was all very vague.'

'But maybe it alarmed someone who thought it would be safer if Yannis was silenced. Nick, those crates. Have you ever looked in them after we've packed them? Perhaps we ought to check that nothing goes in them after we've left the beach.'

He looked at her in surprise. 'I don't see how we can do that. If they are tampered with, then it's after they've left the bay. I know exactly what I put in each crate. I've got a note-book, and each crate is numbered. Every night, I write

100

down what I have done during the day, and what went into which crate.'

'Yes, I know that. But after they've left you, could they be opened up and something illegal, say gold, put in with your amphorae?'

'But that would be too dangerous. Everything that goes out of the country has to be shipped through customs. Every crate is labelled and its contents listed. It would only take one suspicious customs man to open one of the crates and find something illegal inside for the whole lot to be confiscated. If those two jokers out there on the yacht were playing around with gold, they'd hardly put them in a crate which has to go through the port authorities.'

Petra turned away and looked out to sea.

'But I think Yannis did see gold,' she said stubbornly. 'And somehow I think it's connected with that yacht, James Rochester's yacht.'

'Then we shall go and take a look. It's about time I took a look at the site. No diving, not yet. Just a preliminary exploration.'

'Yes, that's right.' She picked up the basket, her face suddenly relaxed. 'Tomorrow. We'll go in Markos' boat. He's leaving early for the mainland so he won't know. He'll be furious if he hears we took it without his permission but it won't take long. Only an hour.'

'Can you manage the boat?'

'Of course, and so can you. It's a diesel engine. He leaves the key with Spiros.'

Somehow the afternoon had lost its magic. They walked down to the car in silence, both lost in thought. He kissed her when they reached the car, and she clung to him with a fierce intensity.

'Nick, what are we doing? What are we going to find?'

'Nothing, my darling. Nothing. Just a trip out to a yellow buoy, and back again. Just something to set your mind at rest. Nothing's going to happen.'

He kissed her gently on the forehead, and they got into the car. 'Petra, we'll find out what happened to Yannis, and then it will be only you and me. And we shall be happy. Don't you feel it too? Or is it just this place?'

101

'No, it would have happened anyway. The gods are on our side. I knew it would happen as soon as I saw you. But first we must find out who killed Yannis. And why.'

In the event, Petra saw Markos the next morning, and he allowed them to use his boat, when she told him that they planned a trip to the cave of Cyclops to explore the interior. With the usual warning about the narrowness of the tunnels, and the danger of a sudden sea surge, he'd reluctantly agreed, then set out himself for the mainland.

But at Patiteri he changed his mind. He knew he was vacillating. He felt like a man lost at sea, at the mercy of the wind and currents. But the hydrofoil was waiting to go to Skiathos, and it seemed simpler to join it and see a man about a delivery of stones than to wait for the Volos ferry and go cap in hand to yet another bank. Never again, he thought, would he be in control of his own destiny. It was far easier to let events take him over.

At five o'clock that afternoon, Nick met Petra on the jetty of Steni Vala. She'd already picked up the key from Spiros, and together they set of towards the south-east and the island of Peristera. Neither of them had any idea what they expected to see but, privately, Nick thought they were wasting their time. Without diving gear, all they would see would be a yellow buoy marking the site. He hoped the two divers would have finished work, and it was for this reason that he had suggested a late start.

Markos' boat chugged steadily over the glassy calm water. The wind had died away as it did most afternoons, and the air was hot and still. *Centaur* was no power boat. Built for stability in deep waters, it could take a lot of gear. It did occur to Nick that it was an unusual boat for a man like Markos to own. He didn't need to fish. He didn't have to transport freight for a living. He wasn't exactly poverty stricken. Somehow, Nick thought, he should have owned something racier and faster. Somewhere in that tense, tightly controlled person there was a flamboyant personality waiting to escape.

It didn't take them long to get within sight of the wreck. Trained to spot navigation marks, Nick recognized the yellow buoy from a long way away. It was just a spot on the water, like the head of a seal. Behind it lay the long whaleback of the island.

Then he saw the red motor boat. He turned to Petra who was leaning over the bows, watching a shoal of fish in the water.

'Hell! The men are still here. I thought they would have gone long ago.'

She turned to look.

'They must be working late. They usually leave around four.'

'So your spies have been at work,' he said with a smile.

'What do you expect? A small island, a wreck, and two unsociable divers. The whole island is talking about them. They worked out the times of the day shift ages ago.'

'Well, we're nearly into August, and I suppose they want the stuff up quickly now. Anyway, they can't object to our taking a look from the surface.'

He opened up the throttle, and the boat drew near the yellow marker. The motor boat was tied to the buoy and there was one man in it. He'd heard their engine and was standing up, waving his arms.

'Is he trying to tell us to go away, or is he just pleased to see us?' said Nick.

Then they saw the second man. He suddenly shot up through the water like a dolphin and climbed into the motor boat. He was in full diving gear, and as they watched he removed his face mask and loosened his can of oxygen. They were now within hailing distance.

'Hallo there,' shouted Nick. 'We've come to join you.'

'Get back,' shouted the first man. Nick thought it was Takis. 'This is private property. Get back. You've no business to be here.'

'Who the hell does he think he's talking to?' said Nick to Petra angrily. 'Don't be so bloody stupid,' he shouted back to the divers. 'It's me, Nick Harding. You see me every day. I won't bother you. We want to see the site.'

'Get back. Get back, or you'll regret it.'

'By now Nick was furious. To be actually threatened, and in front of Petra. 'What a bloody cheek. Hold on. I'm going on.'

He urged Markos' boat to full speed. He had no idea what he was going to do when he reached the divers. Some instinct made him want to ram the red boat, and tip the two men into the sea. Suddenly he saw Takis bend down and take something out of the stern locker.

'Nick, look out,' screamed Petra. 'He's got a gun.'

Sure enough, Takis was pointing a rifle at them. Nick turned *Centaur* sharply to starboard and the gun went off. He felt the bullet cleave through the air, just by his head.

'My God, they're maniacs!' he shouted. 'Get down,' he said suddenly to Petra, who had been thrown sideways by his change of course. He felt a surge of white hot anger. All he wanted to do was to kill the two men ahead of him.

The second shot came very near. He heard the thin whine of the bullet overhead, and the splash as it landed in the sea.

'Nick, go back.' said Petra, suddenly very calm. She had stood up and was coming to take the tiller away from him. 'You can't sink them. They'll get us first. You haven't a gun.'

The third shot was aimed at her. She saw Takis raise the gun, and instinctively threw herself along the bottom of the boat. Just in time. Nick heard the dull thud as the bullet skimmed the top of the gunwale, sending a splinter of wood flying through the air. It brought him to his senses.

'Bastards!' he shouted. 'All right, you can get away with it this time. But not the next.'

Then he turned the boat, and raced back to Alonnisos, a fourth shot speeding them on their way. He looked down at Petra, who hadn't moved.

'Hold on,' he said. 'We're going home.'

A man stood waiting for them on the shore. It was Markos, beside himself with rage. Roughly he pulled the boat up on to the beach, and then looked down at Petra inside it. He turned on Nick furiously.

'Where the hell have you been? Petra, what's been happening?'

She raised herself on to her knees, and Nick saw the bruises on her arms where she had been thrown against the side of the boat. He went forward to help her on to the shore but Markos was there first.

'No, you don't. Keep away. You've done enough damage as it is.'

He carried Petra to the hut and put her in the chair. Nick went to get fresh water to wash the cut on her arm. When he got back, she had recovered enough to take the bowl from him and wash her own bruises.

'Markos, calm down. We went to have a look at the yacht, that's all. But the two men were there and, Markos, they have a gun! They used it, first at Nick then at me. They only got the boat, a large chunk is missing from the bows, but they meant to get us.'

Markos stood there, his face black with anger.

'I warned you not to go there! It's lucky I came back early from Skiathos. I told you those men are evil. And you, Nick, are just bloody irresponsible to take her out there. This is not a pond like your English Serpentine. We don't go on after-noon picnics to look at men with guns. God, I could kill you! And I would, had anything happened to Petra. As it is she's badly bruised.

'Why don't you get the hell out of here? We don't want you here, you and your bloodthirsty friends. Get back to England and your wife, and leave my sister alone.'

For a moment, Nick wanted to hit Markos. He clenched his fist, ready to strike but Petra intervened.

'Look, calm down both of you. You're only making matters worse. Of course we didn't expect the men to have guns. But what do we do next? Those men are dangerous.'

'What about the police?' said Nick, still trying to control his rage.

'This isn't England,' said Petra, still calm. 'In the first place they would have to come over from Volos, and that takes time. And when they get here, what then? There's no proof that the men fired at us. I know the boat's damaged, but how can we prove that those men were responsible? By the time the police come, they will have hidden the gun and will deny the whole incident. If we tell the police that we suspect something illegal is going on out there, by the time they get round to sending down divers the men will have cleared the wreck.'

'She's right,' said Markos, who now had himself under

control. 'We'll have to wait. Sooner or later we'll have enough evidence to call in the police, but not yet. It might just be possible that there is nothing going on out there at all. Just a valuable collection of archaeological treasure, and the men could have been given guns to ward off thieves. They might simply have over-reacted. To give a Greek a gun is asking for trouble.'

'It's the first time I've seen men use guns to keep sightseers away from a site,' said Nick ruefully.

'But how long do we wait before someone else dies?' said Petra suddenly.

'Someone else?' said Markos slowly.

'Yes. They killed Yannis. He must have seen them with something they didn't want him to see. Then he told everyone in the taverna.'

'We've got no proof they killed Yannis,' said Markos impatiently. 'Look, the verdict was accidental death. He's buried now, and the police won't be interested. Try telling them that you suspect that two men murdered a harmless idiot who babbled away in a taverna about seeing gold. Tell them also that the *Meltemi* was blowing, and he was out on the rocks catching squid. No, we shall have to wait until we have more evidence than that.' He looked at Petra. 'Come now, back to the house. Can you walk?'

'Of course. I was winded, that's all. And a bit bruised.'

In spite of her protestations to the contrary, Petra was shocked and the bruises on her arms were extensive. Elisavet was concerned for her, although they told her nothing about the shots. They all agreed that older people shouldn't be told anything about the men or the wreck, otherwise they would have both become deeply alarmed and would keep Petra in the house for the rest of the summer.

That evening, Nick suffered Markos' black looks in silence. By ten o'clock, he'd had enough and went to bed, leaving Markos to his own dark thoughts. Petra had gone to her room as soon as they got back to the house. Elisavet told him that she had gone straight to sleep. Nick felt guilty and upset about leading Petra into a dangerous situation. The whole household seemed to look at him reproachfully, and he reached his room grateful to escape their hurt looks. By half-past ten, he too was fast asleep.

It was around one o'clock in the morning that he woke. He lay there listening to the sound of the wind in the pine trees. He could just hear the noise of the waves breaking on the rocks below.

Suddenly he heard another sound: the creak of a door opening. He sat up and looked around him. There was no-one there. Moonlight filled his room, and his door was firmly closed.

Then the sound again. The door of a room along the corridor. He got out of bed and went outside. It was Markos' room. His door was open, and there was a light shining into the corridor. Suddenly Nick knew he should talk to Markos. To apologise for risking Petra's life. To tell him that he loved his sister more than anything else in the world, and nothing in the world would make him upset her again. He loved and respected her, and he knew she was not for him.

He walked along the corridor and looked into Markos' room. The desk light was on. There was a pile of papers, and a pair of glasses on top. Markos had been working late. But it was not that which made Nick draw back and tiptoe to his own room.

Markos was inside the room, standing by his bed. The drawer of the bedside table was open and Markos had taken out a gun. A revolver. The sort the police used. As Nick watched in horror, Markos filled the gun with bullets and checked the mechanism. Then he laid it on the table.

Back in his room, Nick stood there, his mind in a turmoil. Markos! Fully dressed at one o'clock in the morning, with a gun in his hand. Markos! No wonder he hadn't wanted Nick to inspect the yacht. It wasn't only that he feared for Petra. It could be that he had an interest in the sunken boat. Perhaps he knew more about the 'treasure' than he let on. Certainly he was in a perfect position. Living in a house overlooking the site. Free to come and go without question. Always going away to the mainland and the other islands. Hating Nick, but knowing he was useful. Friendly with everyone on the island. Always in the taverna, talking to Spiros. And now, armed.

Nick walked across to the window and looked down at the peaceful scene. Already another thought had occurred to him. Yannis. Could Markos possibly have killed Yannis to silence him? If so, who next? And who else was involved in that wreck? Elisaver? Andrikos? Had they also got shares in it?

He sat down on the edge of the bed, and tried to order his thoughts but it was useless. His mind was like a kaleidoscope of shifting patterns and combinations. One thing was clear. He could now put behind him all thoughts of going back to England. He had to find out what was going on, and warn Arnold Ponsford. But what the hell had he walked into?

Chapter 11

Bernie watched the fisherman motor slowly up to the ramshackle jetty. A small boy appeared out of the trees and helped him unload his three baskets of fish. So the place wasn't deserted. Somewhere there was a house which might have a room to let for the night. She was tired. She'd spent a week travelling around Euboea, mostly on foot as the buses were unreliable and crowded. She'd stopped at every café along the coast asking if a middle-aged American had called there for water or provisions. At every place people stared at her in disbelief, and touched their foreheads significantly. Mostly they shrugged their shoulders and walked away, thinking that she was one of those eccentric American hippies in search of the simple life.

She was thinking she might have to go across to Volos in Thessaly, the administrative centre of that part of the world. There were few hospitals in Euboea, and if Nelson had been taken seriously ill, he would have had to be transported to Volos, a journey of some thirty miles across the Trikiri Channel. She could also get official help there. Someone might have reported a missing yacht. After all, yachts flying foreign flags weren't all that common in the remoter parts of Greece. But the fact remained that Nelson was notoriously unsociable at sea, and would never have dreamed of giving his call sign to the port authorities in Volos or the Piraeus, as he would have done in Boston or Cape Cod.

The fisherman had now left his boat and was making his way up the beach. He stared at Bernie. Tourists were few and far between on that particular beach.

'*Kalispera, Kyrie*,' she said. He nodded, and stopped expectantly in front of her. The child looked up impassively. She asked if there was a place to stay for the night. She also said she was hungry. Again the man nodded, and told her to follow him. Her knowledge of colloquial Greek had improved during her week's wandering, and she was now able to communicate quite well with fishermen and farmers.

At the top of the beach the man stopped, and asked her if she liked calamari and red mullet. He called the fish *barbounia* and, as she didn't appear to understand, lifted one out of his basket and held it up for her admiration. It was a magnificent specimen and she said she would be delighted to eat it. He seemed pleased.

That evening, over the fish and retsina, she asked the Liakis family if they had seen anything of a single-handed American sailor in those parts.

Andreas put down his glass and said to her surprise: 'Yes, it was several weeks ago now. In June, just before the storm.'

'You saw him here?'

'We didn't see him, but we saw his boat. He didn't stay long. He came in about this time of the day, as it was getting dark. We watched him anchor not far from the shore. It was a beautiful boat. We don't see many like that. We saw the lights go on, and he went below. That was all. When we went back after supper to get our nets ready for the morning, he'd gone. He must have stayed just long enough to eat his meal. He didn't come ashore.'

'How did you know he was an American?' In her excitement, Bernie had forgotten she was talking to a sailor. He looked at her surprise, as if she had said something stupid.

'The flag, of course. The American flag. We don't see many of them around here. Frenchmen and Italians, and recently the English, but they always sail in convoys.'

'Of course! How stupid of me. I should have known. But did you see him leave?'

'We didn't see him up anchor but we saw him in the distance, leaving the bay. He had no navigation lights on, but he might have turned them on later. It seemed foolish of him to sail without them. But people do, you know. Especially if they're without a crew.'

'But not Nelson,' thought Bernie. 'Not Nelson.' He was the most particular man she knew.

Out loud, she asked, 'Could you guess where he was going? To Volos perhaps?'

Andreas shook his head emphatically. 'No, the course was for Skiathos. North-east. He'd already turned when we saw him.'

'Skiathos? Is it far from here?'

'About thirteen miles. Not a bad journey if the weather's good. He might have caught that storm though, unless he stayed in port. I expect he did. People usually stay in Skiathos for a few days. It's nice there.'

Bernie sat thinking for a few minutes, whilst Andreas' wife cleared away the plates and brought bowls of yoghurt and honey.

'Is it possible to get to Skiathos tomorrow?' she said.

'Of course. But you will need a boat to take you there, and there are no ferries from here.'

'Could you take me?'

Andreas shook his head. 'Not tomorrow. Kostas could take you, he's my brother, but he would have to give up a day's fishing and that means a lot to him.'

'I wouldn't expect him to take me for nothing. Tell him to let me know how much he'd need to take me to Skiathos, and I'll pay him that, plus a bit more for his trouble. He won't be out of pocket.'

This altered the situation, and when the meal was over Andreas went off to find Kostas and arrange Bernie's trip to Skiathos.

That night, Bernie slept well in her spotlessly clean bed under the white lace bed-spread which was only used for guests. At last she knew she was on the trail. Someone had actually seen a strange yacht flying an American flag. And that was more than anyone else had seen over the last few weeks. Tomorrow Skiathos, the most important of that group of island called the Sporades. The islands which the ancients had called 'The Gates of the Wind'. Her journey, she felt, was coming to an end.

On August 3rd, Bernie walked into Spiros' taverna in Steni Vala. It was six o'clock, and she'd arrived from Patiteri by

111

taxi. She'd had a row with the taxi driver, who wanted to leave her at the top of the cliff, and had made him drive her down to the harbour by the other road. She was hot and tired. Her hair needed a wash, and her legs were dirty.

The place was full of locals who stared at her in astonishment. One or two got up to confirm that it was a taxi doing a three point turn outside in the garden. The rest of them continued to stare, as if she was an apparition. Finally one of the men, strong and good-looking, stood up and came over to her.

'Good evening,' he said, hand outstretched. 'My name's Karakulas. Marcos Karakulas. Can I help you?'

'Yes, please. I need a bed for the night. Maybe for two or three nights, I don't know yet. And,' she went on, 'I would very much like a bath.'

Another yacht? Another American? Another collector of antiquities? Nick stared at Bernie in disbelief. Was she, he wondered, just another joker in the pack, brought home by Markos to dispel his mounting suspicions about the wreck out there? Or a *deus ex machina*, let down by the gods on to the stage to sort them all out?

He could believe the most recent part of her story. How she had left Euboea in a fisherman's caique, and had landed in Skiathos. How she had heard about the sunken yacht off the island of Peristera. The hotel manager in Skiathos had apparently been enthusiastic in his description of sunken treasure, and how an English archaeologist had been put in charge of the recovery. Nick had winced at that. It seemed highly unlikely that the yacht was her godfather's – but all the same, she had thought it worthwhile coming to Patiteri and then along to the bay.

The meal was over and Petra had lit the lamp but all of them felt disinclined to go to bed. Elisavet had brought out another bottle of retsina, and Nick continued to study the tired girl opposite him. She looked as if she'd been wandering around the intricate coastline of Greece for some time. Her body was lean and hard after all the exercise, and her hair hung down to her waist. It was beautiful hair, he decided. Now that she had washed it, it was the colour of an Irish peat bog. It framed her face like a dark curtain, and she had tucked it back impatiently from time to time during the evening. Her manner, in spite of her tiredness, was direct and vigorous. He thought she was someone who certainly wouldn't tolerate fools gladly. Neither would she be easily frightened. But was she in any way connected with Markos? Certainly he had sat watching her all the evening as if mesmerized, hanging on every word she said. Possibly, thought Nick, to make sure she said the right thing. But why would he need a rich American girl as his accomplice, if indeed he needed one at all? Why had he brought her here? For information? Nick thought of the gun and shuddered. To dispose of her? Perhaps she was the joker he least wanted to see.

Markos hadn't said a word all evening, but now he suddenly sprang into life.

'Your godfather,' he said, 'did he collect ancient pots? The kind of thing Nick here's working on?'

She turned to look at Markos. Nick noticed her dark eyes were impassive, as if she had herself tightly under control.

'It's possible,' she said. 'He collected everything. Last year it was jewellery and the occasional statue, but this year it could be anything. He did say when he last spoke to me on the phone that he was on to something big. He wouldn't say more but told me to wait and see. He sounded in high spirits. He said I would know what it was on my birthday. He always made – ' She paused and then corrected herself: 'He always makes a big thing of family occasions. Particularly my birthday.

'We were expecting to meet up in July, as I said. Then he would have shown me what he had collected this time. But he said nothing about pottery. How much is there on your boat, Nick?' she said, turning to him. She always called the yacht 'his' and he found it amusing.

'There's quite a bit, I believe. It's kept me busy for a month now and there's still a lot to come up, I think.'

'Have you been down to have a look?'

The group looked at each other uneasily. How much should they tell her?

'No,' said Markos. 'It's well guarded.'

'Well guarded! For God's sake, what for? I've heard it's

only a private yacht. Not a Spanish galleon filled with all the treasures of the Indies!'

'No, but for some reason they don't like visitors. As it's a private operation, they're perfectly entitled to set their own conditions.'

Nick stared at Markos in disbelief. Was he really defending those two men out there? That seemed to be taking the role of devil's advocate a bit too far.

'Have you asked them what's on the boat?'

It was now Nick's turn to answer Bernie. 'They don't talk a lot. In fact, they're damned unfriendly. Now the original two have been replaced by two more who bring the work down to the hut when I'm not there. Unless I borrow a boat and go out to them, I'll not be able to ask questions. And it's a bit tricky shouting things across an expanse of sea to a couple of unsociable individuals.'

Bernie was looking increasingly tired and puzzled. At one stage she closed her eyes, jerking herself awake as Markos continued his inquisition.

'Your godfather,' he said shortly, making him sound like the head of the Mafia, 'do you know the name of his yacht?'

'No, not exactly. Nelson only bought the boat a year ago, and we haven't seen much of each other since. This cruise he was planning was to be our holiday. Then I would see the boat, and what he'd been buying around the Mediterranean. I know it was a Rival, because he reckons it's an easy boat to handle on your own. And he didn't like anyone on his boat – except me,' she added.

'I asked him its name when he phoned across to Rome, and he only laughed. He said it was something to do with Poseidon. He was laughing, and said he hoped the Old Boy wouldn't be angry with him for stealing his favourite. Now it looks as if Poseidon got his own back.'

'Poseidon had many favourites,' said Petra suddenly. 'All the gods had cup bearers and handmaidens and so on. I wonder which one he chose – your godfather, I mean. But the colour? What colour was it?'

Again Bernie shook her head. 'I'm sorry, but I don't know. Remember, I was to see it for the first time on this cruise. He liked surprises.'

'So, two yachts, both unseen by anyone we know of. In the case of "our" yacht, we do know its owner. Or rather its dead owner, because our man was drowned during a storm. We know the name of the trustees and – hold on.' Nick had remembered something. He clapped his hand to his forehead. 'Listen, this could help. I get my orders from a chap in London. His name's Arnold J. Ponsford. He's American like you, and he's acting for the trustees of the dead man's estate. He lives somewhere near the British Museum, and I've got his telephone number somewhere. He's the man who paid me, and sent me my air ticket. Now, if you want confirmation from him that he really is working for the man he says he's working for, why not give him a ring? You might detect something from his manner if he's lying. It's only a thought.

'Also, it might be just possible that he heard of another yacht in this area when Rochester's yacht went down in the storm. Two boats could have foundered, and your godfather could have disappeared as well. It was a sheer coincidence that Rochester's yacht settled on a ledge off the island, otherwise no one would have found it either. As it is, no-one has yet found a body, as far as I know. If they have, then someone is keeping very quiet about it. If we had a body things would be a lot easier. There would be none of this uncertainty. Bodies can always be identified, even after they've been in the water for some time. But as it happens, all we have to work on is one unseen boat, and two watchdogs out there, who bite.'

'As a matter of fact,' he went on, 'I wouldn't mind having a word with Ponsford myself. The post office in Patiteri will put the call through for you. I'd like to tell him that I don't like his employees. They might be good divers but I don't like their manners. We could go around eleven as there's a two hour time difference between London and Greece. You might have to book your call.'

'No, I'll take you,' said Markos suddenly. He had jumped to his feet and looked like a man who had suddenly made up his mind. 'You'll need a hand with the Greek, I expect. They speak a strong dialect around here.'

'But I could get away tomorrow,' protested Nick, who didn't want to entrust Bernie to Markos. 'The work's tailing off a bit. And I could do with speaking to Ponsford.'

But Bernie hadn't head him. She was staring at Markos, and she too had made up her mind. 'Thanks for the offer,' she said softly. 'It's good of you to help me.'

Nick felt annoyed and humiliated and puzzled. Why had Markos taken it upon himself to be Bernie's guardian?

That night, Petra came to Nick in his room. He was standing by the window when he heard her knock on his door. He was surprised because she'd never come to him before, and lately he'd thought she was avoiding him. She walked across to join him, and together they looked out at the moon shining down on the waters of the bay.

'Nick,' she began quietly, 'what if James Rochester and Nelson Donelly are one and the same person? What if our yacht is the one Bernie's looking for?'

'Then either one or the other was murdered or removed from the scene. But I don't know why. You don't murder someone for a collection of pots, however precious. Let's hope Ponsford can throw some light on the mystery. I think myself that Bernie's godfather disappeared somewhere out there. It was a fierce storm by all accounts. It's quite possible that she will never find him.'

'This used to be a quiet place,' said Petra, turning to face Nick. 'Nothing ever happened. Now there's mystery, and death, and talk of murder. I don't like it. It's not even safe to sail over to the island. It's just as well your wife didn't come to join you.'

'My wife?' Suddenly he realised how little she had been in his thoughts during the last week or so. 'What makes you think of her?'

'Oh, I don't know. She must miss you, don't you think?' She was looking at him enquiringly.

'If you mean has she written to me since I've been here, the answer's no. She knews this address, because I've sent it to her. she knows about the post office at Patiteri because I sent her a post card from there, with the telephone number.'

Suddenly Petra put her arms round his neck. He could tell she was upset, and held her close. Once again he smelt the sweet smell of herbs in her hair, and he knew he wanted her. But the mention of Marian had brought him back to reality. He kissed Petra gently, and tried to draw away. But she didn't

116

want gentleness. She wanted him to desire her, and show it. So he kissed her again, more fiercely this time, and felt her respond. The warmth of the scented night was all around them, and he could feel her breasts through the thin cotton of her night dress. She unbuttoned his shirt, and kissed his chest. Her hands were stroking his neck and shoulders, and caressing the outlines of his face.

'Nick,' she said, 'make love to me. I know you want me.'

But he knew that it was neither the time nor the place for love. 'No, Petra,' he said, gently taking her hands. 'Of course I love you. Of course I want you in my bed. But, darling, I'm not free. You know that. And I don't want to make you unhappy. We must wait. It won't be long before the work's finished here, and then I shall have to think about the future. But remember, I'm twenty years older than you, almost old enough to be your father. You ought to marry someone more suitable than me, someone nearer your own age. And,' he said realistically, 'this is not the moment to make love. Your parents haven't come upstairs yet, and Andrikos would kill me if he found us like this. To say nothing of Markos.'

But she still clung to him, her eyes fixed on his face.

'Nick, this American girl. You like her, don't you? Do you find her attractive?'

So that was it, he thought. He should have guessed. Petra was afraid of Bernie.

'No, no,' he said, stroking her cheek. 'She's not my type. Too strong. Too dynamic. I'd be left behind breathless. No, I prefer Greek girls, even if they have blonde hair, and come into my room when they shouldn't.'

'But Markos likes her,' she said, slightly pacified. 'He seems to be spell-bound. And he's only known her for a few hours.'

Nick paused. How could he possibly tell her his doubts about her brother? Let her think Markos was fascinated by Bernie's charms. But he would have to watch them both from now on, to see whether Bernie was Markos' accomplice or his victim.

He smiled down at Petra, calming her with his voice. 'Well, let's hope his condition is reciprocated. But believe me, Petra, it's you who fills my thoughts all the time. And now I think now you should go back to your own room.'

117

He kissed her again, and led her to the door. The magic of the islands was all around. Soon, he knew, it would be too strong for him.

Nick and Petra were waiting for Markos and Bernie when they got back from Patiteri the following day. It was half-past one, and they had agreed to meet at Spiros's taverna. Markos had dressed up for the occasion and was wearing a dark blue suit and pale shirt that set off his dark good looks. He looked the prosperous businessman, taking the morning off from his affairs. Nick could see him one day as Mayor of Alonnisos.

'Any luck?' he asked.

Bernie shook her head. 'I got through all right. There was no problem in calling London. But an Oriental guy answered the phone. He said Ponsford cleared out of that address on July 10th and gave no forwarding address. His rooms are still empty, so I guess I was speaking to the landlord.'

Nick looked at her in some dismay. 'Damn! He didn't tell me he wasn't staying in London for the summer. I wanted to get in touch with him about the rest of the amphorae. They need to be catalogued, and I'm a bit behind on the paperwork. They ought really to go to a proper team of experts before they get shipped out of the country. Some of them are still very fragile. Now I don't know who to contact. Damn!'

'So we're no further forward with finding out who the real owner of the yacht is,' said Petra. 'Is there anyone else we can contact?'

Spiros had been hovering in the background during this conversation. Now he stepped forward looking anxious. He had lost weight, Nick noticed, and his hand was still bandaged. He was also tense, and there were shadows under his eyes, as if he hadn't been sleeping well.

'Mr. Harding, sir,' he said, ignoring Markos, 'won't you introduce me to your new friend? Is she going to stay in our village?'

'Yes. Sorry, Spiros. Come and meet Miss Fitzpatrick who is staying with Markos' family for a few days.' Nick made the introductions. Spiros was polite but less effusive than usual, as if something was on his mind.

'I'm trying to solve a mystery,' Bernie explained, sitting down next to Nick and helping herself from a bowl of olives. 'My godfather disappeared back in June. He was sailing a yacht a bit like the one Mr. Harding's working on. My godfather was called Nelson Donelly, an American like me. Have you heard of him?'

Nick watched Spiros. He seemed frightened, and his attention was on Markos rather than the American girl.

'Miss Fitzpatrick, there is only one sunken yacht in these parts. Mr. Harding knows all about it. He knows who the owner is. I know nothing, nothing at all. It's just a simple salvage operation, I believe. That's all.'

'Then why is it guarded?' said Nick suddenly. 'Why are there men out there with guns?' He watched Spiros closely, seeing his growing agitation.

'Because there are valuable things on board, Mr. Harding. Surely you know that. And valuable things have to be guarded. They must protect the yacht from sightseers.'

'Not by shooting at them. Not even sunken treasure ships filled with gold are guarded by men with guns.'

'Not in your country maybe, but out here things are different.' Spiros began to flick away imaginary crumbs from the table cloth.

'I didn't know about the guns,' said Bernie quietly. 'I'm pretty sure that it can't be Nelson's yacht out there. He had nothing on board as valuable as that, I'm certain of it.'

'We didn't tell you last night because we didn't want to alarm you on your first evening here, but the yacht is closely watched and it wouldn't be wise to go out there and see it. Would it Spiros?'

But he wasn't to be drawn. He had calmed down a little, and was waiting for their lunch order. He beckoned Angie to bring more retsina.

'It's better to keep away from private property, Mr. Harding. Out here, people take private property seriously. And you yourself have said that the jars and pots are valuable. Lots of people would want them as souvenirs.'

'Maybe. But no-one has broken into the hut and taken any. They're there for the asking, as you know. There's no lock on the door. Why then guard the yacht? Why not put two chaps

119

on guard outside my hut all night? That would make more sense.'

But Spiros seemed to have lost interest. He turned to Markos.

'Come now, Mr. Karakulas. *Calamari* for your guests, fresh today, and *tzatziki* – very refreshing. We make our own yoghurt,' he explained to Bernie. 'Even though we haven't seen your godfather, I hope your stay here will be pleasant. We are a very straightforward people. Nothing dishonest. Nothing devious.'

'Except a tendency to fire at you if they don't like the look of your face,' said Nick under his breath.

Chapter 12

Spiros was frightened. The midnight call was late in coming. He now hated the whole business, and since the attack on him, detested the Frenchman. But he also knew he was trapped. There was no going back now. He depended on the money. Katerina had just told him she was expecting another child and wanted an annuity, and his wife was pestering him for a deep-freeze just because she had finished child bearing. Sometimes, Spiros thought, life was not worth living.

But the call came at a quarter-past twelve, just as people were leaving the taverna. Spiros stared at the phone as if mesmerized. Prickles of fear rippled down his spine. My God, he thought, how he hated the Frenchman.

'Spiros? Where the hell have you been?' The familiar voice was harsh with irritation. He wished he'd never picked up the receiver. 'Didn't you know I was going to phone tonight? You bloody Greeks are all the same. Drink and women. That's all you care about. Never again am I going to operate in your part of the world.'

Spiros thanked God for that remark. He, too, had had enough of bloody Frenchmen. He was tired of being shoved around and bullied on the orders of Magnus, whom he'd never seen and never wanted to.

'What's up, Magnus? What do you want me to do?' he managed to say at last.

'What you're told, no more. Why did you let that Englishman near the yacht? You know it's not clear yet.'

Spiros was just about to make a sharp retort but thought better of it. Magnus had to be humoured. There was nothing to be gained by antagonizing him at this stage. Although he knew his right hand would always be safe. They needed that for their own purposes. Still, there were other things they could do. Spiros suddenly felt his stomach churn with fear.

'I'm sorry, Magnus, but I'm not Mr. Harding's keeper. I couldn't stop him going out there. I knew nothing about it until Takis told me.'

'It was your job to watch him, as I told you before. He asks too many questions. We can't remove him yet, until all the stuff has gone, but watch him.'

'He's harmless. He won't go near the yacht again. And, Magnus, was it really necessary for Takis to start firing at them? Everyone's angry and suspicious. They could have called in the police, and that would have been the end of it all.'

'No, it wouldn't. We're ready for that. The evidence would have all been removed. All the police would have found is a couple of divers, and a collection of old pots. But it mustn't come to that. I've told Takis to cool off, and I've put the other two on the wreck. Damn Greeks! They're always trigger happy. I should have used Frenchmen, but that would have caused far too much interest. It's bad enough having an Englishman on the spot. And Spiros – who the hell is this American girl? Is she dangerous? How much does she know?'

'She knows nothing. She tried to make some enquiries about the London end, but the contact has left so she got nowhere. I think she's already decided that the yacht is not the one she's looking for. And Karakulas is keeping her occupied.'

'Good. Keep it that way.' The voice had become harsh with irritation. 'I've had almost enough of these distractions. Watch her, Spiros. This girl mustn't foul up the operation. We might have to remove her if she becomes suspicious. Nothing – *nothing*, I say – must go wrong now. Do you understand?'

How he hated the man! His arrogance and indifference to other people's difficulties. How was he supposed to be able to watch everyone's movements, and read everyone's thoughts? But all he said was: 'Yes, Magnus. But we have to be careful.' His voice had dropped to a mere whisper. 'People are getting

122

to know her. We don't have many Americans around here, and she is particularly charming. There'll be one hell of an outcry if she disappears. She's also rich with influential contacts back in the States. Not quite a Sixth Fleet job if she disappears, but almost.'

'Relax. We won't take any action yet. I rely on you to keep her off the scent.'

Spiros cursed his luck. The Frenchman asked the impossible.

'Listen.' Magnus seemed to have relaxed a little. 'Next week, the fourteenth, the dead will rise. Do you understand?'

Spiros' heart missed several beats. So soon? 'I understand. And where will the dead go when it's risen?'

'With the others. Then the yacht will be clear. But we still need Harding. Papadopoulos isn't ready for us yet. More crates have to be cleared.'

'And me? The usual?'

'Yes, of course. Don't fail us. After the fourteenth that will be the end of the business as far as you're concerned. You'll just have to keep things ticking over until all the stuff is away. But watch Harding. He could be a problem. If he asks too many questions, he will have to go. Nothing must stop the operation now. Nothing.'

The phone went dead. Spiros looked down at the receiver as if he wanted to dash it against the wall. He was safe for another week but that was all. Also things were looking bad for Mr. Harding and the American girl. He liked Mr. Harding. Every day he looked at the gleaming pile of neatly pressed shirts which he sent to Patiteri for special laundering. So many people had admired them. Even his wife had admitted reluctantly last Sunday, that he looked handsome in them. It was years since she'd paid him a compliment. Perhaps, thought Spiros as he stood there, still holding the receiver, he ought to warn Mr. Harding to keep clear of the wreck. . . . But maybe he should say nothing. It might only make the Englishman more suspicious. And Englishmen were stubborn. They could never take a hint. He'd want to know why he wasn't allowed to ask questions, and what business was it of Spiros' anyway? It was all too complicated.

In any case, Mr. Harding was safe for the time being. There

was still a lot of stuff to be shifted. And so far he suspected, nothing. He'd be safer if he just stopped asking questions. But then it wasn't easy to stop someone trying to find out why he'd been shot at on an evening's outing with his girlfriend. Somehow, he'd have to get Mr. Harding to accept things as they are, get on with the job and stop asking questions. But it was going to be difficult.

For several days Nick watched Markos closely. The two men scarcely talked to one another now. Nick resented Markos' criticism of his friendship with Petra, and he also suspected that Markos knew more about the submerged yacht than he was prepared to admit. And he couldn't understand his pre-occupation with Bernie.

Nick liked the American girl. He liked her frankness and her cheerful self-assurance. He agonized over whether he ought to confide his suspicions about Markos to her. But she was old enough to look after herself, and Nick knew how much he'd resented Markos interfering in his relationship with Petra. So he said nothing but watched events closely.

Each day Markos went off with Bernie on some expedition or other. Sometimes on foot to look out from the headland. Sometimes in Markos' car. Several times they set off in his boat on trips to the neighbouring islands. Once Bernie told Nick that they had hired a friend's motor launch and been to Skyros, some twenty-eight miles away. They'd also been north to Pelagos and Iura, but always they came back with the same answer. There was only one yacht that people knew about and that was the one off the island of Peristera. If there was another one, then it must have foundered in the storm and sunk without trace. But Bernie couldn't rest until she'd explored every island and bay in the Sporades, and Markos was happy to take her wherever she wanted to go.

Throughout this period, Nick was restless and unhappy. He suspected Petra was avoiding him. She spent more and more time in Patiteri with a party of Scandinavian tourists, and Nick would often go there in the afternoons and, hidden away in the corner of a quay-side café, sit and watch her. He loved to see her wind surfing, her long honey-coloured hair streaming behind her like a flag. She was an expert water-skiier, and people would come from all over the island to watch her demonstrations in the bay of Patiteri.

His work was beginning to diminish, and he could take longer and longer periods away from the hut. The two men who brought him the pots only came once or twice a week now and he hadn't seen the grey van for several days. He expected to be told any day that his work was over. And that was the moment he dreaded.

He had to be home about September 15th for meetings and a conference before term started, and soon he would have to book his seat home as they were hard to come by at this time of the year. In many ways he wanted to get away from the place. He knew he was becoming obsessed with Petra. He felt like Dr. Aschenbach in *Death in Venice* who wanders the streets looking for the boy, Tadzio. He felt he would come to the same end if he didn't pull himself together. But twenty years of marriage, even if it wasn't a particularly happy union, were hard to dismiss. He knew Petra was deliberately distancing herself from him so that she might allay her family's fears and give him a chance to make up his mind.

He could, of course, ask Marian for a divorce. Thousands of people went through the process every year. But then what? Was it really fair to expect Petra to saddle herself with an ageing academic, and not a very rich one at that? Would her family really want her to give up her life in the islands and go off and live with him in England? And there could be trouble with Marian if she wouldn't agree to the divorce. Did he really want to involve a young girl in squalid scenes with an emotional middle-aged woman? It was all an unbearable mess.

It was in moments like this, when he could see no way out of his predicament, that he took himself off for long walks to the end of the headland. There he would listen to the sound of the sea as it surged through the underground passages. Once he saw a water spout hurl itself into the air in front of him, a great jet of water thrown up by the pressure of the sea behind it. After hanging weightlessly in the air for a second, it had dropped back into the ground. There had been no warning, not even a subterranean rumble, just a sudden eruption and then a gentle subsidence. It was a strange landscape, he

125

thought. Beautiful but sinister. Dolphins leaping joyously in the sea. Demons grinning from the craggy sides of the cliffs.

One night, he sat as usual by his open window. It was late; after one' o'clock. As usual, he'd been unable to sleep. The pattern was now familiar. He'd fall into a light doze around midnight and sleep for an hour or two. Then he'd wake up, unable to drift off again until five o'clock. Then he'd fall into a deep sleep, and wake up at his usual time exhausted and depressed.

That particular night, about ten days after Bernie's arrival, there was a bright moon and the air was scented and caressing. It seemed a waste to be inside on such a night, and with thoughts of his imminent return to England he decided not to waste a moment of it. So he put on his shoes and trousers and went out into the garden, down the path which led to the beach. The sand shone whitely ahead of him. The gnarled shapes of the olive trees were sleeping trolls. There was no sound, not even a whisper from the sea, just the faint sound of a bell from one of the goats turning restlessly in the hut where they were locked away each night. Even the dogs slept.

Then he heard the engine noise, the heavy throbbing sound of a powerful diesel. He stopped and looked out to sea. There, coming round the headland from the direction of the sunken yacht, was Markos' boat *Centaur*. And the man at the helm was unmistakably Markos. Nick looked at his watch. It was a quarter to two. What the hell had Markos been doing out there at that time of night, he thought? He hadn't been fishing because when he stopped the engine and pulled the boat up on the shore, he took nothing out of the bottom of the boat. It was hardly likely that he'd been on a pleasure trip at that hour of the night.

He stepped back behind one of the pine trees, and Markos passed him so close that Nick could have stretched out a hand and touched him. Markos carried a torch, nothing else. He strode up the path, and into the house. As Nick watched, first the bathrom light went on then the light in Markos' room. Then darkness fell. Quietly, and even more worried, Nick went back to his own room and tried to sleep.

August 13th was Bernie's birthday. She was thirty-three, a fact she wasn't proud of. Most of her contemporaries in New

126

York had married by now, sometimes twice. Several of her friends had babies. It was an age when, in the past, girls would start to become reconciled to their lot as spinsters.

It was a hot cloudless day with a slight breeze, perfect for sailing, and Petra had left early for her class in Patiteri, promising to be back early for the birthday dinner. Bernie looked forward to the long day ahead of her. Elisavet had been delighted at the opportunity of providing a celebration meal, and she had left the house early in pursuit of delicacies. Bernie had settled herself on the terrace with a book and a jug of coffee, and listened to the sounds coming from the kitchen. Elisavet employed a village girl to help her there twice a week. There was no sign of Markos.

She found it difficult to concentrate on her book. She'd read several pages without understanding a word, but she needed this time to herself. It was an opportunity to think and make decisions. The ten days she'd spent with the family had been very happy, in many ways the happiest time she'd ever known. They had made her very welcome, and she'd relaxed in the sun and the warmth of their friendship. Of course she was still worried over Nelson's disappearance but as the days passed, she was beginning to think she would never find him. It was more than probable that he had drowned when his yacht capsized. Thousands of sailors had come to the same end since time immemorial. However, once she'd fully accepted the fact, she knew she would have to think about returning to New York. Or at least Athens, where she would have to notify the authorities. But she dreaded the thought of leaving the island. It was comfortable, safe, and Markos had been attentive.

But she'd noticed a gradual change in him since she'd arrived. Each day he'd seemed more withdrawn and silent. On the trip to Skiathos the day before he'd hardly said a word, and had looked away every time he'd caught her eye. Something, she knew, was wrong. And it worried her. She liked the strange dark man whom the Elizabethans would have described as 'melancholic', and she had to admit that she found him disturbingly attractive. It was this feeling that she wanted to analyse, as it had been a long time since she'd felt anything like it for a man. Not since the affair with Gerry

127

which now seemed centuries ago. Markos had been very kind, and very patient. He'd taken her to remote places in search of a yacht which she suspected he didn't really believe existed. But suddenly, over the last few days, there was a tension between them which she couldn't understand. And now, she thought, he was beginning to avoid her.

So it was with some surprise that she looked up from her book to see him standing in the doorway. He'd put a basket down on the table and was looking at her shyly, like a schoolboy told to be polite to a middle-aged aunt.

'Happy birthday, Bernie. If you're not doing anything special, why don't we go over to the island and take food with us? We could swim, eat, and come back in good time for your dinner. Everyone else is occupied, and it's a good day to be out on the water.'

She put down her book and got up to go with him. 'What a marvellous idea. No, I've no plans for the day. And it's my turn to steer that great boat of yours.'

Together they went down to the beach to where *Centaur* had been pulled up on to the sand. There was no sign of Nick, or Bernie would have asked him along too.

'Don't you like sailing boats?' she asked, as together they hauled the boat into the sea.

'Not any more. They're treacherous, especially around here.'

'But you don't mind Petra sailing?'

'I'd rather she didn't. But it's impossible to stop Petra from doing anything, once she's made up her mind. But I was happier when Yannis was with her. He knew the wind better than anyone else I've known.'

Bernie said nothing. She'd heard about Yannis, and knew how his death had affected the family.

They set off for the island of Peristera on the other side of the straits, landing in a tiny cove. The heat, as they approached land, was intense. There was no one around, not even the ubiquitous herd of goats. They pulled the boat up on to the shore, and Bernie looked up at the cliffs.

The silence was overpowering. Even the cicadas seemed subdued. Markos picked up the basket and made his way across the beach to the track which led up the cliff.

128

'Come,' he said. 'We'll not go far. It will be cooler under the trees. We can come back here to swim later.'

She followed him up the sandy track, under the scented pines. It was cool and shady, like the nave of a cathedral. Shafts of sunshine pierced the arch of branches overhead creating a stained glass window effect of shifting colours and patterns. There was a smell like incense from the herbs which she crushed under foot.

At the top, they looked over to the island of Alonnisos. They could see quite clearly the harbour of Steni Vala, and the red-tiled roof of the taverna. They saw the clusters of white houses scattered at random over the hillside above Agios Demetrios.

'It's beautiful,' she said. 'Does anyone live here? I thought I saw something over there. It looked like a white building.'

'That was the church. People did live here, but then the earthquake destroyed their houses and they went away. Now just a few tourists come here to swim and snorkel. There are a few deserted huts around. Sometimes at this time of year visitors of the hippy variety come over and sleep in them. But sooner or later they have to go over to Alonnisos for bread and *ouzo*.'

They walked on towards the building, a typical fishermen's church. Four stone walls, a round dome for a roof, and the white stone cross on top.

'You see there was a community here once. They had a church. It's not much but big enough for the people who lived here.'

Markos pushed open the heavy wooden door, and they looked inside.

'Not much to see. No decorations like the ones you saw the other day with Petra in the monastery. The people here didn't have much money. But I like the air of peace, and it's always cool here. It's one of my special places.'

'It's perfect,' said Bernie, who was dazed by the beauty of the place. 'How long has it been here?'

'Long before the Turks came. It survived the earthquake. I think it could survive most things. The walls are very strong, like a fortress. But let's go outside. There's a wonderful garden which the priest used to look after.'

129

The church was surrounded by a cultivated plot which had been allowed to run riot. Olive trees jostled with fig and vine for space. The grass was waist high, and green and moist, which suggested a fresh water spring somewhere. Vines, heavy with grapes, grew rampant like wild things. But they were not yet quite ripe.

Markos found a place under a fig tree where the grass was green and soft. He sat down, put his hands behind his head, leaned back against the tree trunk and looked up at the sky.

'This place has memories for me. They found the boat here, you know. The boat which my wife and Mitsos went sailing in. They never found the bodies. That's why I don't like sailing boats.

'Perhaps I shouldn't come here any more,' he said to Bernie who had sat down next to him. 'Perhaps it's time, like Andrikos says, that I forget the past. Nothing can bring back the dead. But all the same, I still love this place.'

'I've got memories too,' said Bernie quietly. It was the moment for confidences. 'But they do fade in time. After all, the past is over and done with.'

'Did he die too?'

'No, I wish in some ways that he had. He simply said he didn't want me any more. I was too much trouble. You see, he was married and would never leave his wife. Perhaps desertion is worse than death, because the person is still there.'

'But you can't still love a man who has done this to you?'

'No, not now. But at the time. . . She looked around the little clearing. The air was vibrating with the hum of insects.

'I think Nelson is dead. I don't feel I shall see him again. I think now he is at the bottom of that beautiful sea out there. It's not a bad place to be. But I shall miss him. He was more than a father to me.'

'Was he very special?'

'Yes. He's really responsible for what I am. When my parents died, he paid for everything – a good school, my clothes, the university. My grandparents couldn't have afforded it. He never married, so I suppose I was a daughter for him. He'd bought me a birthday present. He said so on the phone that time when I last spoke to him in Rome. He seemed pleased with it.'

130

Markos suddenly jumped to his feet. The movement took her by surprise.

'Your birthday! I nearly forgot. Let's put away all these sad things. Away with the shadows! I've bought you a present too,' he said, suddenly shy again.

He went over to the basket, and opened it. First he took out a white cloth, and laid it on the grass. Then four ripe figs, which he placed on a big leaf. A bunch of grapes, two thick glasses, and a bottle of golden wine.

'First, we drink your health,' he said, and poured out a glass of wine which he handed to her. 'Now the present. I bought it in Patiteri. I hope you like it.'

She opened the package, smiling up at him in surprise and delight. Inside was a string of amber beads, the colour almost of the wine. They were beautiful and flawless.

'They come from the Baltic, I gather. What they were doing in Patiteri, I'll never know. The man said he bought them off a tourist. I thought they would match your hair. Here, let me do it.'

Bernie had laid the beads against the neck of her blouse, but was having difficulty fastening the little gold clasp. She came over to him, and gently he fastened the necklace. Then he stood back and looked at her consideringly.

'They look good? Do you like them?'

She stood with her back to the sunlight, laughing. She looked very beautiful in the pale green cotton blouse and skirt she'd bought in honour of her birthday. Markos stared at her in wonder.

'Behold thou art fair, my love; behold, thou art fair.'

Bernie laughed at his seriousness. 'Thanks for the compliment. But you can skip the bit about my hair being like a flock of goats. The poem goes on about fig trees putting forth her green figs. And look, we have them. We're surrounded by them.'

She picked up one of the figs he'd brought, and bit into the moist purple flesh. It was bursting with ripeness, and the juice ran down her chin.

'Look, figs. Figs everywhere.'

Then Markos took her into his arms, and kissed the juice away from her lips. He was very tense, and she could feel his urgency. Suddenly, she too became serious.

131

'Take off your blouse,' he said almost sternly. She undid the mother-of-pearl buttons. She wore nothing underneath as her breasts were firm and needed no support.

'You have beautiful breasts,' he said as he stood there gazing at her in wonder. Then, gently, with hands that trembled slightly, they undressed each other. He led her to the fig tree, and together they lay down in the shade. Slowly, hesitantly, they caressed each other, marvelling as lovers do over each other's perfection. Markos was a gentle but strong lover, like no-one she had ever met before. She felt as if she was experiencing sexual desire for the first time. She didn't dare to call it love. Not then. Gazing up at the sun filtering through the flat green leaves of the fig tree, she felt like a new Eve in the Garden of Eden.

His strong hands, slightly roughened by manual work, stroked her breasts. He kissed her face, drawing her hair round her like a cloak. She could feel him trembling with excitement; she felt his lips on her breasts. She felt her own desire and knew that she wanted him inside her, and to share his excitement.

At first he was too eager, like a boy with a girl for the first time. So she had to guide him to the place. Then he was uncertain, as if he didn't know whether she really wanted him.

'Are you sure?' he whispered. 'Do you really want me?'

His breathing was coming quickly now, and he was stroking her thighs. Then his hands were between her legs, caressing and stroking her, but not wanting to hurt her. It was as if he didn't trust his strength. For an answer she simply seized his hand and held it there until he felt her desire. Then he bent down and kissed her rounded stomach, and licked the tiny circle of her naval.

'Is it good?' he said, wanting to please her.

'Very good,' she said. 'You are a wonderful lover.' Then his control deserted him, and he took her fiercely. She cried out with that eerie cry of a woman experiencing an intense sexual climax. She was trembling and held him to her, not wanting him to stop. She loved his powerful body, and the dark head between her breasts. She loved the feel of his penis, that marvellous instrument of pleasure, between her legs.

132

It was over too soon. He was shaking with excitement, and it was a long time before he lifted his head and looked at her.

'My dear,' he said, 'I didn't intend this to happen. Not today. I've always wanted you, of course. You must have kown that.'

'But what better day is there? My birthday. Look, I'm still wearing your present.'

Sure enough, the amber beads were still in place. They glowed against her sun-burnt skin. He bent down and kissed her neck and then her breasts, as if he was reluctant to be parted from them.

'They look very well. But nothing can match your beauty.'

'Even though I'm too tall, and too strong.'

'Like Aphrodite. All those goddesses were tall and strong.'

'And they live in this place. They are being kind to us today.'

Reluctantly he helped her to her feet. The feast of grapes and figs was still there. The wine untasted in the glasses. The garden had cast its spell over them, and they spent the afternoon sitting together on the grass, sharing the grapes and drinking from the same glass. They made love again as the sun began its descent over Skiathos. This time they took longer, still marvelling at each other's perfection. This time she gave herself to him completely, crying out with joy when they climaxed together.

The bottle was empty, and it was getting late. They packed up the remains of the lunch and walked down to the beach.

'We shall come back,' said Bernie, as she turned to take a last look at the glade. 'This is my place now, as much as yours.'

When they got to the inlet, they raced into the sea, laughing and splashing each other like children. Both were strong swimmers, and they swam to the out-crop of rocks which marked the entrance to the tiny harbour. They lay down on the table-flat surface of one of the larger rocks, and Markos turned to kiss her. She tasted of salt and retsina.

'Happy?' he said.

'Yes. The happiest I have ever been. A wonderful day.'

It was the sound of Petra's singing which brought Markos to his senses. He had gone up to his room almost as soon as they came back from the island. On the way home his mood had changed. Maybe it was the last sight of the bay where the boat had been found, perhaps it was the glimpse of the distant buoy which marked the resting place of the other boat, but by the time they had reached Agios Demetrios he was depressed and full of remorse. He'd left Bernie almost immediately and went to his room where he lay face down on his bed. In spite of Petra's entreaties he had refused to come down for the dinner, saying he had work to do. Fortunately, they were used to his moods. But the joy of the afternoon had gone. What had he done? What would Bernie think of him now? What would be her reaction tomorrow, when the magic of the place had worn off? What could he possibly hope to offer her? What was he but a middle-aged Greek, an impoverished builder? And she, rich and independent, and beautiful.

And to have seduced her in such a place! The place where his wife had died. They had swum together in the little harbour where her body had been found. They had kissed on the rock against which her body might have been battered by the waves. And his son, Mitsos! How could he have looked at another woman, and seduced her so quickly and with so much delight?

But Petra's song brought him back to reality. She had a clear soprano voice, and the song was about love and a young girl on an island in the summer. Andrikos always played the *bazouki* after these celebrations, and he usually liked to play alone. The songs were mostly about war, and Greek victories over the Turks. But that evening he had been in a softer mood, and he'd asked Petra to sing with him.

So when the song ended, Markos crept down to join the family on the terrace. He looked shyly across at Bernie, who was still wearing the same blouse and skirt she'd worn that afternoon. The beads were still around her neck. She smiled at him, a smile full of sympathy and understanding. It told him all he needed to know. That she knew why he was unhappy. That she understood about his wife and son. But, the smile seemed to say, the place had been enchanted. And now it was over. And need never happen again. Everything was as before.

Andrikos put down the heavy musical instrument.

134

'A good birthday, eh?' he said to Bernie. 'You haven't been disappointed?'

'The happiest of birthdays. I don't want it to end.'

'Happiness should never end, child. But it's up to us to see that it lasts.'

Chapter 13

'Can you handle diving gear?' asked Markos.

It was three days after Bernie's birthday, and Nick was sitting at the table in the hut cataloguing the weeks's finds. The deliveries had stopped the day before, and he was now keen to get the paperwork finished; partly for his own purposes, as he wanted a full record of that extraordinary summer, and partly to send a full account of the contents of the crates to the Rochester Estate.

He wasn't expecting to see Markos. The coolness between them had increased over the last few days, and Nick had deliberately avoided talking to him. He was almost convinced that Markos was the leader of some modern gang of wreckers operating in the Aegean, bent on the destruction of rich people's yachts and on stealing their contents. Also he still didn't trust his interest in Bernie.

Now he looked up at the tall figure blocking out the sunlight and nodded.

'Yes. I'm no expert but I had a few lessons last year in the English Channel, off Newhaven. Why?'

'I think we could go down to the wreck now,' said Markos, still standing in the doorway as if reluctant to invade Nick's territory. 'What about this evening? The men seem to have given up for the time being. I've kept an eye on them. There was a lot of activity two days ago, but they've given up the night watch now. How about your side of things? Is there much more to do?' He glanced towards the half empty basket of pots in the corner.

'Nothing yesterday. Mostly paperwork now. But there are

still a few more to do over there. Interesting ones, too.'

'Then we ought to go now. It should be clear out there. We must try and find out the name of the boat. It shouldn't be too difficult. It all depends on which way she's lying, and where they painted her name. But once we've identified it, we are on the way to finding out the real owner. Whoever owned that boat – Rochester, or the other Irishman – must have registered it somewhere.'

Markos, not entirely familiar with America's immigration history, insisted on attributing Irish nationality to Nelson.

Nick felt a stab of excitement. It was what he needed, some physical activity to take his mind off Petra and the uncertainties of returning to England.

'OK' he said. 'Have you got a spare suit?'

'No, but I can get one. What depth did you reach in England?'

'A hundred and fifty feet. The limit, I think?'

Markos shook his head. 'For your waters, yes, but we can go down to two hundred out here. The mixture is different, oxygen and helium. Can you manage that?'

'Yes, I've tried it. We can stay down a bit longer, is that right?'

'We'll need to. We'll have about twelve minutes, at a push. Two to get down, and four to get up. That leaves us with five minutes on the site, and a bit to spare. I'll go inside the hull, if we have to. Could you hover around and get me out of any difficulties.'

'Of course. At least it'll be a bit warmer than Newhaven in April.'

Just before six, Markos was back with the suits and the air cannisters. They changed in the hut, and walked silently down to Markos' boat which was pulled up on the shore. He started the engine, and the boat chugged out into the straits and towards the yellow buoy.

There was no-one there, just as Markos had predicted, and no other sign of life. Just the tips of some mainsails in the distance, part of a flotilla fleet making its way towards the most easterly of the islands, Iura. Even if the boats decided to come back this way they wouldn't interfere with Nick and Markos, as they always kept near the Alonnisos shore when they were in the straits.

137

They tied *Centaur* up to the buoy, and both men put on the rest of the gear. Markos gave Nick a hand with his stabilizer jacket, which held the air cannister in place. He clipped the buckle together, and tested it to see that it was quite secure. Nick did the same for him. Markos gave Nick a knife and a torch, and they both checked their watches then the masks and the air check. With a nod to Nick, Markos stepped off the side of the boat and Nick, with a last look at the blue sky and the cliffs of Alonnisos, followed him.

Down he went through water that was still bright with sunshine. Huge red fish with yellow stripes glided in front of him, as if escorting him to the remoter regions. Fish with huge faces scrutinised him. Faces with blubbery lips, and cold indifferent eyes. They seemed unconcerned at the invasion of their kingdom by two intruders with webbed feet, and back packs of air.

A colony of squid-like creatures scurried past Nick, like a group of London commuters in the rush hour, running to catch their trains. He stretched out a hand to touch them, but felt nothing. They were as unsubstantial as the shades in Hades.

Then the sunshine vanished, and he was in Stygian darkness. It was getting colder, and he knew they were almost there. He saw Markos ahead of him, the light from the torch guiding him, and followed him down. His own torch light fell on a different species of fish, larger and fleshier. They floated past him, colourless grey shapes, like phantom ships. The silence was eerie – just the sound of his own breathing. He felt a surge of exhilaration. He was a god sharing a new element. As powerful a god as any who explored outer space. Just ten minutes of air. Ten minutes to be a god.

Suddenly, below him, he saw the shape of a huge Leviathan lying on its side. It was the yacht, settled with its bows towards him on its starboard side. He glanced at his watch. It had taken them exactly two minutes to get there. Just as predicted.

Markos had disappeared, and Nick swam closer to the wreck to be there if he should be needed. He turned sharply to explore the port side of the boat – and then it happened.

He felt a tug at his back. He tried to swim forward, but something was stopping him. Desperately he looked round,

138

and the torch shore on something that is the nightmare of all divers. A net! The yacht was covered by a net! And no one had warned him. Frantically he turned and twisted, trying to free himself, but he was a fly trapped in a spider's web. The more he threshed about, the tighter he became enmeshed. He felt his heart thundering in panic. He wanted to shout out but no sound came. He reached down for his knife, which all divers have for just such an emergency, but dropped his torch. Instantly he was in total darkness and there was no sign of Markos. He hung there in the cold and blackness, suspended from the hull of the boat by the cannister of air on his back. It was a punishment, he thought wildly. A punishment for challenging the gods. Nick Harding, a second Prometheus!

He still had the knife in his hand, and he slashed around in the dark, trying to cut the net. But he couldn't reach behind him and all his efforts were useless. The he knew he was going to die. He thought of Petra, and Marian, and then his parents. He was gasping for air, suddenly realising that all his movements to try and free himself had used up almost twice as much of the vital oxygen as the time submerged warranted. There were limits to his godhood and he had almost reached them. His end would be here, in the cold and dark, watched by millions of indifferent sea-creatures.

Reality began to recede. He was aware of pain across his chest. Soon he stopped fighting to free himself, as the effort was too much. He knew he was just seconds away from unconsciousness.

Then he felt the arms round him. Two arms that gripped him tightly in the darkness, and lifted him off the side of the wreck. Someone had cut him free. He was dimly aware of the ascent. Someone was sharing air with him. First some for him, then for the other person. Then the sunlight and the warmth. Just as the two men surfaced, Nick passed out. They had made a perfect assisted ascent, and had made it only just in time.

Minutes later he came to. He was lying in the bottom of the boat, and Markos was speeding towards the bay of Agios Demetrios. His face gear had been removed, and someone had unfastened the neck of his wet-suit. He felt aches and pains in all his limbs and tried to move, but the effort was too much.

'Hold on,' said Markos, grim-faced at the helm. 'We'll soon be there. Just keep still.'

Back on the shore, Markos lifted him out of the boat and helped him into the hut. Nick collapsed in the arm chair, and took several deep breaths. Markos went to fetch water. In minutes, Nick felt better. Then he turned on Markos.

'Why?' he said. 'Why the net? And why the hell didn't you tell me?'

Markos' face darkened in anger. 'Because I didn't know there was a net. At the stern of the boat, there's a bloody great hole cut in the hull. Large enough to get in and out without getting caught up. They must have wanted to camouflage the yacht to stop it being seen from the air. They didn't want a crowd of photographers and sightseers obviously. But you're lucky to be alive. Had you been down there on your own, you would be dead by now.'

'But where did you get to? You were a hell of a long time coming.'

'I was inside the hull, you fool! Do you think I wanted you to die down there? Believe me, if I'd wanted to get rid of you, there are easier ways of setting about it.'

'Yes, like flinging people over a cliff – like you did to Yannis.'

For a moment, Nick thought Markos was going to hit him. Instead, he walked over to the door of the hut and stood there in silence. It was then Nick noticed that Markos was holding something in his hand. Something he'd not seen before.

'I'm sorry,' he said. 'That was stupid of me. But I thought I was going to die down there. I should have realised you were inside the boat. Did you find anything?'

Markos glared at him.

'Maybe. I don't know. But I brought this up, if you're interested. If you hadn't made such a mess of your dive, I would have gone down again.'

He held something out to Nick, who was now able to focus on it. It was a spherical object, made of brass and heavily encrusted with sea growths. Nick turned it over and saw that letters had been carved on the back. Six capital letters. He rubbed a finger over their outline.

'N.E.R.E.U.S. Strange. What does it mean?'

'Nereus, the cup bearer of Poseidon. One of the old fellow's favourites. Don't you remember?'

'Oh God, yes. That first night, when Bernie arrived. But how many favourites did the old chap have?'

'Several hundred at a guess, but none of them as well-known as Nereus.'

'So we're still not sure. Why the hell didn't Nelson leave a call sign and the name of his yacht with the port authorities in Volos? It would have saved all this speculation.'

'He was an individualist, didn't have a civil service mentality. But do we tell Bernie? It will only upset her, and we're still not sure.'

Nick, weak but recovering, was struggling out of his wet-suit.

'I think we've got to tell her. It's a clue. she might be able to work on it.'

'I'll tell her tonight. But not about the diving, Nick. You nearly lost your life, but we don't want the family to know. How are you now? I'm damned pleased we don't have to fly you to Volos to put you in a decompression chamber. You're lucky.'

'I only know one thing: from now on I stay up here, in the fresh air. The fish can live in peace. I'm fine, just tired. But thanks for coming to the rescue.'

It was the least he could say.

When Nick got back to the house, he went straight up to his room, pleading an overdose of the sun as his excuse for not joining the others for the evening meal. He didn't see the two letters waiting for him on the table in the hall. When Elisavet brought him up a tray of food later in the evening, she deliberately left the letters where they were. She was worried by his exhausted appearance and drew the curtains in his room to keep out the sun.

Nick slept for twelve hours, and woke up feeling almost back to normal. Coming downstairs, he saw the letters and looked at them in disbelief. The first he'd received since he'd come to the island. Someone must have collected them the day before from Patiteri as there was no delivery to Agios

141

Demetrios. The English stamps looked strangely anachronistic, and for a few seconds he stood there, turning the letters over in his hand, afraid to open them. They reminded him of a world he'd forgotten.

One letter looked official – a long white envelope, a neatly typed address. The other was from Marian. He recognized her copper-plate handwriting. He stared at it as if it were a hostile thing, then took them on to the terrace to read over his coffee. He decided to open the official one first. It could be anything. A letter from his university asking him when he intended to come home. A communication from the elusive Arnold J. Ponsford giving his new address. Income tax. Anything. But probably nothing upsetting. From his experience, only harmless things came in long white envelopes with typewritten addresses.

So he opened the official one first. He read it uncomprehendingly and had to read it a second time before the meaning sank home. It was from his wife's solicitors at a London address somewhere in the City. The language was formal, slightly archaic, the meaning shrouded in circumlocutions. It was quite a few seconds before Nick understood that the term 'my client' referred to his wife, Marian, but eventually the meaning penetrated. Marian was petitioning for a divorce on the grounds of the irretrievable breakdown of the marriage. She wanted him to come over and collect whatever he wanted of the furniture. The house was already on the market. Half of the proceeds would be his. They would need his signature to sell it. The letter was only ten lines long. Plus the reference number, of course. He was interested to see his marriage was filed under the code MH 18. Were there, he wondered, seventeen other couples with the initials MH?

Reality was receding. It was fortunate that he was eating his breakfast alone on the terrace as he wouldn't have been capable of coherent conversation. Was this how twenty odd years of a relationship ended? A polite letter from some strangers in the City, expert at sorting out furniture and houses? He had been so proud of the swimming pool which they had hardly ever used, and the double garage. Now they suddenly meant nothing to him. His first instinct was to write a letter straight away to this firm with the ridiculous name of

Potterton and Blackthorne – like a central heating firm – and tell them to sell anything they liked and give it all to his wife. He had all he wanted here. He glanced round him. A small room in a house overlooking the Aegean. A single bed with a white lace bedspread, and a desk. He'd settle for that.

But there was still the other letter. The one from Marian. At least she had taken the trouble to write to him personally. He'd know that handwriting anywhere. She'd taken lessons in calligraphy early on in their marriage so that she could design her own business and Christmas cards. There were two sheets of paper inside. Her usual thick cream paper which she ordered from a special stationer's in Brighton. The address was engraved in the top right-hand corner. Nick had always disliked the paper. It seemed unnecessarily pretentious. His frugal Newcastle upbringing balked at the extravagance. He always bought his own paper in Smith's, or used the university cards.

'*Dear Nick,*' he read.

'*I'm sorry to disturb you at your important work.*' (That's a lie, he thought. She's not at all sorry. She never liked my work or understood it.)

'*But I thought I ought to say something by way of explanation about the solicitor's letter which no doubt by now you have received.*'

God, it was catching. She'd taken to writing like Potterton and Blackthorne. Or perhaps, he thought with a rush of emotion, she found it easier to write about a painful subject in semi-formal language. Formality eases one through the sadness.

'*For a long time now, I have been aware that all was not quite right with our marriage, and I think the time has come to put an end to it. I'm sure you will agree. You might even be thankful that I have taken the initiative. Simon and I thought we might make a go of it. After all, he knows about the business side of things, and we have now decided we love each other.*'

He dashed away a tear that was threatening to trickle down on to the sheet of paper. For a second he couldn't read any more and looked fixedly out to sea. Then he felt a surge of anger that she could treat the subject so dispassionately. How had she come to the conclusion that she loved Simon? At a business meeting?

143

*'The house is up for sale, as of course I shall need my share
of the proceeds. I think you ought to come home as soon as
possible and choose what furniture you want.'*

At least she still calls it 'home' he thought.

*'Could I have the sideboard in the hall? I'm not sure who it
belongs to – I think we bought it together – but I could make use
of it in the cottage we're buying outside Lewes. I could also
make use of the 'fridge and the deep freeze, if that's all right. I
suppose you will be eating out most of the time. I think I bought
them with my own money.*

Seen you soon,
Yours affectionately,
Marian.'

It was unreal. It wasn't happening to him. Here was his wife
talking about a deep freeze when years of marriage were
ending. And why did she write *'Yours affectionately'* at the
end of her letter? If he ever wrote back, then he would say, as
he always did, *'with love'*. Because he had loved her. He
wanted to remember Marian as the girl he'd loved so desperately when he was an unsure and earnest young man, acutely
conscious of his social shortcomings. He had been dazzled by
her sophistication and county background. Looking back
now, he saw only too clearly that he'd married for the wrong
reasons, and now he was paying the price. Solicitors letters
and disputes about sideboards! Not if he could help it. He
would let her have anything she wanted. He only wanted for
himself the knowledge that she was grateful to him for making
things so easy for her. It was the least he could do.

He went up to his room, and spent the next hour writing
letters. One to Potterton and Blackthorne agreeing to the
divorce. One to his wife telling her to have everything she
wanted. Nothing was really his. Just his books, and then only
the academic ones. He suggested she put them in some crates,
and get them delivered to the university if the house was sold
quickly. He would sign anything she wanted. If he was still
away, then she could make use of that legal machiavellianism
called a Power of Attorney to get round the problem of his
signature.

The last letter was to the University of Athens. He told
them what he was doing in Greece and listed his academic

144

qualifications. It was just possible that they might have heard of him. He told them what he knew of the wreck of the Roman vessel in the bay on the island of Iura, and asked if they were proposing to carry out any recovery of the amphorae? If they were then he would like to help them, if they needed any assistance, as he would like to work in Greece. Then he gave them two addresses: one in Agios Demetrios c/o the Post Office in Patiteri; and the other, his professional address in Brighton. Already he no longer regarded Lavender Cottage as his home.

Then he went out into the heat of the afternoon, started up the engine of the Volkswagen and drove into Patiteri. It was only three o'clock, and the post office was shut, so he sat down in a small café and drank coffee until four o'clock, thinking about nothing at all but fighting off a desperate tiredness. He must have dozed for half an hour or so as it was the noise of someone opening the shutters which jerked him awake. Then he went into the little post office, handed over the letters to a sleepy figure behind the counter and paid the postage. He'd done it. He'd broken with the past. The old clerk looking at him in irritation because he'd disturbed his peace seemed an unlikely messenger of the gods.

Then Nick drove back to the bay and swam a mile out to sea. He swam as he had never swum before. Turning round, he saw the table-like rocks at the mouth of the bay. He made for them and pulled himself out of the water, lying there gasping for air and feeling the sun soak into his body.

He looked up at the sky, streaked by striations of cloud which meteorologists call 'mackerel', and tried to collect his thoughts but it was no use. Images of Marian clouded his brain. Marian in her wedding dress, an unusual one made of old Victorian lace. Marian buying the house in Rottingdean, choosing the furniture with such loving care. Then Marian in bed, always uneasy without clothes. Always conscious of her wide hips, and full breasts. Marian, uncomfortable over his early passion, submitting with grace but without enthusiasm.

Where had he gone wrong? Too much enthusiasm in those early days? Too little consideration for a girl whom the nineteenth-century novelists would have described as 'gently brought up'? Had his Celtic ancestry and working-class

145

upbringing been too much for her? Then, lately, rejected in bed, he had become cold and distant. Again and again she had reproached him for giving her no emotional support, but it was difficult to give that support when she herself had suggested the separate rooms. Now she wanted to marry Simon. A younger man, and one whom Nick had always suspected of being afraid of women. In fact he'd thought him definitely effeminate. But perhaps that's how she wanted it. She would mother him, and spoil him, and he would be undemanding and grateful. Perhaps she needed a passive man.

He rolled over on to his stomach and gazed down at the swarms of fish lazily gyrating around the rock, like a troupe of ballet dancers. For a moment he concentrated on them, trying to drive out the images of his wife from his mind. But it was impossible. At least he could concentrate on the good parts of the marriage. The successful side. His house, his profession. He remembered his lectures with a sudden twinge of shame. The quick witticisms aimed at the gallery. Those ingenuous boyish mannerisms with which he had charmed television audiences. Had they been no more than a cry for attention, an adult version of the need to show off?

But now those days were over. There was time to start again, in a new job if possible. The next thought saddened him. A new wife? One day. And children? He would have liked a child, but Marian hadn't been enthusiastic. Perhaps, he thought ruefully, with that flash of insight that comes to everybody at such moments, he was only now growing up. But it hurt, as growing up always does.

That evening he joined the others for dinner. There were only four of them: himself, Petra, Elisavet and Andrikos. The others were quiet and concerned, and didn't expect him to contribute much to the conversation. He felt Petra was looking at him curiously, and after the others had left she stayed with him for a while on the terrace.

'You weren't in the hut today, Nick,' she said. 'I looked for you.'

'I had things to do, unfortunately. Professional things. Letters to the university. I had to go to Patiteri.'

Suddenly he wanted to tell her everything. To pour out his

146

feelings of anger and guilt over the two letters. To tell her about his share in the marriage break-up. To confide in her his childhood anxieties. He also wanted to take her in his arms, make love to her and cradle his head on her breast. But he knew it would be wrong. Now wasn't the right moment. Not when he was in emotional turmoil, and she had something to tell him. Something that wasn't personal.

She had been out sailing that afternoon, running up the coast to Iura. The wind had been changeable, and several times she'd thought about turning back. Then, just as she'd made up her mind, she'd seen the red motor boat. The two men were motoring along the coast, very near the edge of the cliffs. She had thought they were dangerously near, and wondered whether she should warn them. Then the wind had shifted, and she'd had to tack. When she was back on course, the boat and the two men had disappeared. She was quite clear about it. One minute it had been there; two minutes later, it had gone.

'Now boats can't disappear, Nick,' she said. 'They either go out to sea, or into harbour, or along the coast. Well, this boat didn't do any of these things. It vanished into thin air. And there was only one place it could have gone. Into a cave.'

Her face was serious and puzzled. Nick, too, had forgotten his own troubles. The yacht again. Was it really only yesterday he'd gone down there with Markos? And where was he this evening? He hadn't been in to supper. Had he taken Bernie out to the yacht? And the barometer? Had he told her about it or had he wanted to conceal the fact that he now suspected that the yacht out there was her godfather's. Nick concentrated on Petra's words. There was a mystery to be solved, and he'd wasted a day in selfish introspection.

She went on to describe how she had hung about waiting for the boat to come out but it had not reappeared.

'You must agree it's odd, Nick. The boat must have gone into a cave and stayed there. Those two men aren't tourists. They weren't out for a joy ride. Something is going on. But I couldn't do any more this afternoon, as the wind had freshened and I had to get back.'

'Who was in the boat?' Nick asked. 'The usual couple?' His mind was racing. Had Markos told anyone about the barometer? Probably not, as he wouldn't want the family alarmed – especially Petra, who obviously didn't know about their diving expedition. She thought he was ill from too much sun, something she was familiar with through her teaching of Northern Europeans.

'I couldn't see,' she went on. 'They were too far away. But it was their motorboat all right. There isn't another like that around here.'

Nick was still lost in thought. 'Did they see you?'

'I don't think so. I was a long way away, and they disappeared so quickly that I thought for a moment I must have dreamt the whole thing.'

Nick thought quickly. So the two men had left the wreck, and were taking pleasure trips along the coast. There was only one thing to do, and that was to go after them.

'Could you identify the cave? The one they vanished into?'

'There are only two possibilities. Further along the coast there are literally thousands of caves but in that place there are only two: Cyclops' cave, and another marked by a bush above the entrance. I remember thinking it looked like an eyebrow. Both are huge, and go back well into the hills.'

'We could take a took tomorrow, if you're still willing. We could take the sailing boat, because that has the great advantage of being silent. Also we would look as if we were just out for a joy ride. We'll take torches, and use oars inside the cave. I suppose it's pretty dark in there?'

'It is if you go back far enough. The tunnels can go on for miles. But they're not wide enough for a motorboat. There's nothing inside, you know, and there are no dry places for storing things. I believe they used some of the caves during World War Two for hiding ammunition but they had to build ledges to keep the stuff dry. There's no room to store boxes of pottery.'

'I doubt if they'd bother with pottery but they might want to hide something else. So let's take a look tomorrow. Say around three.'

Petra looked relieved. 'I'm glad you agree with me that it's all a bit odd. But you, Nick? Are you all right? You do look a bit all in. It was stupid of you to stay in the sun so long. You've never done it before. You should have known better by now.'

148

He laughed. 'I was always inside the hut! But the work's nearly over now. I took a long swim, and fell asleep on one of the rocks out in the entrance to the bay. It was stupid of me. Must be advancing senility. Anyway, Markos was very severe with me and told me I deserved everything I got.'

She looked at him sharply. 'Markos? When did you see him? He's been away today. Somewhere with Bernie. No-one's seen him. He also spent last night in his room. There's something strange going on. What is it, Nick?'

He tried to look unconcerned, although his mind was racing ahead. 'Nothing that I know of. He seemed all right when I met him, as I came up from the beach yesterday afternoon. But tomorrow we'll try and clear up the mystery of the motorboat. A good sail tomorrow will chase away the cobwebs.'

'I hope so. There are changes in that quarter too.' Nick looked at her in surprise. What other changes was she referring to? Once again, he fought back the impulse to tell her about the change in his circumstances, but it was getting late and her mind was on the red motorboat and Markos. Later, when the moment was right, he would tell her everything.

'Well, we shouldn't be out too long. We'll have to keep an eye on the weather though.'

He thought of the sky he'd been staring at for most of the afternoon. Those clouds usually meant changes were on the way – changes of a meteorological nature.

'Yes, the wind played around quite a bit this afternoon. But it might settle down.'

He wanted to stay with Petra and talk the night away. There was so much to tell her. But she was particularly solicitous about his well-being, as she knew the dangers of too much sun. Reluctantly he allowed her to steer him up the stairs and, much to his surprise, fell instantly into a deep sleep the moment he fell into bed.

Chapter 14

There was no doubt that the weather was changing. By three o'clock the next day the sun had disappeared behind a thick cloud. The air was hot and humid. Sweat trickled down Nick's back, even at sea. The air was filled with a fine grit which got into everything. Even the waves had lost their energy. Too lethargic to rise and fall, they languorously rolled around in all directions at once. It wasn't a day for sailing. Even the caique seemed listless, its sail flapping impotently against the mast. When the wind eventually came, there were only a few feeble puffs, then nothing.

They made slow progress along the coast, Nick labouring to make full use of all the favourable wind shifts. It was fortunate they didn't have far to go.

'That one, over there,' said Petra suddenly. She was in her usual place in the bows, watching the coastline. 'We're a bit earlier than yesterday, so probably we won't see the other boat. Just as well. But we oughtn't to stay out much longer. Anything could happen at any time in these conditions. Let's get closer in to the shore.'

Nick steered the boat towards the yawning mouth of the cave. It was an eerie sensation. The outcrop of vegetation over the entrance gave it a human appearance. He felt as if he was guiding the boat into the mouth of some monstrous giant. Once inside, the mouth would snap shut like Jonah and the whale.

'We'll drop the mast and sail when we're inside,' called out Petra, unperturbed by the sight of the cave.

Into the giant's mouth went Nick, straight as a dart. Inside all was quiet. The only sound was the gentle soughing of the waves. There was no sign of the bats. They were either asleep, or hadn't colonized this particular cave. The water was a brilliant turquoise and the boat glided over shoals of dazzlingly striped fish which darted around in a frenzy of fear as the caique passed over their heads.

Above them the vaulted ceiling, supported by the perpendicular columns of stalagmites and stalactites, rose up to cathedral heights. Hundreds of half-formed stalagmites formed the pillars of the nave. It wasn't hell they'd drifted into, but paradise.

They lowered the mast, and Nick took hold of the oars and rowed amongst the pillars, astonished at the variety and the beauty of the calcium carbonate deposits. It reminded him of the caves he'd explored in Somerset, or the expeditions he'd made with his father to the Pennines when he was a boy.

But Petra was anxious not to delay. 'There's no-one here,' she said, whispering as if she was in church. 'But the cave goes back a long way, and if they're hiding stuff in here they would find a place down one of the tunnels.'

At the back of the cave, a tunnel dwindled into blackness. It was wide enough to take the caique, and high enough to give them plenty of headroom.

'That's where they would have gone to the other day. There might even be another cave along there, maybe with a room leading off above the water line.'

'Right, we'll take a look. Get the torch ready,' said Nick, feeling like the leader of a troop of boy scouts.

Then they were off into the tunnel, swept along by a current. They were soon in darkness, and the light of the torch shone on the fantastic rocky convolutions of the limestone walls. Strange twisted faced with demonic grins leered down at them. Groups of hideous dwarves, carved by some diabolic sculptor, formed startlingly vivid frescoes. Demons mocked them at every turn in the tunnel. It was not a place for the fanciful.

It was also cold, and eerily quiet. Just the sound of individual drips of water, and the occasional splash of an oar. Nick and Petra, dressed only in their swimming gear, began to wish they had brought pullovers. Petra was shivering. It was a strange world they were in. Nick felt as much of an intruder here as he did in the underwater world of the fish. But the fish had been indifferent. Here they were in demon country, and the inmates didn't like intruders. There was still no sight of a boat, or the men. In fact there was no evidence that anyone had been there for the last thousand years.

'Would it be possible to bring a motor boat up here?' said Nick, as they rounded another bend in the tunnel. There was only just room for their two oars. Soon he would have to use the paddle as the tunnel was narrowing by the minute.

'Not for much longer,' said Petra, her teeth chattering. 'Their boat's wider than ours.'

They crept along for a few more yards, Nick pushing the boat along with the paddle against the walls as he had been taught on the canal boats when he was a child. Suddenly he looked up. Was he imagining it, or was the roof getting nearer? The tunnel seemed to be shrinking. The boat was also moving along under its own momentum, and Nick had hardly any work to do. Suddenly he realised that the current was very strong. It was pushing him along inexorably. The roof of the tunnel was now only a few feet above his head.

'I'm going back,' he said. 'I don't like this. It's going to be a hell of a job going against this current. Where's it coming from? I thought there were no tides in this part of the world. Hold on, I'm going into reverse.' There was no room to turn the boat, but he could crouch like an Indian in the pointed stern, and push the boat back along the way they'd come. The ceiling seemed to be getting closer every minute.

Suddenly Petra exclaimed: 'The wind, Nick! The wind's changed. I hoped we'd have time but it's beaten us. It's coming from the south, and strongly. That explains all the grit in the air. It blows from the Sahara. Now it's pushing water up the cave. It happens sometimes. Go back quickly! These passages can fill rapidly. It's all my fault. I knew the weather was changing, but I hoped we would make it before it blew up too strongly. I should have known better.'

Nick could now touch the ceiling without stretching. There was no sign now of the demons. They had all disappeared beneath the water. There could only be about three feet of tunnel above him. He began to paddle with all his strength, but with a mass of water moving against him, his progress was slow. Petra had become very calm. She had been trained never to waste energy by panicking, and deliberately shone the torch on the water ahead of them, not on the ceiling. Fortunately, they hadn't gone too far down the tunnel, but now he could touch the ceiling, even though he was crouching in the boat. They no longer felt the cold. In fact the exertion was making Nick stream with sweat. What air there was, smelt old and stale, and he began to feel sick. He fought back the urge to vomit. Prickles of fear ran down his back, and again he thought of death by suffocation. But this time he had Petra with him, and the thought intensified the agony. The demons were certainly enjoying their revenge. How much longer, he thought desperately, before the air gave out?

He too knew it was fatal to panic, and dangerous. He looked at Petra crouching in the bottom of the boat, ready to start paddling when he gave the order. His fear turned to a surge of anger. He didn't want to die. Not here, of all places, in a tunnel of the Kingdom of the Trolls. Not with Petra, whom he loved more than any other person he'd known.

But now it was becoming difficult to breathe. Inexorably, the boat was being lifted by unseen hands and forced towards the convoluted roof of the tunnel.

'Here, Petra,' he panted. 'Take one of these oars. Give me the torch. Now push against that wall. It's not far, now. Just round the bend, and then we'll see daylight.'

She reached out and seized hold of the paddle. The ceiling was no more than a few inches above their heads. But they were making progress – just.

When they turned the bend, they saw it – a tiny sliver of light. It was enough to make them re-double their efforts. Now Nick told Petra to lie down in the bottom of the boat. He remembered those holidays in the Pennines, and on the inland waterways of England. His father had hired a long boat and they had explored the canals and tunnels that intersected England. It was then that he'd learnt the techniques of the old nineteenth-century bargemen. You lay down on the flat top of your boat, and pushed against the ceiling of the tunnel using your feet.

He couldn't lie down because the mast was in the way, but

he could lean back against the high stern and wedge his feet on the roof of the cave which was now very close. With all the strength in his long legs, he pushed against the rocky surface. With Petra pushing from the bows, the boat began to gather momentum. Finally, in the manner of the canal navvies of a hundred years ago, the boat shot out of the tunnel into the main cave. They cleared the ceiling by a couple of inches.

For a moment they said nothing, just sat there gulping down great mouthfuls of air. But there was no time to waste. The wind was indeed blowing almost straight into the cave, and they would have a job to get away from the rocks. They were on a lee shore, Nick thought; the shore which put the fear of God into sailing men in days gone by.

Together they raised the mast and hoisted the sail. The wind wasn't blowing directly from the south, and they were able to angle the boat sufficiently to fill the sail. Once outside, they ran back along the coast with the wind almost behind them.

Back in Agios Demetrios, reaction set in. Both were exhausted and frightened. Petra was shaking with cold and shock. Nick put his arms round her and, half carrying her along, made her run to the hut.

'Quick, there's a blanket there and some towels. There's also a pullover somewhere; the one I use if I swim at night. God, you're freezing.'

Back in the hut he made her take off her bikini top, and rubbed her down with the towel. She offered no resistance, and allowed him to dry her hair vigorously. Then he laid her on the rug which he used for sun bathing and wrapped her in the towel. He held her close to him, warming her with his own body. Slowly the shaking stopped and she began to relax. He stroked her damp hair, and felt her body warm now against his. She turned her face to him, and as if in a dream, he kissed her eyes and then her lips. Suddenly he wanted her, and he knew she wanted him. They were two people who had survived danger and now wanted the comfort of each other. He stroked her breasts, warm now and smooth as marble. He felt her turn to him, her hands stroking his back.

'Nick,' she said. 'I want you.'

He remembered in a flash of lucidity how he'd once read

154

that people who had survived a dangerous experience felt sexual desire. Hadn't Aeneas seduced Dido in a cave whilst sheltering from a violent thunderstorm? Should he take advantage of someone he loved who was recovering from a bad experience? But she was insistent, and he realised it would soothe her.

Still keeping the towel wrapped round her, he stroked her breasts and felt her body arch against him. Gently he removed the bottom part of her bikini, and stroked her thighs and firm belly. Her skin was like satin. She pulsated with life, and her face was glowing with love and desire. He bent down to kiss her face and throat, his hands between her legs. She was warm and moist and ready for him.

'What the hell is going on here?' said a voice. It was Markos. He stood in the entrance to the hut, looking down at the two bodies wrapped in a towel on the floor.

Nick leapt to his feet, furious at the interruption. He rushed towards Markos, and pushed him in the chest.

'Get out! This is nothing to do with you. I love her. We were nearly killed out there in the caves this afternoon. Now get out.'

But Markos leapt at Nick, who took the full force of the blow on his shoulder. Splinters of pain ran down his arm.

'Damn you, you bloody Greek,' he shouted, beside himself with rage. 'Who the hell do you think you are? You seem to think you're the only one who has the right to fuck around here. Get back to your friends, why don't you, and leave us alone.'

Markos lowered his head like a charging bull and leapt on Nick. Together they rolled on the sand in front of the hut, panting and groping for each other's throats. Petra had come out of the hut, still clutching the towel around her.

'Stop it you two,' she shouted. But neither took any notice of her. It was quite impossible to tear them apart. They were like two mad dogs.

Markos stood up and aimed a kick at Nick's stomach, but he rolled over and in one swift movement got to his feet. Once again the two men stood facing each other. Petra tried to hold Markos back, but roughly he pushed her aside. Nothing could stop them now.

Then Markos charged. Suddenly, Nick remembered his Judo training of years ago. As a boy, he had gone every night to the Community Centre to compete with other boys from Newcastle. He'd been one of the best, and had got to the black belt class. Now he was re-experiencing exactly the sort of attack he'd faced years ago. But this time it was for real. A huge mass of energy was charging straight at him. To meet force with force was useless. So, stepping quickly to one side, he took Markos neatly on his right hip and threw him to the ground. It was a classic Judo movement; one he'd perfected long ago.

His rage had suddenly left him but there still remained the blow to his shoulder. As Markos rose to his feet, Nick punched him full in the face. Then, leaving him to Petra, he went back into the hut to put on his shirt and wash his face.

Several minutes later, he took the bucket of cold water out to Markos who was still sitting on the ground, clutching his head. He looked up at Nick. Blood was trickling down from his left eye, which was already closing. A dark bruise was beginning to appear.

'Here,' Nick said, handing Markos the bottle of *ouzo* which he kept in the hut. 'Drink some of this. You're going to have a classic black eye and this shoulder's going to give me hell over the next few days. Let's call it quits, shall we? And I'll have some of that, if there's any left.'

Nick took a gulp of the pungent spirit, and helped his opponent to his feet. But Markos brushed aside the helping hand and walked off towards the house. Nick made to go after him but Petra held him back.

'Leave it, now. He'll get over it. Sometimes it takes a long time. You shouldn't have fought him. You were like animals.'

Nick took her hand and pressed it. He felt too weary to talk. Somehow he had to face Andrikos and the rest of the family, but he was glad he'd punched Markos. He'd been asking for it for some time.

Walking back up the path to the house, Petra pale and tense by his side, he thought ruefully how quickly his life was changing. To have experienced the fear of death through suffocation two days running. To learn that his wife no longer

156

wanted him. To hold Petra in his arms. To fight her brother. Now to confront the rest of the family. Nick Harding, the cool academic, was experiencing life in no uncertain terms, and he was not sure that he like it.

At the top of the cliff, Petra turned to look at him.

'Well, one thing's for certain, Nick,' she said. 'Those men weren't in the cave. Or if they were, they won't be alive now.'

Andrikos was waiting for them when they reached the house. One look at his face and Nick knew that he would be asked to leave the family house immediately. The old man could hardly speak for rage, and his hands were shaking. 'So Markos has told him,' thought Nick.

'What's been going on, Mr. Harding? I must speak to you now. There are things I must say.'

Nick looked wearily at him. It was useless trying to pacify him now. Later, when he'd washed and put on clean clothes, he'd tell him everything.

'Give me ten minutes, Andrikos,' he said. 'Ten minutes to make myself respectable, and then I'll meet you on the terrace and try to explain. But let me say this now: I love your daughter, and the last thing I want to do is to harm her. I also have things to show you that might make you feel better.'

Later, over drinks and a substantial dish of cheese and olives, Nick told Petra's family about the contents of the letters. He hated talking about them, but it was now essential to inform Andrikos and Elisavet about his personal situation. It was also vital that Petra should know everything about him.

'I understand,' he began formally, 'that you are worried about my intentions towards your daughter.' He addressed the speech to Andrikos, and Petra put out a hand to try and stop him. He tried to smile at her reassuringly, but found the situation very difficult. He felt like the villain in a Victorian melodrama confronting the avenging father and weeping mother. Except Elisavet wasn't weeping. She was calmly filling glasses and fetching more food from the kitchen. Nick had the strong impression that she had more faith in her daughter than her husband did, and he also had the feeling that Andrikos was enjoying himself enormously. Perhaps it didn't happen every day that his guest gave his son a black eye, and he had the opportunity of throwing his daughter's lover out of the house.

157

'I love your daughter,' he went on, talking now to both parents because of the feeling that he might possibly have an ally in Elisavet. 'And I would never want to harm her. I believe she has some regard for me.' He stopped at this point, looking across at Petra for support. Andrikos was fixing her with an accusing stare, and she seemed to be having some trouble in controlling her facial muscles. For an awful moment, Nick thought she might suddenly burst out laughing.

'Is this so?' said Andrikos ponderously, addressing his daughter.

'Of course I love him, Father,' she said, demure now and in control. 'I loved him from the first day he came here. Even though he gave my brother a black eye.'

'Markos was only doing his duty. But you know Mr. Harding's married, my child?'

'Yes, he told me. He'd hidden nothing from me.'

'Doesn't this make you feel guilty?'

'Not guilty, but sad. You know my views on marriage are not the same as yours.'

'Unfortunately not. The younger generation are all the same these days. No respect for the old order which aimed at protecting women.'

'Perhaps times are changing, Father. And we don't need so much protection. After all, you trained me to be independent.'

Nick thought the moment had come for him to intervene and stop a family argument. He got up and went over to Andrikos.

'This letter came from my wife's solicitors yesterday. You might remember there were two letters for me which Markos picked up in Patiteri. Please read it. It doesn't alter the situation all that much, but it might make you feel better.'

Andrikos read the letter in silence, then passed it over to his wife.

'The second letter was from my wife. She wants to marry someone called Simon, and she wants to keep the sideboard and the deep freeze.'

Then he walked across to the edge of the terrace, and looked out across the sea. There were no stars that night, and

158

the moon had disappeared. The wind still blew from Africa.

The family said nothing for a long time. Then he was aware that Markos had got up and left the group. Petra was standing beside him, and he felt her hand in his.

'I'm so sorry. You should have told me.'

'I was going to, but your head was full of motorboats and wrecks. It doesn't matter. I still love you, and always will. This letter might just make things a little easier. But what happened down there in the hut this evening has nothing to do with these letters. That was just you and me. Nothing else.'

Elisavet handed the letters back to him. 'Thank you for showing them to us,' she said. 'It does make things easier for us. Andrikos doesn't approve of divorce, but he loves his daughter and I believe you will make her happy. He will come round to it, in time. Please stay here as long as you like. You are still our guest. And I hope things work out smoothly for you. Our daughter is just a bit strong-minded.'

Here she put and arm around Petra, and Nick was struck by the likeness between mother and daughter. Suddenly there was an interruption.

'Good God, what's been going on here?' said a strong American voice. 'And what the hell's the matter with Markos? He dashed past me like a mad bull, and it looks as if someone's punched him in the face.'

It was Bernie, back from Volos where she'd been to make enquiries about Nelson's boat. No-one there had heard of a yacht called *Nereus*, or of an owner called Nelson Donelly so she was no nearer a solution. She stood there looking at the family group, and Nick pushed a chair towards her. She looked tired and dejected.

'Sit down my dear,' said Andrikos. 'There's a lot to tell you. You begin, Petra.'

Chapter 15

The taverna was empty except for Petra and Nick, sitting at a table in a corner of the terrace. It was still too early for most Greeks to think of eating. They were discussing the disappearance of the red motor boat when Bernie came in and joined them.

'Has anyone seen Markos today?' she said as she sat down and helped herself to the bowl of olives which Spiros had brought over. 'My God,' she continued, 'what pathetic cats. Why doesn't Spiros feed them properly?'

Two wraith-like cats, apparitions from the underworld, rolled in the dust between the tables. One looked about to give birth. They both had the long pointed faces which Nick had seen on friezes in Egyptian tombs.

'He'll be back soon,' said Petra, and Nick looked at her sharply. Did she know her brother's movements? Certainly she seemed unconcerned.

'If he's not back tonight, then I'll have to go on my own.'

'Not back to Volos?' said Nick.

'No, Athens.'

'Athens! So you've given up Volos?'

Spiros had come forward to fill up their glasses and Nick told him impatiently to leave them alone. He was looking ill, Nick thought. His usual bonhomie had deserted him, and he was becoming intrusive and a nuisance. Apparently he'd bought an enormous swordfish from a fisherman that morning, and was proposing to barbecue it that evening. They could hear the sounds of several people hacking at the flesh in the kitchen.

'We'll eat when it's ready, so go away and leave us in peace.'

Spiros reluctantly left them and shuffled away to his place in front of the bead curtain.

'Yes, I found out nothing there,' continued Bernie when Spiros was out of ear-shot. 'If Nelson did come to these waters, then he didn't bother to register with the Volos authorities. That could mean any one of three things. He couldn't be bothered to tell the authorities where he was, or he didn't intend to stay long, or else something happened to him. In which case, he wanted to vanish, or he died in that storm, or he was kidnapped.'

There was silence for a few moments.

'But why,' said Petra, 'should anyone want to kidnap Nelson? They didn't want to steal his boat – if that is his boat out here. We're not sure of that yet. If they wanted the collection of pots, it wouldn't be worth their while killing a man for them. I know you think they're priceless, Nick, but thieves aren't interested in things that have no value outside a museum. And again, why should they want to spend all that money bringing Nick out from England to do a job any museum would be glad to do for free?

'They'd kill for drugs, or gold, or art treasures. But you don't kill a man and sink his boat for a collection of broken pots. A private collector would want them, though. And pay to have them repaired and shipped to wherever he wanted them. I think we have to assume that James Rochester exists.'

'He certainly paid my air fare, and sent me a cheque. At least his agent did,' said Nick sardonically. 'In fact, this whole business only makes sense if that boat out there does belong to James Rochester. But I suppose there could be two boats in this area – both named after one of Poseidon's favourites. It might be that Nelson had a heart attack whilst he was caught in that storm. Did you check the hospital in Volos, Bernie?'

'Of course. One of the first things I did. And even if he was too ill to give his name when he arrived, then the hospital would have notified the American authorities in Athens. That's if he carried a passport. The hospital seemed pretty efficient.'

'I admit it's all very strange,' said Nick. 'Two boats sink in

161

storms. Two boats carrying collector's items. We don't know what Nelson had bought. Then two men disappear. But we're left with only one boat. One of the men has an heir who wants to recover the amphorae on that particular boat and pays me to come out and get the stuff ready to be transported to the States. So they employ some men to recover the pots from the wreck but they're a pretty unfriendly lot. They warn people away with guns. They go out for joy rides along the coast, and disappear into caves. And now they don't care who goes out to look at the wreck. They even let Markos and I go out and poke around.'

Spiros had come forward to bring the plates and bowls of salad. He lit the oil lamp as the evenings were beginning to draw in now. The taverna was filling up, the fish steaks were grilling on the charcoal grid and the air was alive with insects. Spiros was wanted everywhere at once.

His wife appeared bringing them a plateful of swordfish. There was the usual ritual of filling glasses, and exclamations over the fish. Nick, suddenly contrite over his previous impatience with the over-attentive Spiros now offered him a glass of wine. But too many people were shouting for him, so reluctantly, he drank down the wine and dashed off.

'What now?' said Petra, after they had all eaten for a few minutes.

'I'm going to Athens,' said Bernie. 'It's the obvious place. Don't you see? Look, Markos found that barometer – he told me that other evening when you went to bed, Nick. He told me about the whole episode. By the way, it was very rash of you to go down there. I hear you nearly got killed.'

'It takes a lot more to polish me off. But, yes, it was unpleasant.' Petra put out a hand to touch him. He'd told her most of the details, but had omitted the danger he'd found himself in. She instinctively understood. She knew all about the perils of scuba diving.

'But the barometer could be vital. If *Nereus* was the name of Nelson's boat, then we're on the right track and I can get the police to investigate. Look, Nelson knew a man in the Piraeus customs. I've forgotten his name – Papadopoulos, I think. Yes, that's it, Demetrios Papadopoulos. He set me off in this direction. We didn't discuss the name of Nelson's boat

162

but he'll know it. There'll be a record of it somewhere. By all accounts, Nelson arranged with Demetrios to get the stuff put into one of the warehouses whilst we went off cruising. That was the plan. Then later, he would get it shipped back to Boston. Demetrios is bound to know the name of the boat. At least he could tell us if it was called *Nereus*. If not, then that's Rochester's boat out there and we can all go home.'

'It certainly would establish the name of Nelson's boat. If it was *Nereus*, then we can go to the police. They will probably order the wreck to be lifted, and if it's Nelson's boat, and not Rochester's, then they can arrest Takis and Co. And me too, probably. I'll be an accessory to the murder of your god-father! My God, Bernie, what a situation!'

It was an appalling thought, and for several minutes they sat there saying nothing. It was Spiros who brought them down to earth.

'Coffee, Mr. Harding? Or anything else?'

Nick forced his mind back to the present. 'Coffee, Spiros. Three large coffees.'

Bernie's mind was still spiralling out of control. 'Your car, Nick. Can I borrow it tomorrow? Just to get to Patiteri. I'll leave it there, and it can get me back again. I should get back the same day, if the flights to Athens aren't all booked. But the day after at the latest.'

'Yes, of course. But the car's not mine. Spiros here has been very tolerant. He'll never make any money as a car hire firm.'

Spiros had stopped to listen, and now he turned to Nick.

'Don't worry, Mr. Harding. Your shirts are more valuable than Greek drachmae. You can always make money but not buy shirts like these every day. Not from London tailors.'

'Shirts?' said Petra, suddenly amused. 'Did you have to sell your shirts, Nick, to pay Spiros' bill?'

'That's another story,' said Nick. 'No, not to pay the bill. Only to readjust my life, that's all. And Spiros happened to be in on the act.'

'I'll leave tomorrow, early,' said Bernie, whose mind was still working on the details of her plan. 'A pity Markos has gone off, but it won't take two of us to speak to Demetrios. In actual fact, Demetrios might clam up if he saw Markos. Another Greek, you know.'

163

Spiros came back with the coffee, and this time he didn't linger. In fact he seemed suddenly distant and withdrawn, as if he too had things on his mind, Probably, Nick thought, his wife had shouted at him for talking too much. The sounds of chopping had been replaced by the loud voices of demanding customers, angry over the delay in receiving their supper. Spiros, decided Nick, had an unenviable life.

Bernie set off from the bay of Agios Demetrios at a quarter to eight the next morning. All the signs were that it was going to be fine so there should be no delays on the hydrofoil. In spite of her preoccupation with Nelson's yacht, Bernie loved the hydrofoil. It was the only practical way to get from one island to another, and there were regular services to Skiathos, Volos, but not yet to Athens. She would have to catch a plane from Skiathos.

The hydrofoil was a familiar sight in those waters. It had its regular course, and never got in anyone's way. But it was always there, patrolling its territory, like a creature out of classical mythology. It travelled at high speeds, rising out of the water on stilts like a praying mantis. It hugged the coastline wherever possible, and made spectacular entrances into the small harbours, causing consternation amongst the visiting yachtsmen.

Bernie was glad to be taking a positive step towards tracing her god-father. Instinctively she felt he was close, out beneath the waters of the North Aegean. A practical girl not given to fantasising, she nevertheless felt that he had come here and probably met his death out in the straits between the two islands. Once in Athens, now equipped with the name of at least one boat, she ought to be able to find out for certain.

She would have liked Markos to be with her. She found she was thinking a lot about him now, trying to fathom his strange moods, trying to sort out her feelings and what she wanted from life in the future. The thought of him was with her this morning, stored away in a safe compartment of her mind, to be brought out and examined in quiet moments.

But not then. The road, and the strange car with independent brakes and gears, took all her concentration. The road was no more than a roughly macadamised track, full of pot-

164

holes and dipping precariously down the sides of steep hills. Therefore when she saw the woman waving to her from the side of the road as she rounded a bend, she was not inclined to stop. But the woman seemed agitated, and waved her arms frantically at Bernie. She was a local woman, dressed in the long black skirt of the peasant with a shawl wrapped over her head. She was young, and obviously needed help.

Bernie was a sensible person who knew it was dangerous to give lifts to hitch-hikers. But Alonnisos wasn't New York, and she remembered the kindness she had received when she was travelling on foot round Euboea, so she stopped and wound down the window.

'What do you want?' she said in Greek. 'How can I help you?'

The woman had now wrapped the shawl round her face, and was sobbing desperately.

'My mother,' she said. 'She's ill. Very ill. I must go to the doctor quickly. Would you be so kind as to take me to Patiteri, or at least part of the way? She's been ill all night, and seems worse this morning. She just lies there breathing heavily, and her face is blue.'

'Wouldn't it be quicker to telephone? She sounds bad.'

'*Kyria*, we have no telephone. Perhaps if we pass one we could stop. Perhaps – ' she said, suddenly shy – 'You could show me how to use it. There are no houses near us.' She pointed up the hill, and sure enough there was no house to be seen.

'We live there. The hut behind those trees.'

'Well, get in. We'll see what we can do.'

As the woman seemed so distressed, Bernie got out to help her to the passenger seat. She left her own door open, and stepped out on to the dry grass at the side of the road. Suddenly, two men appeared from behind the olive trees. They were dressed in jeans and western style denim shirts. They had tied scarves over the bottom parts of their faces. The woman melted away into the scrub land.

Before Bernie had time to cry out, one of the men seized her from behind. She felt an excruciating pain as her arms were twisted roughly behind her back. Then the other man came at her, and she took the blow full on the face. The sunlight faded. She could no longer hear the noise of the cicadas, and she felt herself falling, falling, into a pain-filled darkness.

When Bernie didn't come back the first night, Nick and Petra were disappointed but not unduly worried. After all, she had been optimistic to think that she could see Papadopoulos and fly back to Skiathos all in the same day. By the second evening there was still no sign of her, and neither had she telephoned. On the third day, Nick was distinctly alarmed, and when he went down to breakfast, found that Petra had left the house early, before anyone was up. He didn't want to confide his fears to Andrikos and Elisavet, who seemed unconcerned at Petra's departure, so, after breakfast, he wandered disconsolately down to the hut. Somehow he felt Markos was responsible for Bernie's disappearance. The memory of him standing by the bed in the early hours of the morning, gun in hand, was still fresh, and Nick now definitely suspected Markos of being in league with the two men guarding the yacht. For days he had been looking tense and strained, and his disappearance, together with Bernie's, seemed to confirm Nick's suspicions.

The hut was now his office. Most of the jars had been collected and no new ones were arriving, but he still had a lot of writing to do and had borrowed a typewriter from Spiros. It was the sort of ancient machine used by typing schools – an upright Adler. It was adequate for his purposes, although the ribbon was so worn he had to go over the text at the end of the day with a biro.

Around ten, Markos walked into the hut. The swelling from Nick's blow had gone down, but there were dark shadows under both eyes and he was unshaven. His clothes were creased, as if he'd been sleeping rough, and he smelt strongly of *ouzo*.

'Nick, where is she? Petra tells me she's gone.'

Nick got slowly to his feet. 'She hasn't come back here, if that's what you mean. I should have thought you'd know where she is. After all, you wanted her out of the way, didn't you? Just like you wanted Yannis silenced and me drowned.'

For a moment, Nick thought Markos was going to hit him

166

again. Instead, he turned wearily away and looked out across the sand.

'My God, Nick, you're a bigger fool than I thought you were. Can't you see I'm as worried as you are? More, I suspect, because I know these islands, and the people. Can't you see that I don't want Petra harmed, nor my parents worried? I also care what happens to you, as you are my father's guest. But the way you're going on, I don't rate your chances of getting back to England in one piece very high.'

'Thanks! But don't you see that you've been behaving bloody mysteriously lately? Where have you been hiding during the last few days? And what about that gun?'

Markos turned round and looked carefully at Nick.

'So that's it. You saw me checking the gun, and you think I'm going to use it on you and Bernie. As it happens, I think we *shall* have to use guns soon, and I shall want you to help me. It was the gun I proposed to give you, that you saw me with. I haven't used it for years. Let's hope you know how to use it when the time comes, and you don't muck things up again. So you want to know where I spent the last couple of days? Well, come with me. Petra knows, as she came to find me this morning. And thank God she did. The car's at the top.'

They climbed the track to the top of the cliff. Markos' grey Renault was parked in the shade, and the two men got in. In silence, Markos drove towards Patiteri. Halfway there he stopped the engine and got out, obviously expecting Nick to follow. It was a desolate part of the coast. Sandy cliffs dropped down to the sea. There was no bay or harbour, just a steep drop down to a jagged edging of rocks. This was an arid part of the coast, where few trees grew; just a scattering of olive trees clinging to the sandy soil.

Still in silence, Markos plunged down a track, disappearing from sight almost instantly, Nick felt a twinge of nervousness. If Markos was going to get rid of him, here was the perfect place. A sheer drop, only the rocks below. But he couldn't turn back now. After a second's hesitation, Nick plunged after him, his shoes slipping on the sandy ground. The sun beat mercilessly overhead. Soon his shirt was soaked in sweat, and he was dazzled by the bright, white-hot light.

The path twisted and turned, skirting boulders and finding the level places. Suddenly, he turned a corner and saw in front of him a shepherd's cottage, clinging precariously to the side of the cliff as if it had been carved out of the sandstone. It was a simple white-washed building with a tiled roof. There was a patch of garden at the back, with a handful of hardy vines and a bed of tomatoes. Markos opened the plain wooden door and beckoned Nick inside.

It was very simple. Just a bed, a chair and a table, which looked hand-made. In one corner was a rudimentary kitchen and bathroom. A table with a bowl and jug on it, a calor gas cooker, a saucepan and kettle. That was all. The floor was the natural stone of the cliff, and there was a worn rug near the bed. It was a monk's cell, thought Nick, except for the bottle on the table and the empty glass.

'My other home. The place I come to from time to time when I have to get away from the others. Petra hates me coming here, but she understands. It's my retreat. I think here, and plan, and sleep. Lately I've been drinking.'

At this point, Markos strode across to the table, picked up the half-full bottle of *ouzo*, took it to the front door and poured the contents out on the sand.

'But no more,' he went on. 'We'll all have to have clear heads to see this through.'

He emptied the jug of water into the wash-basin, and splashed water over his head. Then he dried his face with a towel, and combed his hair.

'I come here to sort things out. Not the things you're thinking of. I don't spend my time plotting the murder of visiting professors, or yachtsmen for that matter. Only personal things. I feel close to my wife here, and to Mitsos. He was only eight when he died. A fine sailor, and full of promise. They are both very close to me here.

'There are many things on my mind at the moment. You and Petra, and then the news of your divorce. I'm sorry I distrusted you, Nick. I can see Petra loves you, and perhaps I was just a bit jealous. I have always thought of myself as her protector. But of course she must have her own man, and I think you're right for her. But I don't want to see her hurt, and sometimes I thought you irresponsible and uncaring.

Like the time you took her out to the wreck, and then into the cave. After Soula died, Petra was all I had left and I didn't want anything to happen to her. Of course I worried about her.'

Nick said nothing. Suddenly he felt a wave of sympathy for Markos. They were friends after all. They were concerned about the same people. Their interests were the same. He walked over to Markos and held out his hand.

'I'm sorry I've been insensitive, but I'm still not sure just what I've walked into. And there's Bernie. She could have found out something by now.'

Markos took Nick's hand and pressed it hard. 'Yes, there's Bernie. It's quite likely she's delayed in Athens but we can at least ask the company whether she booked on to the hydrofoil. Let's get into Patiteri. We can also phone the airport, and see whether she got to Athens.'

They left the hut, and climbed up to the car. Nick, following the broad figure of Markos, wondered at the complexities of the man. Capable of great feeling, passionate and impulsive. A man of energy and vigour. Yet also a solitary, needing the loneliness of a shepherd's hut to restore his equilibrium.

The official in the booking office was polite but firm. No-one answering to the name of Miss Fitzpatrick had booked on the hydrofoil recently. There had been plenty of spare seats so there would have been no difficulty in getting a place. Markos then telephoned the airport at Skiathos. No, she had not booked on to any of their regular flights to Athens.

Markos was now becoming frantic. They sat down at a table in the main square, and it was with difficulty that Nick persuaded him to drink some coffee.

'Nick, this is bad. Where is she? If she's not in Athens, then she could be here. On this island.'

'Look, someone must have realised she was going to Athens to check on the name of Nelson's yacht. That someone didn't want her to get there. But who, besides Petra and I, knew where she was going? You weren't there when we discussed this.'

'This place is full of spies. Too many people are watching us, and that yacht.'

But Nick was't listening. Suddenly he jumped up and pointed towards the quay. 'Look, Markos. Over there! That's my car!'

Sure enough, the Volkswagen was parked neatly at the far end of the water-front, in the shade so as to be inconspicuous. They went over to it and found the doors unlocked. There was no sign of the keys. Markos looked desperate.

'Nick, she got here but then what? She didn't get on the hydrofoil. She wouldn't have bothered with a boat as it would have taken too long. Nor would she have left a car unlocked. We would, but not an American. She also knew it was your car, and that would have made her doubly careful.'

'It looks bad, Markos. Look, let's get back to the house and find out if there's been a message. If not, then we'll get to the police. I can fetch the car tomorrow. Spiros has a spare key, but this is getting beyond us.'

For once, Markos didn't argue with Nick, and they drove quickly back to Agios Demetrios. As soon as they arrived at the house, Markos dashed inside to see whether Bernie had telephoned. So it was Nick who found the letter on the table on the terrace. A white envelope, wedged under the oil lamp which they lit in the evenings. He picked it up. There was no stamp, so someone had delivered it by hand. It was addressed to him, and not to Markos, and was written in English, in tolerable handwriting.

'*If you go to the police,*' it said, '*we shall kill Miss Fitzpatrick. She is safe for the time being.*'

That was all. Nick stared at it in horror. So it was all true. Everything they had suspected was true. Bernie had been kidnapped because she wanted to find out the name of Nelson's boat. She had asked too many questions. Probably now they were all in danger. And he, a harmless Professor of Archaeology at the University of Sussex, had walked into a gang of thieves. But what were they after? Not the amphorae for sure. Only a museum would be interested in them, and museums didn't pay much. There had to be something else.

'Markos,' he called softly. 'Come here a moment. Bernie's safe. But we're in one hell of a fix.'

Chapter 16

That same night, Petra came to Nick's room. He had been half expecting her. Markos had shown her the letter, and she had been shocked and horrified. That night the house seemed full of an uneasy silence. Andrikos and Elisavet were the only ones who slept peacefully, as they were in ignorance of the day's events. Markos and Petra had decided not to tell them about the letter as there seemed no point in alarming them yet. At the moment they assumed Bernie had been delayed in Athens – a perfectly normal thing to happen to anyone travelling by hydrofoil. It was for this reason, said Andrikos, that he never went to Athens.

It was around twelve that Nick heard the tap on his door. He had been thinking about Petra most of the evening, wondering what he'd do if it had been her whom the men had kidnapped. He would have had to tell her parents, and probably Andrikos would have gone straight to the police. Then the unthinkable could have happened.

She came in wearing a thin cotton robe, her face pale and mysterious in the moonlight which flooded his room. He came over to her as she stood uncertainly by the door and kissed her. Then they sat together on the edge of the bed, looking out across the bay. Below, in the shrubbery, a cat called out its challenge to another, a tense eerie sound, that sent shivers down the spine. The call of one lost soul to another.

'Nick, why should anyone want to harm Bernie?' she said. 'What's wrong with her trying to find out the name of Nelson's boat? It seems a perfectly natural thing to do.'

'I don't know either. I don't know lots of things. I also want to know where I fit into all this. But what a perfect night, Petra. Far too good to waste in sleep. Look at the stars. This is an enchanted island.'

'Yes. Circe lives here, and Cyclops. There are sorcerers out there as well as wood nymphs. Sorcerers who kill men with guns, and who killed Yannis. And why did they kill a harmless idiot because he was telling everyone that he'd seen gold? This Nelson, Nick, do you think he could have been up to no good? Do you think he could have been buying gold ingots, and using the amphorae as a cover? Maybe Takis and Co. knew about him, and murdered him for the gold. Then Yannis came along and saw them landing the stuff further along the coast.'

'But then what? They didn't bring it ashore to gloat over it. They would want to get it off the island as quickly as possible. And from what Bernie says, Nelson had no need to smuggle anything. He was almost a millionaire. A legitimate one. He made his money out of a chain of hotels and restaurants. The pots and jars could have been his, though. It's the sort of thing millionaires like to collect, although I think they belong in a museum. But I agree with you, they are not the sort of things thieves murder for. Neither would they run the risk of kidnapping an American tourist if the pots were the only things on that yacht. However, I can't see a man like Nelson, retired and wealthy, bothering to run gold ingots into Greece or anywhere else. It just doesn't make sense.'

Petra got up and walked to the window. Outside, the garden and terrace were flooded with moonlight. The cypress trees looked like rows of sentries standing guard.

'I wonder what Markos is doing?' she said. 'He was like a caged bear this evening. I hope to God he hasn't taken on Takis and his gang single-handed.'

'I don't think he would be so rash. Also, I haven't seen them now for several days. I don't think they'll show their faces again.'

She turned to face him.

'And what now, Nick? Your work is over, isn't it?'

'It's back to England to start with. I shall have to give in my notice there. I might have to stay on until Christmas.'

'Nick, you can't do that! Leave your job, I mean.'

'Why not? I love this place, and I love you, Petra. And you belong here. I might have to live for part of the time on the mainland; that is if Athens wants me. But I could write and work here.

'At the moment, I have only half a house to live in,' he went on jokingly, 'so I haven't much to offer you. That's why I must go back and sort out my affairs.'

She came and sat beside him. She took his hand, and looked thoughtfully into his eyes.

'Nick, it's a big step. You know it can be foul out here in the winter. The wind can blow for days, and we're stuck on the island. You'll miss England. It's primitive out here, and harsh. You'll miss your fine house and comfortable life.'

'I've done with all that, Petra. A house way above our means. It was all false. I was a slave to the credit companies, and for what? To prop up a failing marriage. To cover up an emotional vacuum. Petra, I can see myself out here, working for Athens on marine archaeology and sharing my life with you – if you'll have me.'

She was still holding his hand, and her gown had fallen open to the waist. Her perfect breasts gleamed satin-smooth in the moonlight. Her hair was loose, and cascaded down her back – a bright path of gold. Then he knew she wanted him to make love to her. It was inevitable. The danger, the fear over Bernie's fate, had brought them together.

He turned towards her and took her in his arms. He kissed her pale face, and traced the outlines of her mouth and eye-brows with his lips. She slipped the robe off her shoulders and lifted her arms to cradle his face to her breast. Gently, he laid her down on his bed and kissed her neck, her arms and then her breasts. Her skin was cool and perfumed with the familiar scent of rosemary and thyme. Her nipples were dark circles in the pale light, and for a moment he drew back to wonder at her beauty.

But she wanted him, and pulled him down on top of her. He felt her arms round his neck, then her hands caressing his back. Her body arched to his and he wanted to take her there and then. But the moment was too beautiful to lose. He wanted to hold on to it forever. He bent down and kissed each

173

breast, and curled his tongue round each perfect nipple. Then his passion increased and he tore off the gown which had slipped down to her waist, and bent down and kissed her rounded belly and the dark hollow of her navel.

He had forgotten his own clothes, and it was Petra who helped him out of his shirt and unzipped his jeans. Now the two naked bodies were together, desperately trying to become one. Two people fusing their own identity. One flesh, one mind, the thought flashed through Nick's brain as he caressed her.

'Are you sure, Petra?' he said. 'Do you really want me? You know this is forever.'

For an answer she drew him closer to her, and it was she who guided him to the right place. Then he forgot everything in the joy of making love to this beautiful woman whose body gleamed with a supernatural phosphorescence in the moonlight. Her hair tumbled on to the pillow, and she lay smiling up at him with her dark eyes.

Then he took her, and they rocked together in the age-old rhythm. They shared the same climax, and lay panting in each other's arms. It was a long time before either of them spoke. He covered her with a sheet as the night air was getting chill. Then, in the manner of all lovers, he had to ask, 'Petra, my love, was it good?'

And she, drowsy with pleasure, murmured, 'Too good. Why did you have to stop?'

'There will be many more times like this. One day we shall sleep together every night. We shall grow old together. This is an enchanted place.'

It was dawn before she left him and went back to her own bed.

That night, Magnus rang earlier than usual. Spiros had been waiting impatiently for his call. Too much was going on and he needed more instructions. He hadn't seen Takis and the others for a long time, and things seemed to be getting out of his control. He felt worried and uneasy. Bernie's disappearance only increased his anxiety.

The taverna was still packed with locals. One or two tourists had found their way along the coast from Patiteri and were calling out for music and dancing. He'd had to rouse Angie, who was asleep, to get more bottles out of the cellar. It was going to be a long night.

'Spiros?' There was an urgent note in Magnus' voice. 'Are you sure no-one can overhear us?'

The din coming from the taverna had risen to such a pitch that Spiros was able to answer quite truthfully 'Quite sure'. And then his control snapped and he shouted angrily into the mouthpiece: 'Why did you take the girl? All hell's broken loose here. Karakulas is going round like a mad bull saying he'll murder Takis when he finds him. He thinks he's responsible for kidnapping the girl. What's going on?'

'Calm down, Spiros. It will soon be over. Just do as you're told, and keep your stupid mouth shut. You talk too much. Keep your ears open, and don't do anything foolish. That's all.'

The voice was unemotional, almost amused. Magnus spoke with the guttural accent of the back streets of Marseilles. However hard he tried to conceal them, he betrayed his origins every time he opened his mouth.

'That's where you were born.' thought Spiros bitterly. 'And that's where you'll die.'

His stomach was churning with fear. He felt sick, and had to control an urgent desire to rush to the lavatory. Why, he thought angrily, did Magnus have this effect on him?

The voice went on. 'Listen, in five days the stuff will be off the island. Demetrios will be ready for us on the twenty-ninth. He can get those damn dogs out of the way that night. A lot of the stuff is already in the warehouse but the next few days are crucial. We'll get the stuff out first, then the other, then the Alexandrian treasure. We've got to get that over to Rio where I've found a buyer. The other goes to the States.

'But, Spiros, the timing is crucial. Nothing must foul up the works now. I've got my doubts about the Englishman. We've finished with him now, his work's over. We've got enough crates but he's a nuisance. I understand that he's in love with the Karakulas girl?'

'Yes, and the family will go beserk if anything happens to her.'

'Don't worry. No-one's going to the police. Kostas will

shoot the American girl if there's any trouble. Karakulas knows we mean what we say. He won't get anything from Takis, even if he finds him.

'Now, Spiros, keep your ears to the ground and your bloody Greek mouth shut. Harding will go if he makes any trouble. He's too damned clever. Whatever happens, the police mustn't get a whiff of this until after the twenty-ninth. Then I don't mind what you all do on that island. They can come over in boatloads for all I care.

'For now, keep everyone out of trouble. Tell them to stay in their beds, with anyone they like. Five more days, and then you can do what you please. A good operation, I think. Good takings. A good retirement for us all.' As usual, he rang off abruptly.

Spiros put the receiver down slowly. His mind was racing. Five more days and then peace. Five days. It seemed an eternity. Tomorrow the Englishman and Karakulas would be rampaging around the island, asking questions and alerting the police. Someone would tell them about the kidnapping, that was certain. Then Magnus would hear of it, and the American girl would be murdered. Then all hell would break loose. The island was crawling with spies, and he couldn't trust anyone. He had to watch the Karakulas household, but someone for sure was watching him, Spiros.

Markos was safe. He was too well-known and respected in the community for anyone to harm him. Rumour had it that he might be elected Mayor of Alonnisos next year. But Nick Harding! He was in real danger. If he disappeared, then no one would be particularly concerned. He would be just another tourist who had come to grief in the treacherous waters around the Sporades. The furore his death would cause would divert all attention away from Takis and the others. In fact, he wouldn't put it past Magnus to engineer the disappearance of Nick Harding in order to create that diversion. Time was now of the essence.

But Nick Harding, whose shirts he was wearing. He was a friend!

That night, Spiros found it impossible to sleep. He tossed and turned restlessly all night, and Alexia left him at three o'clock in the morning to find a more peaceful place next to Angie.

*   *   *

176

Nick was up early the next day, in spite of a strong inclination to lie in bed and think of Petra. But he wanted to finish the job as it would be September the following week, and Bernie or no Bernie he still had work to do.

He went down to the beach before the others were up. Even so, he caught a glimpse of Markos' car setting off in the direction of Patiteri, and knew he and Petra weren't the only ones unable to sleep last night.

The hut was just as he left it. The chair, the piles of pottery shards, the table, the two half full crates. He went over and looked in them. They were just as they had been the day before. No-one had been to collect them. He was puzzled, as the crates contained two beautiful Minoan storage jars, and for a moment he considered writing to Ponsford to tell him about them. Then he realised he had no address to write to. It was all very strange. Everyone seemed to have lost interest in his work, but he knew he was not finished until he received the second cheque, and his return air ticket.

He was standing there, contemplating the crates, when he heard the sound of a motor bike. It was a familiar sound, and he left the hut wondering why Spiros was bothering to come and see him. It was the first time he'd been down to the hut since Nick had started work. He watched the slim unathletic figure scramble down the path, slipping and sliding on the loose stones. Spiros ran over the sand towards Nick, perspiration streaming down his face. He was breathing heavily and seemed to be in a state of extreme agitation.

'Inside, Mr. Harding. Quickly! We mustn't be seen.' He almost dragged Nick back into the hut. Once inside, he shut the door.

'What's up, Spiros? This is the first time you've been down here. Why the rush?'

'Nothing, Mr. Harding. Nothing. It's just that I have to be at a meeting at nine o'clock. But your work?' He glanced swiftly round the hut. 'It's finished? No more pots?'

'No more new ones. But there are several over there in those crates that ought to be collected sometime. No-one has actually told me to stop yet and I don't know whether the yacht's clear. I've been told that there are still a few left out there but I don't know how many.'

177

He watched Spiros closely. For a long time he had wondered how much the taverna owner knew. Spiros now appeared to be in a state of extreme agitation.

'How do you know that, Mr. Harding?'

'We've been out there, Markos and I.' Nick looked steadily at the frightened man. Spiros knew something, he was certain of it. But how to get him to talk? Probably, thought Nick, he knew what had happened to Bernie, and where Takis had hidden her. Already Nick, like Markos, was coming to believe Takis and his surly companion were Bernie's kidnappers. But he had to go carefully. One false move and Spiros would shut up like a clam. At the moment, Spiros liked him. Nick didn't want to turn him into an enemy. So he perched casually on the edge of the table, and pretended not to notice the Greek's agitation.

'You shouldn't have done that, Mr. Harding,' said Spiros in a voice high with what appeared to Nick to be sheer terror. 'There are people on these islands who watch what goes on – spies. They won't like you poking around out there.'

'Why not, Spiros? We did not harm. Who could possibly object to an archaeologist visiting a site? Who are these "spies" anyway? Who employs them? Don't be so melodramatic, man. And, incidentally, what have you done with Miss Fitzpatrick?'

It was a shot in the dark but Nick wasn't disappointed by Spiros' reaction. He positively jumped with fright. Then he backed towards the door, and Nick cursed himself for saying too much.

'Mr. Harding,' said Spiros, one hand on the door flap as if to dash away if Nick should resume his interrogation, 'I don't know where Miss Fitzpatrick is, and that's the truth. I know very little,' he said bitterly, 'but I do know she's safe. Those men won't harm her yet. But they will, if things get too hot.

'Now listen, and then I must go. You are my friend. You gave me these wonderful shirts. Everyone admires me now. But you are in danger. No, please be serious,' he said, as Nick began to laugh. 'Don't ask me how I know this. Just take it that I do know, and I am warning you to be careful. Look, your work is done here. Now please take a short holiday – a week or so. Take Miss Petra to Skiathos, or the mainland. Go

178

and see Mount Athos. Greece is a beautiful country. But go away from here. Come back next week, and then everything will be fine again. I will give a good party – lots of music and *ouzo* will flow like water. Perhaps I will get a dancer from Skopelos. But please, go away. Today.'

Then, before Nick could ask him any more questions, he tore open the door and ran over the beach to the path. Nick heard the roar of the motor bike's engine, and Spiros had gone.

Nick stood there uncertain what to do next. Part of him wanted to do as Spiros had said: take Petra to Skiathos. A week of making love and being with her all the time, then to come back here when everything was calm again. Given a choice, Nick preferred a quiet life. He was an academic, not the stuff of which heroes are made. But another part of him knew he would not leave Agios Demetrios now. He couldn't leave Markos. He couldn't leave his work in this unsatisfactory state, half-finished. He knew Petra would never run away, either. He was certainly no coward, and he didn't believe that he was in any sort of danger. After all he had been paid to come out to the island and to do a job, and as far as he was concerned, the job wasn't over yet. So he'd stay, and see the thing through. But first, he'd have another word with Spiros. Nick doubted that he was a real crook. If he was, then he was only small fry. He was too weak to mastermind an international gang of theieves, but he was most certainly in the pay of someone who used him for his own purposes. Nick intended to extract as much information from Spiros as he could before the day was out.

All was quiet now in the bay as Nick shut the door of the hut; only the familiar sound of the goat's bells coming from somewhere up the cliff. He didn't see the flick of a black skirt, nor hear the rustle of bare feet on the pine needles further up the path. Maria, the local girl who had so successfully stopped Bernie on her way to Patiteri, had watched the scene from halfway up the cliff. She'd watched Spiros go into the hut with Nick. She'd seen him leave on his motor bike. Now she turned swiftly, pulled the shawl across her face to keep the insects away, and walked back along the road to Steni Vala.

*   *   *

Spiros took his siesta at half-past three as usual that afternoon. He'd spent the morning at a meeting of the town council in Patiteri, and had got back late for lunch. It was a Friday. His wife had gone to see her parents as she always did, and Katerina was snoring by his side. She was already swollen with pregnancy, and took up too much room in the bed. Spiros was uncomfortable and hot. He'd also drunk too much at lunch-time. His stomach ached, and he felt a little sick. Impatiently he kicked his companion to stop her snoring. She humped herself over on to her side, and the noise stopped.

Spiros lay very still. He was tired after a restless night but still sleep eluded him. His mind was working away over the implications of Magnus' last phone call. Now he was glad that he'd warned Nick. If anything should happen to that stupid Englishman in the future, it wouldn't be Spiros' fault. He'd done all he could to protect him. But he felt uneasy. He thought back to that morning on the beach. Had anyone seen him talking to Nick Harding? He knew Magnus had spies everywhere. He employed people to watch other people. Spiros knew some of these shadowy people. Most of them were his friends, but he knew they were grateful for the extra money. Had one of his so-called 'friends' been watching him?

However, he'd seen no-one that morning. The beach had been deserted, and he had passed nothing on the road home, not even a tourist. Nick had been on his own, too. So he felt pretty certain that his trip to the beach had gone unobserved. At last he turned over, pushed the mound of Katerina over towards the wall, and went to sleep.

Fifteen minutes later, he was woken by the sound of someone outside in the garden calling his name. At first he ignored it, hoping Katerina would rouse herself. But she slept on – the sleep of the physically exhausted.

'Damn the woman,' he said to himself. 'She's as lazy as a mule.'

'Spiros, Spiros!' It was a woman's voice. Wearily he got out of bed. He sat on the edge for a few moments, trying to collect his thoughts, then he pulled open the shutters noisily, hoping to awaken Katerina. It was he job to get up. He needed his sleep. Outside he saw the slim figure of Maria, Sarantis' wife, a pretty woman who looked after herself and so far had avoided having children. Not like the woman in his bed. He wondered for a second why he always had such bad luck with women. Why was it that he only had to look, at them and they became pregnant?

'What is it?' he asked Maria, who was standing on the rough grass beneath his window.

'It's the child, Angie,' she said. 'She's hurt herself. She was playing over by the showers, and slipped and fell. She's hurt her back, I think, and can't move. It looks bad. Come quickly. She screams if I try to lift her.'

'Damn her,' said Spiros, whose first instinct was to go back to sleep again and see to the child when he woke up. But he was soft-hearted where children were concerned, especially his grand-children, and the little girl was one of his favourites. Many a time she had worked with him in the taverna until she was almost dropping on her feet, and she hardly ever complained.

'I've told her many times to keep away from that place,' he called out as he pulled on his trousers. 'It's not finished yet. There are holes there, and slimy places where the wash basins will be. There are piles of rubbish and dangerous bits of equipment all over the place, but still the kids go there. Hold on, I'll come.'

Spiros was building a camping site not far from the taverna. It was on a rough patch of ground where a few fig and olive trees grew. It was to take about fifty tents, and he was planning to have all modern conveniences. So he'd ordered a wash house to be built, with showers and lavatories and sinks. It was to have hot water, and the campers would then stop using his one wash basin in the taverna. There were no kitchens on the camping site, as he still wanted them to eat in his café.

He'd started the project last year, but it wouldn't be finished until next spring. The plumbing was causing problems because of the lack of water pressure. He would probably have to abandon the idea of running hot water, and then the campers would still pile into his one washroom. However, he was confident that the German tourists would love it, and he would soon become the most prosperous man on the island. Then there would be no more telephone calls from Magnus.

He went into the garden, the heat greeting him like a blast

furnace. Even the cicadas seemed subdued. Cursing all children, he stumbled across the grass, past the neat row of petrol cans which his wife had painted red and filled with geraniums. Through the vegetable patch where tomatoes and aubergines grew in profusion. Then through the rough part of the garden where the two olive trees stood like arthritic old men. At the far end of this patch stood the concrete building which was to be the new wash house. Maria had vanished. He couldn't hear anyone crying, and he couldn't see the child. He hurried over to the building, turned the corner by the first shower cubicle, and then stopped.

They were on him before he had time to cry out. Two men with iron bars; the kind warehouse men use to open crates, one end flattened like a sword blade.

Takis struck first. He aimed at Spiros' legs, and with one blow crushed his knee cap as if he was chopping up meat in a butcher's shop. Spiros screamed in pain, one high-pitched cry, like a rabbit caught in a snare. Then Takis struck again. This time it was across his face. There was a crack of splintering bone and Spiros fell to the ground. He couldn't cry out any more as his mouth had vanished.

Then, as he lay curled up in the foetal position, they went for him with knives and stones. Soon nothing remained of his face. It was just a mass of bleeding flesh and bone. It was Giorgios who delivered the coup de grace by plunging his knife into the genitals.

The blood lust was soon over. Takis was the first to recover. He wiped his knife on Spiros' trousers and looked at Giorgios who was leaning against the wall of the shower cubicle, breathing heavily.

'Come on,' he said, 'let's get this fool out of here.'

There was a car parked under the trees. It didn't take them long to drag Spiros' body over to it, and haul him feet first, into the back seat.

'What about that?' said Giorgios, pointing to the pool of blood on the sand.

Takis went over to it, and kicked fresh sand over the stain. He looked up at the sun.

'It'll soon dry,' he said.

They drove the car out along the road towards the headland

182

then turned off into a field in the shade of some pines. Together they pulled Spiros out of the back seat, and dragged him over the rough grass. Together they heaved him towards an opening in the ground. It was a dangerous place, the hole almost concealed by tall grass. It would be almost impossible to find unless a person knew it was there.

Then they lifted the limp body and stuffed it down the shaft. They heard it fall several feet, but they didn't hear the splash as it landed in the cave of Cyclops.

Chapter 17

'For God's sake, where are the bastards?' shouted Markos. Tense and white-faced, he'd had no rest since he came home. It was Saturday, and the three of them were on the terrace going through the motions of eating breakfast.

'All day yesterday, we searched the island for the four of them. And not a sign. Nothing. But how can four men, all of them strangers here, vanish? And the boat? No-one has set eyes on it recently. Am I going mad?'

He sat down, and clasped his head in his hands. Petra went over to him and stroked his dark hair, matted and unkempt from neglect.

'Markos, stop. You'll kill yourself. Try to be rational. Here, have some coffee.' Angrily he pushed the cup away, spilling the coffee on the table.

'Look you're not helping anyone by being so extreme,' she went on. 'Just because people around here say they haven't seen the men doesn't mean that they're not here. Someone could be hiding them for money. We don't know what we're up against.'

'But *who* is paying the islanders to keep quiet? A gang? A conspiracy? And what do they want with Bernie?' He leapt to his feet again, and began to pace up and down the terrace like a caged animal. Markos was essentially a man of action and enforced waiting didn't come naturally to him. Tense with worry and pent up fury, he was ready to attack anyone who advocated caution and procrastination.

'My God,' he went on, turning to Nick who was annoying him by the calm way he was drinking coffee, 'we can't sit

184

around here all day doing nothing. Waiting for some unknown bunch of thugs to decide what to do to Bernie.'

Markos was single-minded in his worry. He thought only of Bernie, and what the men might be planning for her. Nick, however, was trying to piece together the other bits of the jig-saw. Bernie's disappearance, he realised, was only one part of a much bigger operation. Also he knew she was all right. Spiros had told him. Scared and worried, perhaps, but safe. He hadn't told the others yet about Spiros' visit as he didn't want to focus alarm on himself. Petra would be bound to want him to go away somewhere and hide, and he would have to refuse. He had to see this through, get back Bernie, and find out what was going on out there on the yacht.

'Markos,' he said impatiently, 'no-one is "sitting round doing nothing". For God's sake have something to drink, and stand still for a moment. Don't waste your strength. We may need it later.

'Look, we know Bernie's safe. We haven't yet gone to the police, and the note assured us she was all right. Now be rational. It's the next move we're trying to work out.'

Markos picked up the cup of coffee which Petra had poured for him, and tried to drink it. He knew he was becoming impossible to live with. Both his parents had left the breakfast table, taking their coffee to their own room and hoping the others would calm him down. They thought he was fretting for Bernie, and prayed that she'd put in an appearance soon.

Then something occurred to him. 'Spiros! What the devil's happened to him? We could do with him at the moment. He knows most things that go on around here. Apparently, all hell broke loose in the taverna yesterday evening. He didn't come home for dinner, and no-one knows where he is. Katerina and Alexia are fighting like a couple of demons. It seems he was in bed with Katerina in the afternoon, and suddenly took himself off, leaving her asleep. When she woke up, Alexia had come back and found her in Spiros' bed. She managed to drag her out of it and into the passage, even though she's half the size of Katerina. Then she beat her up with a broom, Katerina kicking and screeching like a wild cat.

'It's too bad of the man to take himself off now. He must know something about Takis and Co., although come to think of it, I've never seen them drinking together so they're not all that thick. Spiros is no crook, but he's not above taking the odd handout or two.'

'Spiros is no crook,' echoed Petra, who up till then had said very little. 'He might make a bit illegally on the side now and then. And he needs money at the moment. What with his camp-site, and his women and children, I sometimes don't know how he manages to struggle on.'

'When he comes back we'll have to tackle him,' said Nick, suddenly finishing his coffee and standing up. He walked across to the edge of the terrace and looked down to the beach. A flock of goats had wandered on to the shore and were standing looking uncertainly at the water. Another hot day, he thought. No wind, a cloudless sky. A thought struck him.

'Look, we spent the whole day yesterday searching the surface of the island. Why don't we go underground today? Petra was the person who last saw the boat, and she thought it went into one of the caves.

'We only went into one of them, and had to come out pretty quickly. Why don't we take your boat and have a look at the other cave – Cyclops' cave, you call it? They are ideal places for hiding men or illegal goods. My own feeling is that the gang has left the island, but I might well be wrong. They might still be here, waiting for orders to ship the "stuff" off the island. Let's have a look at Cyclops' lair.'

Markos was already making towards the door. 'I agree, Nick. Let's go. We only need to look at the big cave, where the tunnels are large enough to take *Centaur*. Where *Centaur* can go, the red motor boat can go. It's pointless to explore the smaller ones. The wind's all right today. We'll need torches, and one other thing, Nick. We'll take guns. Just in case.'

Then he glanced at Petra, who was busy clearing away the cups.

'You've got your Regatta today, haven't you? No need for you to come. They'll need you.'

'Then they will be disappointed. I'm coming with you.'

Both men stared at her in horror. 'Petra, I forbid it,' shouted Markos. 'These men could be dangerous. You know they have a gun. This is not women's work. Nick and I go on our own.'

186

But Petra was stubborn. She was glaring at Markos and, looking at her, Nick was reminded of her father. Gone was the golden woman he'd caressed in bed. She was now a tigress, snarling at her brother with anger and contempt.

'Women's work! You talk of women's work. You know nothing about women if you think I'm staying here waiting for you and Nick to come home. Bernie is my friend, too, and I *love* Nick. So like it or not, I'm coming with you. Besides, you know I'm used to guns. You taught me to fire one.'

She turned away from them with a contemptuous flounce of the hips. She was suddenly very Greek. Nick had a vision of her out on the hillside with Andrikos, fighting the Turks.

'Whilst you get the torches and the guns, I'll go and get the boat. I'll meet you on the shore. Take something warm to put on. It's cold in those caves.'

Without one look at the two men who were standing there speechless, she was off. For a moment, Nick wondered who was in charge of the expedition. Ruefully he looked at Markos, who smiled at him sympathetically. Then they went to get the torches.

The cave of Cyclops was the largest of the caves that honeycombed the southern shore of Alonnisos. Sometimes tourists came there to admire the stalactites and stalagmites, and the fantastic sculpture made by the limestone formations. It was also the home of a large colony of bats. Now, as Markos reduced speed and took the boat into the enormous entrance hall, they called out their warning in a continuous high-pitched whine, like an ultra-sonic frequency.

'Listen to them,' whispered Petra, 'the spies of Cyclops. They're telling him we're here.'

'As long as he doesn't tell his friend Poseidon to send the sea up again,' said Nick nervously. He hated these caves, and the feel of the chill dank air.

Markos motored round the huge cavern, looking for a suitable tunnel which could take the boat. He found one at the back of the cave, to the right-hand side. He plunged into the darkness, calling out for torches, and the bright shafts of light shone on the rockface high above them. There was ample room for a paddle steamer. Nick noticed that there were demon faces in the rock there, too. Grotesque faces leered down at them from the tunnel walls. Cruel mocking faces that taunted them.

Regardless, Markos took the boat along a dead straight tunnel that penetrated the bowels of the cliff. Other tunnels branched off at regular intervals, like sidings on a railway line.

'Markos,' said Nick suddenly, 'do we stay here or take one of those side tunnels? You know the caves.'

'I'll go along a bit further, and then take one of the turnings. There's nowhere here that the men could hide a boat. Too many tourists come here at this time of the year.

'But Bernie won't be here, so what the hell are we looking for? They can't hide her on a ledge, or do you think they'll tie her to a rock, like Andromeda waiting for Perseus to come and rescue her, or Simon Stylites sitting at the top of his pillar? For God's sake, Nick, what's the use? There's nothing here. Just bats, and a lot of malevolent faces looking at us.'

He revved the engine in exasperation, the water surging up over the bows.

'For Christ's sake, calm down, Markos,' said Nick angrily. It was then he realised how edgy they all were. The cave had an extraordinary effect on them.

'We're looking for a boat, and four men, remember? I'm sure they won't keep Bernie down here.'

'And what if we round a bend, and come across them? What do we do? Open fire? Or say "Good morning. Nice day for a trip to the caves". We're like a pack of children, Nick, playing at adventures.' He urged the throttle forward angrily, and water swirled higher up the tunnel walls, drowning the demon scruptures. Petra, sitting in her usual place in the bows, and now soaked by Markos' irritable acceleration, shouted at him.

'Slow down! You'll have us all drowned. Keep away from the rocks, or else you'll crash the boat. Who knows what we're looking for? Anything that can help us find Bernie, remember.'

Her words seemed to calm Markos, and he reduced speed. Two minutes later, he throttled back still further.

'Watch out,' he said, 'I'm turning left here. Not for long. If there's nothing here, I'll turn back. We could search this labyrinth for weeks and find nothing.'

The boat nosed its way into the smaller tunnel. It was very cold now, and the air smelt of stale sea water and the acrid tang of bats' droppings. Nick flashed his torch upwards to see how much head-room they had. There was more than enough. The beam lingered on the strange convolutions of the rock. He felt as if he was inside some giant sea beast, gliding along endless miles of intestines. All around him were weird depoits of calcium, worn into tight folds and pockets.

And then he saw it. A sack, he thought at first. A sack wedged on a shelf of rock just above his head. Then he thought it could be an out-crop of fungus. But then he saw the arm.

'Markos, stop. Over there,' he whispered. 'What is it?'

Markos had seen it, too. 'The torch, Nick. Keep it there. That's right. My God, it's someone up there. A body.'

Markos guided the boat underneath the shelf of rock. Then they were sure. It was someone who had fallen from above, and whose body had been caught by a shelf of rock which jutted out from the wall. It lay there, spread-eagled on the ledge, one arm hanging down.

They stared up at what had once been a human face. Now there was nothing. Just a purple mess of flesh, and a white bone where the nose should have been. A bit of black hair still clung to the top of the head.

The hand that hung down had no fingers. Each one had been neatly severed. The rest of the body had been hacked with knives. The leg, twisted under the rest of the mass, was obviously broken. The other leg had been shattered in many places by some blunt instrument.

Markos could look no longer. He sat down in the boat, stunned. Then he leant over the side and was sick. Nick took a last look at the body, already fixed into its ghastly position by rigor mortis.

'Oh, God,' he said, 'it's Spiros.'

'Are you sure?' said Markos, still trying to control his stomach. 'There's no face.'

'No, but I'd recognize his shirt anywhere. It's the one I gave him. At least the bastards left his clothes on. Petra, are you all right?'

189

She'd slumped forward against the bow of the boat. For a second Nick thought she'd fainted. When she looked up, he noticed she was shivering with shock.

'Of course I'm all right, but let's get out. I can't look at him.' Nick heard her voice tremble, and handed her his pullover.

'Put this on. It'll stop you shaking. Let's go, Markos.'

'Yes, outside quickly,' said Markos, putting the engine into reverse. 'Now I know what we're looking for. The devils who did this. And they've got Bernie! My God, what have they done to her?'

'Relax, Markos,' said Nick, 'I'm sure she's safe. They wouldn't harm a foreigner, especially not a rich New York lawyer. She's not an insignificant islander like Spiros, poor devil.'

They backed towards the main tunnel then turned the way they'd come. In the sunshine at the cave mouth, Markos turned off the engine and looked at the others.

'Who next? And what now? The police? Then Bernie dies. But I'm not turning back now. I go on until I catch these bastards. But Spiros! Why him?'

'He came to see me yesterday,' said Nick softly. 'Down at the hut. I didn't tell you as it didn't seem important at the time. He came to warn me, to tell me to take a holiday. Only for a week, then I could come back as it would all be over. But he wouldn't tell me what would be over. He seemed to think I was in some danger if I stayed on. I couldn't get much out of him at the time as he seemed very nervous and I had to let him go. I swear no-one saw him come down to the beach. There was no sign of anyone when I went back to the house. But someone must have seen him and that's why he was killed – yesterday afternoon, when he left Katerina. And we were laughing about it, just a while ago.'

'Now we're all in danger. My darling, you shouldn't have come.' He turned to Petra who was still shivering, in spite of his pullover.

'Nick, I'll come with you wherever you go. You've got a Greek woman on your hands now, not one of your docile Englishwomen. I shall always be there, even in danger. Women, you know, are used to death. We still lay the bodies out here in Alonnisos. There's no undertaker. I helped the family with Yannis, you know. Everybody is involved when death happens out here.

'Yannis was the first to die, don't you see now? They got him before Spiros because he couldn't keep his mouth shut. And Spiros wouldn't, because you were his friend.'

They sat there in the mouth of the cave for a few moments, their thoughts in turmoil. It was Nick who spoke first.

'Markos, this is not an ordinary salvage job. We're dealing with smugglers. Twentieth-century smugglers, but just as desperate as their earlier counterparts. They won't hesitate to murder anyone who gets in their way.'

'And I believe that they're using your crates to get the stuff out of the island.'

'They're always sealed when they leave the hut. I've checked on several of them. You know, sometimes I went back to the hut after dinner. I actually opened one or two, to see if all was as it should have been. There was nothing wrong.'

'Then they must open them later. You know what this means? They're not in the slightest bit interested in your side of things. It's the crates they want. Now they've got enough, your work's finished and you're expendable. God, Nick, you're in real danger. No wonder Spiros was worried. There's not much time now before they catch us. Somewhere on this island they've got a store; for what, we don't know. Probably gold or drugs. Now we've got to find it. The yacht's empty. Whatever Nelson had on board, it's gone from there but it could still be here, on the island.'

'So you think it was Nelson on that yacht?' said Petra, who seemed brighter now.

'I don't know,' said Markos. 'But it looks more and more likely. Rochester could just be a substitute, to stop people asking about Nelson.'

'Until Bernie came along,' said Nick bitterly.

'Yes. But I find it hard to believe that Nelson was a gold smuggler,' said Petra. 'Or any kind of smuggler for that matter. If they wanted his boat for a dump for their stuff, then they didn't have to murder a man for it. Any boat would have done. Any pots would have kept you occupied, Nick, and

191

filled up their crates. No, Nelson had something they wanted badly. Something they have happily killed for, and for which they will kill again. What it was we'll never know. He was a collector, wasn't he? Then he must have bought something somewhere that they wanted. And how did they know about it?'

'And they made use of me,' said Nick suddenly. He could see it all now. A young professor. A popular archaeologist. Someone who needed money, and was vulnerable to flattery. 'They're not interested in classical pottery,' he went on with increasing bitterness. 'Ten thousand pounds they paid, to get some fool out of England to act as a cover for their activities. A fool, who just sat there for weeks doing what he was told while all around him people get murdered and kidnapped. And now, when the job's over, and whatever it is they want is out of the country, they'll get rid of him too. In case he talks too much, or goes to the police. No wonder they picked on me. They recognized a fool when they saw one.'

'Don't be so bitter,' said Petra, leaning forward and taking his hand. 'You found me. The summer hasn't been a total loss.'

'Yes, I found you.' And he put his hand over hers.

'But you're still in danger, Nick. At least Spiros thought so,' said Markos suddenly 'And that could mean that the men haven't finished whatever they're doing. The stuff's not yet off the island otherwise they wouldn't give a damn what you're up to and Spiros wouldn't have cared. He was murdered yesterday afternoon, we think, after he disappeared. Then they dumped his body in the tunnel, but from above. He got caught up on that ledge. They must have known about the shaft leading into that cave. It's a big one, and the body would have found its way out to sea eventually, and then it would look as if someone else had fallen onto the rocks.

'There are hundreds of these shafts to the sea. If I was hiding something, I would need a dry place with access to the sea so I could get the stuff away by boat. Also a boat could bring the stuff to the bottom of the shaft to be hauled up for storage. Petra saw a boat going into a cave, and it didn't come out whilst she was watching. They could have gone into one of the tunnels, left the boat there, and climbed up to the place

192

where they were storing the stuff. Nick! We know of just such a place. The monastery, St. Michael's monastery! There's a shaft there that goes down into this cave. That's how the monks used to escape in time of persecution. They built it.

That's where we ought to go now. We've either got to go back into the cave and look for a shaft that leads up into the monastery – but for that we'll need more time, and a compass, and we still might be too late. Or we could go to the monastery itself and work downwards. That way, we'll only have one shaft to explore. It would take us a long time to discover which shaft it was they pushed poor Spiros down. The place is riddled with them. No, we want a shaft leading to a dry room where things can be stored. A place where no-one goes.'

They were looking at Markos with mounting excitement.

'And one more thing,' he said, feeling in the pocket of his trousers. 'We'll need these.' He handed a small black gun to Nick. It was the same one he'd seen him with the night after he and Petra had come back from the expedition to the wreck. The day the men had opened fire on them. Quietly Nick put it in his pocket. Then Markos took out a second gun, and checked the mechanism.

Chapter 18

There hadn't been many occasions in Nick's life when he had felt really angry. A white-hot anger, where he could have killed someone without any hesitation. There had been that time when his mother had been punched in the face in a street in Newcastle, and two men had run off with her hand-bag. Then there had been the incident with the Jack Russell. He'd come across three men tormenting the creature on some waste land near his home. He would never forget the smoking patches on the dog's fur where their cigarettes had burnt him, and the can tied to his hind leg to stop him running away. Only thirteen, Nick had punched and scratched the overweight bully who led the others, and it took two policemen to prise him away. The anger had quickly evaporated, but he would always remember the grief when he saw the Jack Russell had died. It was from shock, the policeman had said.

Now, on the road to the monastery, he was experiencing the same anger. Markos looked at him in alarm as he took the sharp bends at high speed, pushing the old Volkswagen which he'd collected from Patiteri at midday on Friday. The child, Angie, had found the spare key for him. Now he cursed the car's lack of acceleration, and regretted not using Markos'. Thoughts swirled round in his head like a swarm of bees, fuelling his rage. Spiros was dead. Spiros, his friend. They had killed Yannis, too, a harmless idiot. They'd got Bernie, and they'd made a fool out of him. They'd made a mockery of his profession, and his pride had been badly wounded. They despised his work. The crates were more useful to them than his efforts. For all they cared, he could have filled them with

194

saw-dust. He was proud of his work. Proud of his first-class degree from King's College, Cambridge. He'd had to fight to get there.

They left the car where they had parked it before, in the shade, then walked up to the monastery. It looked like an oasis of calm. Impossible to imagine it a den of thieves and murderers. Nick felt a twinge of uncertainty as he stood for a moment outside the wooden gate, looking up at the white dome and thinking of that first time he'd come here with Petra. Was it possible, he thought, that they were making a terrible mistake?

But Markos seemed unpreturbed. He pushed open the gate and strode in. Inside, all was peace and tranquillity. The cool courtyard, shaded from the afternoon's heat by the clump of pines, seemed a long way away from the grisly scene in the cave. They made their way into the church. Once again the birds were there, twittering anxiously. Christ looked down at them from the inside of the dome. Nick felt like an intruder. This was a holy place, not a robbers' den. The spirit of the place dispersed his anger. He felt the rage ebb away. Outside there were wars and plagues and famines, but here, none of that mattered. Here was peace, and the presence of that good spirit which some people call God.

It was Markos who broke the spell. 'Come on. We'll search the place. I'll take a look at the crypt. Perhaps you'd look outside, Nick, at those buildings. They're the monks' dormitory and refectory. There might be a tunnel leading down from the dormitory. After all, they would have to get away quickly if there was a night attack.'

His calm voice brought Nick back to reality. He shouldn't succumb to the lotus-eating seduction of this place. This wasn't reality, only one side of it.

Petra, who had been quiet and withdrawn throughout the journey to the monastery, went outside with him. In silence they wandered round the outer buildings. They were interesting, but unsuitable as a storage place. The roof had fallen in over the dormitory, and the walls were damp and covered with algae from the overhanging trees. Bushes and plants were everywhere, growing out of the crevices in the walls and pushing their way up through the stones in the courtyard.

Nick knew how quickly nature took over when left to its own devices. He remembered the time when he'd marvelled at the sight of an enormous clump of yellow flowers sprouting out of one of the flying buttresses of Malmesbury Abbey. Where there was space, and a scraping of soil, the plant world moved in. Even in the dank and slimy places in the refectory, strange crops of fungi grew, shunning the sunlight.

In the refectory, they found a trap-door. Nick climbed down into a small room that had obviously been a cellar. There was nothing there now, just a smell of old wine and the rustle of a small creature, disturbed by the light. He climbed out.

'Nothing. It's damp, and there's no way down to the sea.'

As they walked back to the church, they met Markos running over the grass towards them.

'Nick, I need your help. There are steps going down in that shaft But I need a torch. Anything in there?'

'Nothing. Just mould, and rats, and a wine cellar.'

They went back into the crypt. Nick peered into the shaft that he'd found with Petra the last time they'd been there. He could just make out the first rungs of what looked like an iron ladder.

'I'll go, if you like,' he said. 'I'm no hero, but I've been down a few pot-holes in my time. I'm also a bit thinner than you,' he said, turning to smile at Markos. 'Look, I'll need that rope in the car. I'm just enough of a coward to need a rope. I don't mind climbing down into the sea, but I'm damned if I want to fall in it.'

Petra went to get the rope. Then, in true pot-holing fashion, Markos tied one end round Nick's waist, and held on to the other.

'I might be heavier than you,' he said, 'but I think I'm stronger. I won't let you go.'

Then Nick climbed into the shaft and began his descent.

'It's all right,' he called up to them. 'The ladder's safe. Someone has put new brackets on the wall. They look like stainless steel to me, so it wasn't the monks. Someone else has used this passage recently. Hold on. Don't come down yet. There's a passage going off to one side. I'll have a look.'

Then the light from his torch disappeared. The rope in

Markos' hand was slack. He fastened it to an iron hook in the wall of the crypt, and peered down into the darkness.

'He's all right,' he said to Petra, who was standing uneasily by his side. 'He doesn't need help at the moment.'

Nick made his way along the side tunnel, holding the torch between his teeth as he had to crawl along on his hands and knees. Just ahead of him was a wooden door. He pushed against it, and found it offered no resistance. He crawled into a small room, just high enough for him to stand almost upright. It was a cellar of some sort. The ceiling was at ground level. At the top of one of the walls there was a small window which let in just enough light for Nick to get his bearings.

He was in a room about ten feet square, and level with the crypt. So the tunnel had sloped upwards, but he hadn't noticed it at the time. Now he couldn't work out where he was. Somewhere under the church probably.

He flicked the torch round the room, and then felt his heart lurch with excitement. The beat steadied to a strong rhythm which made his breathless. Stacked from floor to ceiling were wooden boxes. Most of them were the same size, but some were simply sacks. Some of the boxes were oblong. All of them were tightly sealed. He walked across to them, and pulled aside some of the sacking. It came away easily. Inside was a sticky brown substance like tightly rolled tobacco. He knew what it was, cannabis resin. He'd attended a series of lectures to warn teaching staff on the dangers of drugs, and show them what the stuff looked like. So the gang were drug runners! And he'd thought he was working for a dedicated collector of antique pottery. Once again he felt a surge of anger so violent that he could hardly breathe.

Quickly he went back to the tunnel, and this time noticed that it did slope downwards. Markos and Petra saw his head appear at the bottom of the shaft and soon he stood on the second rung of the ladder, breathing in great gulps of fresh air.

'Well?' said Markos, looking at Nick's tense face. 'Is it there?'

'It's there all right, most of it. God knows how much has gone already.'

'What is it?' said Petra, white-faced from strain. 'What have you found?'

197

'I only looked at one bundle, I couldn't open the others. Cannabis resin. We're dealing with drug runners, Markos. They probably get it from North Africa or Turkey. Neither is far away. And they're using me to get the stuff shipped off to America. In my crates.'

He unfastened the rope and handed it to Markos. 'We don't need this. They've made it safe down there. Very comfortable really. Come and have a look. The ladder's OK.'

He led the way to the room. Markos and Petra gazed in astonishment at the piles of boxes. Then Markos went over to one of them, wrenched a hole in it with his knife, and stepped back quickly. A stream of white powder trickled to the floor.

'Oh, Christ,' said Nick. 'That will be heroin. There must be millions of pounds worth of the stuff in these boxes, but how many millions have already left the island?'

But Markos wasn't listening. He went over to the pile of smaller boxes. They were piled neatly one on top of each other, almost to the ceiling. Quickly, he tore off one of the lids.

'Nick,' he said, his voice hoarse with excitement, 'look, ingots. Gold bars, hundreds of them. They must be from some bullion robbery.'

'And Yannis saw them,' said Petra softly, 'and we didn't believe him.'

'What is this place?' said Nick. 'Where are we? Somewhere just below the ground, it seems. A cellar of some sorts.' He flashed his torch around the room.

'I think we must be at the eastern end of the church,' said Petra, 'under the altar, I suspect. A sort of priests' hole. The monks could hide here. Then, if in real danger, they could make their way down the shaft to the sea. Even during service, they could make their escape. Whoever it was who brought the stuff here, knew about the monks' hiding places. Convenient for them. Look, there's another trap-door up there. Do you see? In the corner. That's how they get the stuff down here. It saves them using the sea route all the time. They could drive a lorry up to the church and then, if necessary, use the tunnel to make their escape. It's wide enough to take these boxes.'

Markos had crossed over to the furthest side of the room –

the side opposite the wooden door which led to the tunnel. He was studying two more boxes: one about three feet square, the other about eighteen inches long and a foot deep. They weren't with the others. The oblong box was propped up against the wall, as if the thieves didn't want to pile anything on top of it.

'Nick, over here,' he called. There was an urgency to his voice, as if he'd found what he had been looking for. 'This is not the same shape as the others. What is it? Hold the torch.'

This time, he prised the lid off gently. Nick watched him, knowing instinctively that this was the key to the mystery, the vital piece of the jig-saw puzzle. Otherwise Bernie, if they ever saw her again, would have to live with the fact that her god-father had been a drug runner. Markos lifted the lid and started to unwind the thin material which covered the object like a winding sheet. Nick took one look and fell on his knees in front of the box.

'Dear God,' he exclaimed. 'Petra, come and see.' He gazed down at the timeless face of the goddess Selket. Gently, almost reverently, he took off the last of the wrapping.

'Who is she?' whispered Petra.

'The scorpion goddess who protected the dead in ancient Egypt. She guarded one of the four gates of the Underworld and led the dead into the next life. She watched over the tomb of Tutankhamoun, and was often found guarding other pharaohs and dignitaries. She was stolen from the Cairo Museum last December. It was in all the newspapers. It caused a tremendous uproar in the antiquarian world. My God, now we've found it. I can't believe it.'

'Is she made of solid gold?' asked Markos. 'If so, she's beyond price. They'll never be able to get rid of her.'

'No, not solid gold. Almost certainly gold leaf, probably on wood. Heavy gold leaf, though. She's a good weight, I should think.'

'Of course, they could never sell her; not on the open market anyway. But they could dispose of her to a private buyer, who would pay a fortune for her. That's probably why they haven't got rid of her before. They would have to wait for a buyer to come along before they could ship her off the island. That's why they didn't want anyone to see the boat and

199

it explains the guns. With this on board, no wonder they didn't want any visitors.'

He gazed at the statue in wonder, Although he hadn't found her in a tomb, nevertheless, for that moment, he felt at one with all the great archaeologists of the past. He now understood what Howard Carter must have felt like, and the men who opened the boat-tomb at Suffolk Hoo.

'She's perfect,' he said to Petra on her knees beside him. 'But she must go back where she belongs. To Egypt. To the Museum.'

Carefully, he lifted her out of the box. She stood about sixteen inches high with a small delicate face, and a pointed chin, just like a modern Copt's. The hair was tucked into a golden head-dress covered with rubies. The eyes, outlined with black onyx, looked surprisingly modern. It was a timeless face, beautiful in any century. Blank expressionless eyes gazed fixedly at Nick. Gently he ran his fingers over the folds of her dress.

'It's gold leaf all right, but very thick. They could strip it off and melt it down but it wouldn't be worth their while. Not with all those gold bars over there. No, they've got a private buyer for it''

And the other box?' said Markos, already starting to prise open the lid. 'My God, Nick. Look.'

Gently, calm now, Nick put Selket back in her box. Already he was wondering how to approach the Cairo Museum from Alonnisos. Then he went over to where Markos was staring down into the other squarer box. This time he saw the glow of saphires, and the gleam of gold. Not leaf this time but solid gold.

'The Eye of Atum,' whispered Nick, 'made into a royal necklace. One of the most precious objects in the Cairo Museum. It too was stolen in the raid last December. It's the Eye of the Sun-God,' he said to Petra. 'The symbol of royal power in Egypt. The pharaohs were believed to have descended from Atum, or Ra as he was called later on. This Eye was his emblem.'

Almost reverently, Nick lifted the huge necklace out of the box. Six strands of rubies and sapphires held the mighty pendant in place. The symbolic figures, a cobra and a vulture,

200

stood on either side of the enormous eye. Nick put the necklace against Petra's breast.

'That's where they found it. For thousands of years it rested on the breast of a dead pharoah, or his queen. It was discovered in the Valley of the Kings just after Howard Carter found Tutankhamun's tomb. It's from the same dynasty, but it was always over-shadowed by that other discovery. They found it in a tomb cut into the rock-face, but the mummy was badly decomposed, so they never discovered who she or he was. But the owner was certainly royal. The cobra here is on the headdresses of all the pharaohs. It's a symbol of royal power.'

Carefully, he put the necklace back into the box. The great eye made of gold, the iris a huge sapphire, stared up into space.

'Strange,' he said to Petra, 'how this symbol of pharaohnic power has survived into modern times. You paint it on the side of your boats to bring you good luck.'

'All the fishermen decorate their boats with it. It is supposed to bring them good catches of fish. No boat would be complete without it. But this is the real thing. Not just a good luck sign but the original.'

'They won't be able to sell this either,' said Nick suddenly. 'Not on the open market. It's too hot. They'll have to wait for a buyer. But, Markos,' he said, the excitement in his voice barely controlled, 'Nelson bought them! Someone must have shown them to him, and he wanted them. Maybe when he was in Egypt. Someone was waiting for a Nelson to come along.'

'Of course – Bernie!' said Markos, who had now joined the others and was staring down into the box. 'Her birthday present. Don't you remember? Nelson told her on the phone that he'd bought her a present, and that's why they killed him. Nelson, I mean. This, and Selket. These things were meant for Bernie.'

'No,' said Nick emphatically. 'They belong to Egypt. Selket must go back to the musuem. I don't care how much Nelson paid for them, he had no right to buy them. They must be returned. The Eye of the Sun-God must go back to the land if its birth.'

Suddenly, they all heard it. A tiny sound. Not the rustle of a bat, nor the scampering of a mouse. It was a metallic sound. The noise of a shoe on metal.

'Markos,' whispered Nick. 'They're coming. Quick, switch off the torch. Get back. They won't see us straight away. Get back, Petra.'

There was no time to hid the statue of the goddess, or the necklace. There was scarcely time to retreat into the shadows of the boxes. The door leading to the tunnel opened and Takis came in, followed by Giorgios. They obviously knew their way around. They went straight to the pile of wooden boxes, and began to drag them underneath the trap-door in the ceiling. Then they turned round and saw the gleam of gold. Quick as a flash, Takis turned on his torch.

'Who's there?' he said in Greek. 'Come our, or we'll drag you out.'

Chapter 19

Nick reached for his gun, but Markos put out a hand to restrain him.

'Don't shoot.' He mouthed the words. And then, 'Bernie. They know where she is.'

It was the faintest whisper, but the two men heard it. They whirled round instantly, and Takis flashed his torch towards the corner where the three of them were hiding. The piles of boxes protected them like a barricade.

'Stop,' said Markos in their own language. 'Don't come any further. We've both got guns. We're aiming at you now. Stand quite still or else we'll shoot.'

The two men were visibly shaken. Markos' deep voice was amplified by the confined space. He spoke slowly and deliberately, like an Orthodox priest intoning a liturgy. The effect was hypnotic. The two men stood tranfixed.

'Why did you kill the American? Why did you kill Nelson Donelly? Why did you kill him and sink his boat?' The repetitive phrases had a liturgical ring and the two men answered without hesitation, as if they were in the confessional.

'Because he took what was ours. Because he stole the necklace and the statue,' whispered Giorgios.

'Stole?' Markos continued. 'The American wasn't a thief. He wouldn't steal things. He bought them. Where did he buy them, Takis? You answer this time.'

Markos was putting a spell on everybody. His voice was inexorably.

'From Yussef in Alexandria,' said Takis obediently. 'But

203

they were ours. We sold them to him, and he was to keep them for us until we found a proper buyer. We were to share the profit. But when we returned, we found he'd double crossed us. He'd already sold them, to the American.

'Donelly made off in his yacht, but he didn't know we were after him. We caught up with him in the Bay of Chambra. He'll never double cross anyone again.'

'And the boat?' The words dropped into the silence like stones in a pool.

'Out there, off the island.'

'And Yussef? Where is he?'

'The last we saw of him he was face down in a canal. They found him a week later. They'll never find the American.'

Takis was still shining the torch on the place where the voice came from but he couldn't see them behind the barricade. Still intoning his cross-examination, Markos pushed Petra further along the wall, away from the men. Nick heard the sound of a safety catch being released, and knew that the two men were armed. It was now a war of nerves.

'And the statue?' said Markos, risking one more question. 'Where did you find her?'

'A pity museums aren't more security-minded,' said Takis, watching the pile of crates intently. 'We removed her from the Cairo Museum last December. Now she's to go to Rio and no-one's going to stop her. Not you, Karakulas, nor the stupid Englishman.'

The spell was broken. Nick, gun in hand, began to edge round the shield of boxes. Takis saw the movement. Dropping his torch, he fired. But the shot went wide, landing in the side of one of the wooden boxes. A stream of white powder fell on to the floor. Cursing, the two Greeks rushed the barricade. Boxes fell around them in heaps, like children's bricks. Before Takis could focus on the two men properly and take aim, Nick had hurled one of the sacks at him. It missed Takis but caught Giorgios on the side of the head. He went down like a felled ox.

Quick as a flash Markos was on him, pinning him to the floor, his hands round his throat. Takis fired wildly at the place where he'd last caught a glimpse of Nick but he had moved. He was now against the opposite wall, diverting attention away from Petra who was still crouching behind a barrier of boxes under the trap-door.

It was like a diabolical game of hide and seek, but a game played by adults who wanted to kill each other.

'This way, Takis,' shouted Nick as he raised his gun to try and shoot Markos who was entwined with Giorgios on the floor. The Greek whirled round, only to receive a box of cannabis resin full on the shoulder. With a curse, he dropped his gun and clutched his arm.

'It's all up, Takis. Don't move or I'll shoot.' For a second he stood there, still holding his arm. Then, with the speed of a panther, he dived for the doorway into the tunnel. Nick fired. The first time he had ever aimed a gun at a living target. But in the gloom of the cellar, it was difficult to aim straight. He heard the door slam shut and Takis was gone.

'Quick, after him,' shouted Markos, now kneeling on top of Giorgios. 'Don't let him get away. Spiros! Remember Spiros and Yannis. Get him.'

Nick needed no urging. He was already making for the tunnel. Without a word, Petra came out of her corner and followed him.

'Petra, stop,' her brother shouted. 'The man's dangerous. He'll have a knife.'

But without one look at Markos, Petra followed Nick.

Markos was left alone with Giorgios, almost crushing the breath out of his body. Quietly and deliberately he pointed the barrel of the gun at Giorgios' forehead. The man was white with terror.

'Where is she? Where's the American girl? I will kill you happily, you know that. I'm Greek not an Englishman. Don't expect any mercy from me. If necessary, I will kill you slowly, bit by bit, like you killed Spiros. Unless you tell me where she is, I shall start here with your left ear.'

He moved the gun to the left. Giorgios began to writhe in terror but Markos was a powerful man and had a firm grip on him.

'You didn't use a gun on Spiros, did you? You prefer cutting people up with knives. You like knives, don't you, Giorgios? Is that how you killed Nelson? A pointed knife, I expect, in the throat. Am I right?' He pressed down harder on

205

Giorgios' chest. The man moaned in pain but managed to nod his head.

'I thought so. Now I have a knife here. A knife with a sharp blade. I use it to gut fish. Where shall I start on you? You should know the best places. You've had enough practice. Where does it hurt most? Where did you start with Spiros? Come on, man. Tell me.'

Like all cowards throughout the ages, Giorgios broke.

'It was Takis. Takis did it.'

'And you helped him. You'd never start anything, would you, Giorgios? You just run behind people. You'd torture a man who was marked for death. You'd chop up a man for fun. Did you enjoy killing Yannis? He couldn't put up much of a fight, could he?

'Listen to me. I know how to use a knife, and I would enjoy using it on you. Tell me where the American girl is hidden and I'll let you go. Then you'll only have to put up with prison. No-one will let you roam free again but at least you will have your life. If you don't tell me then, believe me, I shall kill you in slow stages. There's Turkish blood in my family, as you know. I'll use the knife first. And then the gun, when I've had enough.'

Markos could feel Giorgios going limp beneath him. For a moment, Markos thought he might faint. He was almost paralysed with terror. Markos put a hand on his heart and felt only a faint pulse rate. He didn't want the man to die, so he pressed down suddenly on his chest and shouted, 'Tell me, you bastard! Tell me. Where have you hidden her?'

'Kostas. Kostas and Sarantis have got her,' he whispered, his eyes dim with terror.

'Where? Damn you, where?' Markos was terrified he might die of shock.

'On the island. Peristera. Jakovas' hut. Where he used to live.' And then he fainted.

Markos looked down at the limp body of the man whom he hated at that moment more than he had ever hated anyone in all his life. His instinct was to put his hands round the man's throat and squeeze the life out of him. But something stopped him. Some spark of compassion made him hold back.

He still had round his waist the rope which Nick had

handed to him in the crypt, before they went along the tunnel. Now he undid it, hauled the man over towards the wall, and tied his hands and feet together. Then he took off his own shirt, ripped out the sleeves, wound the two pieces of cloth together and tied them firmly over Giorgios' mouth. Finally, he tied the end of the rope to the wooden support in the wall. He stood looking down at the body for a few minutes.

Which way, he thought, had the men come? Up the shaft from the cave of Cyclops, or by van? Then he remembered. When the men had first come into the cellar, they had started to stack boxes under the trap-door in the ceiling. Probably they had come to load the stuff up to take away in the van. He'd go that way, and see if the van was still there.

Leaving the body of Giorgios tied to the wall, he went along the tunnel, up the iron ladder, and into the crypt. Then he went out into the blazing heat of the late afternoon sunshine. There was nothing there. Just a hum of insects, and the scent of thyme.

He walked round to the side of the church. The van was there, parked at a strange angle as if someone had started to drive away but had changed his mind. Then he noticed the back tyre was completely flat. Bending down, he saw the bullet hole and knew Nick had stopped Takis just in time. But where were they now?

Then he thought of Nick's Volkswagen. Nick wouldn't have driven off without him. He set off through the gate, and down the sandy track to the road. The men must have brought the van by a different way. They could never have got it through the gate, and there was no sign of any tyre marks on the sandy path. They must have their own way in.

Nick's car was still there. He hadn't bothered to lock the door, and the key was still in the ignition. Quickly, Markos got into the driving seat, turned the key and made off towards Steni Vala. He'd need his boat to take him over to Peristera.

Chapter 20

Bernie's first reaction when she came round on the evening of her kidnapping, was that she was in hospital. She'd had an operation and the process of coming round, like the time she'd had peritonitis, was slow and painful. First, she opened her eyes. Then she was aware of pain; in her head to start with. A throbbing pain, like the incessant beating of tiny hammers. She shut her eyes, and immediately the pain was a little better.

Then she tried to move her arms, but found they were tied behind her back. This puzzled her. Moreover, her shoulders and neck hurt where the men had wrenched her arms behind her. Then she tried to wriggle her toes, remembering this was the first thing she had been told to do when coming round from the previous operation. But this time she couldn't move her feet. They had been tied together. It was all incomprehensible, just like coming round from an anaesthetic.

She needed a small task to concentrate her mind. So, still with her eyes closed, she felt the floor beneath her. She was lying on straw and it smelt fresh. But underneath the straw? Gently she scratched away with her fingers, feeling her nails fill up with some sticky substance, rather like clay. Then she realised that the floor underneath the straw was of bare earth. She lay there for a long time, trying to work it all out, but the temptation to drift back to sleep proved irresistible.

But, just like a patient in hospital, she returned to consciousness after a short sleep. This time she knew where the pain was, and was wary about moving her head. She was now

208

ready to take in her physical surroundings. Just as the patient becomes aware of the paraphernalia around him – the tubes and drips, the other beds, the windows, the radio and television – so she began to take in the surroundings.

Very slowly, she moved her head. She was in a small room with white walls, and a low ceiling. Raising her head a few inches and trying to ignore the pain, she looked across to a rough wooden door. There was nothing else to see. No furniture so no-one lived there. Even the meanest cottage would have had a table and a chair.

She gingerly lowered her head back on to the straw, and turned to examine the wall just a few inches away from her face. It was made of blocks of stone, roughly shaped – she could still see the chisel marks – and piled carefully one on top of each other, in the manner of the Great Pyramid, so that there were no gaps between them.

A patch of mildew had formed at the base of the wall near her face. She traced its progress up to the ceiling, moving her head as little as possible. No-one had lived in that room for years, she decided. Not even animals. She would have noticed the smell immediately.

The room was hot and airless. She was very thirsty. It was strange how no-one came to bring her water. Nurses were always there when people came round from an anaesthetic. Her blouse, she noticed, was soaked in sweat. That, too, struck her as strange. She wondered why they hadn't put her in hospital clothes, but had still left her in the blouse and jeans she'd put on that morning.

Slowly she turned her head in the other direction, and saw the tiny window. It was high up on the wall, immediately opposite where she was lying. A tall thin window, with a pointed arch at the top. It was the sort of window which architects would have described as 'Gothic', or 'lancet' if they wanted to sound technical. It made her feel as if she was in church, or in a room of a castle; the sort of place where soldiers would shoot arrows out of windows like the one she was now looking at. It was too narrow for a person to get in or out of, but it was just enough to let in the light.

The light! It was a blinding light, which made her head hurt to look at it. The sun, a fiery ball of scarlet and gold, had moved into a position where it shone exactly through the little window, just as at certain times of the year the sun shines on the altar stone at Stonehenge. Rays of light streamed down through clouds exactly like an illustration in a Victorian religious tract. She turned her head away and closed her eyes. Immediately the pain lessened. Now she could at least tell the time of day, she thought. The next problem was to know which day it was. Her first task, though, was to establish whether the sun was rising or setting. That established, she could then tell which direction the hut was facing. So she turned her head, and watched the sun with both eyes half shut. She waited, measuring the distance between the top of the ball and the top of the window. There was no doubt. Gradually the gap was widening. The sun was sinking. Soon, it would be dark. So the window faced west; the wooden door, north.

But what day of the week was it? And how did she come to be in that place. She thought back desperately to the events of the last few days. It was no good. She could remember nothing about the immediate present. She remembered the island. And Markos! The name sent the hammers in her head pounding with renewed energy. Markos! In a sudden surge of panic she looked down, bending her head painfully to see. It was all right. The necklace was still there. Markos' amber beads were safe. So she hadn't been robbed. But where was she going when the man attacked her? She presumed they were men, although she could remember nothing about the incident. If they hadn't robbed her, then why should they attack her and bring her to this place? There was no sign of the tapestry bag she used as a handbag. That had been removed. Fortunately there wasn't much money in it but it did contain her cheque book and passport. Damn. Her brain was so tired. It was all too much.

The sun had dropped below the window. She moved around on the straw until she found a more comfortable position, and fell asleep.

It was daylight when she awoke. Her first thought was that the pain in her head was better. She could move it without setting off the hammers. She moved her hands; they were untied. Her legs. She could move them as well. She could sit up.

210

Then she saw the man standing in the doorway. A huge ape of a man, dressed in jeans and a shirt which was open to the waist, revealing a mass of tangled black hair. He looked as if he hadn't shaven for days, and his bare feet were encrusted with dirt up to the ankle. He was carrying a wooden tray. She could see the rim of a metal plate, and the top of a mug. So this was her jailer. He moved nearer her, and she could smell the pungent odour of his sweat mixed with a smell of stale cigarettes.

'Are you all right?' he said in his guttural Greek.

'Yes. Where am I? Who are you? And what day is it?'

'*Kyria*, it is Thursday morning. You slept a long time. My name is Kostas, and you are on the island of Peristera, in the hut of Jakovas, the goat herd. He killed himself a long time ago.'

In spite of herself, Bernie couldn't resist asking, 'Killed himself! Why?'

'Because his wife left him. She preferred a fisherman from Skopelos.' It was unreal, discussing the personal problems of a man she'd never heard of before with a disgustingly dirty man who was holding her captive. He came over to where she was sitting hunched on the floor. His smell was overpowering. She willed him to keep away. He put the tray down on the floor near her, and walked over to the window. 'Eat,' he said.

There was coffee, and bread and cheese, and two ripe figs. She realised she was ravenously hungry; she couldn't remember when she had last eaten.

The man remained at the window, as if he didn't want to embarrass her by watching her eat. Her hands and arms were stiff and awkward through being tied behind her back, but she picked up the bread and dipped it in the coffee. Both tasted surprisingly good. It took her only a few moments to finish the food.

'Water? Can I have fresh water for drinking and washing? It's very hot in here.'

He nodded. 'It'll come.' He pointed to a metal pail in the corner, almost hidden by the straw. She hadn't seen it before. 'That's for the other thing. We'll empty it tonight.'

'So there were two of them, she thought.

He turned towards the door, having picked up the tray.

211

'Stop,' she called out. 'Why am I here? What have I done? I'm not worth holding to ransom. I'm not rich.'

Kostas turned to look at her. She noticed the thick face, the low, neanderthal brow, the heavy eyebrows. Before he answered, she knew it was useless to expect him to know anything. He was the type of man who merely did as he was told.

'You ask too many questions. You are here because I was ordered to bring you here. You were in the way. No-one will harm you if you stay here quietly, and sleep. Don't try to escape, because we have orders to shoot you if you cause any trouble. So sleep, eat, and I will bring you water for washing. And your bag. We took nothing.'

'How long am I to stay here?'

The man shrugged his shoulders. 'Who knows. Until we're told to let you go. I only obey orders.'

She wanted to ask him who gave him the orders, but she knew it was useless. To ask any more questions would only antagonise him. She watched him go out of the door. She caught a brief glimpse of long grass, a sandy path, and a blaze of scarlet from a patch of lilies growing wild by the door. For a second she smelt the sweet scent of the wild thyme, mixed with the tang of the sea. Then the door shut, and she was back in the heat and dust of the goatherd's hut, now contaminated by the presence of Kostas.

Minutes later, the second man came in. He scarcely glanced in her direction but put an enamel water jug down by the door. Then he threw the handbag over to her.

'Everything's there. We took nothing. Not even a single drachma.'

For one wild moment, she wondered whether it would be worth her while to try to bribe these men. But the man must have read her thoughts because he said, 'Don't try to offer us money. It would cost us our lives if we let you go.'

He was physically the weaker of the two men, tall and painfully thin, his clothes ragged and dirty. His face was long and pale with an unpleasant growth of black stubble around his chin. The mouth was narrow and bloodless. When he spoke she noticed his teeth, uneven and heavily stained with nicotine. There were gaps at the side as if he'd lost a few either

212

through decay or in fights. He smelt sour and unwashed, a stale smell of cigarettes and vomit. She saw his hair, thin and greasy, with a bald patch on top of his head like a monk's tonsure. He couldn't be more than twenty-five, she thought. A poor specimen, badly in need of food and sleep. He was very much the underling. Kostas bullied him, probably, she thought. A dangerous man, though; he would enjoy killing.

'What is your name?' she asked him. He looked at her with contempt.

'That's my business,' he said, 'you ask too many questions. Just keep quiet. We'll come when we want to. Don't try to escape. The door's locked, and the window's too small. We're outside, and we've got guns. Keep quiet, and nothing will happen to you. Make any noise, and we'll shoot you. We have our orders.'

With that, he turned and left her. She could hear him talking outside to Kostas. Then everything was quiet. The men had either gone away or gone to sleep.

The food had renewed her strength. Stiffly, she stood up and paced out the distance of the room from one wall to the other. Thursday, Kostas had said. Thursday morning. The sun would tell her when it was evening. She forced herself to walk round the room again. Her legs felt weak. She'd been tied up for almost twenty-four hours and the muscles were stiff. But it was important that she exercised her legs. She would need them if she was to escape from this place.

Then suddenly her head cleared. It was as if someone had wiped the slate clean. Everything came back to her. She was going to Athens. She'd borrowed Nick's car. Then the woman had appeared at the side of the road, and she's fallen for her story of a sick mother and her need to get a doctor. Then the two men. Then blackness. But Athens! She'd been going there to see Demetrios in Piraeus to try to find out the name of Nelson's yacht. Somebody, not the two jailers, wanted to stop her from going. Somebody must have found out she was going. Probably it was someone in the taverna the night before. There had been lots of people near their table.

Then it looked as if her worst fears were realised. It had to be Nelson's boat out there, otherwise no-one would have bothered to stop her going to Athens. And now it looked

213

highly probable that Nelson was dead. But why should they bother to kill him for a collection of pots? It didn't make sense.

Her head was beginning to hurt again. She felt exhausted and depressed. There was no-one around who would answer her questions. It was more than likely that the two jailers knew nothing about Nelson, or why she had been kidnapped. She washed her face with the water they'd brought her. Then she opened her bag and took our a comb and some make-up. This made her feel better, though the bruised face that looked back at her in the pocket mirror she scarcely recognized as her own. There were deep shadows under her eyes in spite of all the sleep she'd had.

She used the bucket in the corner, curled up again on the straw and went to sleep. There seemed little point in staying awake to exhaust herself by asking questions which no-one was prepared to answer.

This was the pattern of her existence throughout Thursday. The men came three times, and brought her food. It was simple but good. In the evening, they brought fresh water and emptied the bucket. She didn't try to repeat her earlier attempts at conversation, and neither of the men spoke a word. They seemed remote and hostile, merely concerned to keep her alive.

It was on Friday that she made the mistake of trying to escape. After breakfast, she heard someone outside. Usually the two men talked for a few moments. Once she'd heard Kostas laugh. But that morning, there was nothing. Kostas had brought her the bread and coffee so maybe, she thought, he was on his own. It was then that she began to think about escaping.

Bernie was finding captivity intolerable. She felt a surge of sympathy for all creatures trapped in zoos. She remembered the solitary gorilla she'd once seen in Antwerp zoo. He'd sat all by himself in a corner of his cage and, as the crowd stared, he'd made himself vomit just so that he could play with the liquid. She'd watched him make patterns on the floor, and had felt so sorry for him. He'd looked at her with such hatred in his eyes. Not because, she'd felt, humans were ill treating him, but because they were the cause of his hopeless boredom.

214

Bernie had been blessed with an energetic and enterprising brain. Now that her strength was returning, it was quite natural that she should plan her escape. She thought of the books she'd read, and the films she'd seen. But apart from *Escape from Alcatraz* she'd not seen many escape films. Neither did she read many thrillers, and war films always bored her. Somehow, people in fiction always had files, or iron spikes to dig away at loose stones in the wall of their prison. Somewhere she'd seen someone digging a tunnel into the air conditioning system with a spoon he'd smuggled into his cell from the dinner table. But she had nothing. Only her bare hands. Not even a nail file in her handbag. And the men always took away the fork they gave her to eat her food with. There wasn't even a rope conveniently left behind by a previous prisoner.

She studied her four walls. There were no weak places; no loose stones; no ventilators. She couldn't reach the window, and there was nothing to stand on.

But underneath the straw was an earth floor. Perhaps she could start digging a tunnel under the wall, and cover it up with straw when her jailers came in, as she'd seen someone do in a film. She looked at her hands and decided they were made for digging. She scratched away at the earth for half an hour or so but soon gave up. She decided she would need paws like a mole's if she was to make any impression on that hard floor. All she'd succeeded in doing was to break her nails and make her fingers bleed. And so she gave up.

She thought again of her gorilla. Like him she couldn't complain of her treatment. The two men brought her food three times a day. They brought her water, and emptied the bucket. They had never laid a finger on her. In fact they looked at her with contempt, certainly not with desire. She wasn't worth raping. But like her friend in the zoo she could never forgive them for depriving her of her freedom.

The idea came to her quite suddenly, just as Kostas came in with her midday meal. He opened the door with one hand, and carried the tray in the other. It was then that, acting on impulse, she leapt on him, knocking the tray to the ground. And then ran out into the glorious sunshine, straight into the arms of the younger man. Cursing her, he held her tightly.

215

They dragged her back into the hut, and threw her to the floor. This time they tied her hands together and gagged her as she was shouting with anger and frustration. Then they kicked her on the legs and arms and she fainted with the pain. They left her lying there, slamming the door behind them in rage.

They left her alone for the rest of the day. No-one brought her food or emptied her bucket. She lay there watching the sun stream through the window, then sink below the sill. Another day over. Tomorrow would be the third day of her captivity. It was thinking about her friends on that other island which caused her the most pain. Markos would think she'd gone to Athens and stayed on there without telling anybody. He would be worried and hurt. She began to sob with weakness and the feeling of helplessness, almost choking on the gag they'd forced into her mouth. The only release from the pain, now both mental and physical, was in sleep. Again she slept the time away – a fitful and nervous sleep. Once during the night she woke up worried in case she should go mad in that place. People did go mad in solitary confinement, she knew. Or perhaps they would starve her to death as a punishment. Heroines in books and films never failed to escape. Why should this happen to her? She felt inadequate, and angry with herself for failing.

On Saturday morning, they removed the gag and untied her hands. Her mouth was bruised and swollen and it hurt her to swallow the water they held to her mouth as her hands were too weak to hold the mug. But she was very thirsty, and the water tasted like nectar.

Both men came in together, one covering the other as if she was a wild beast. They left some bread and meat by her side, and went out without speaking. They had stopped bringing her coffee. She ate the food mechanically and lay back on the straw. She had never felt so helpless before. Another day, and she would contemplate suicide.

It was late in the afternoon of Saturday that she heard the two gun shots. One, a long way away. Then the other, close to the hut. She sat up, wondering whether to call out. But it might only be one of the men shooting a goat for supper. They would only come in and hit her if she shouted. So she listened and waited.

Then there was the sound of someone running – the soft pounding of shoes on sand. Then another shot. A shout, and the sound of someone moaning in pain. Now she was on her feet, waiting for the door to open. Perhaps it was the arrival of another gang. Perhaps the two men had enemies on the island. Then she heard the sound of a key turning in the lock, and braced herself for whatever was to come.

And then Markos burst into the room. Markos, white with anger and worry. He took one look at her, and took her in his arms. He held her tightly for a long time without saying a word. He heard her sobbing with relief and shock, and stroked her hair to calm her.

'Are you hurt?' he said at length, when he was able to speak coherently. 'Did those thugs hurt you?'

She shook her head, trying desperately to control her tears. 'No, I'm all right. Just a few bruises. But I'm so glad you've come. I thought I would go mad here. Where are the two men?'

'I've caught one in the leg. He's outside on the grass. I think he's fainted. For the other one, I used these.' He showed her his hands. 'I've knocked him out, but for how long I've no idea. We'll have to get them in here and then go to the police. Are you all right to walk?'

She nodded. Her tears had stopped. Markos took her hand and led her outside. She stood in the bright sunshine, trying to adjust her eyes to the light. Then she saw her two jailors. Kostas was lying on the sandy path, blood trickling from the wound in his leg. The other was a few yards away, lying very still. She tried to help Markos drag the two men into the hut, but she was painfully weak. Markos laid them out on the straw, next to each other, and turned to leave. Bernie stopped him.

'Wait,' she said. 'I can't leave him like that.' She was wearing a blouse with long sleeves. It had once been white. Now she took it off, tore out the sleeves and, using them as a tourniquet, bound up Kostas' leg.

'There. It's not very professional, but it'll do until the police get here. I can't let him bleed to death.' Markos said nothing, but bent down and checked that the two men had no weapons on them. He found a knife on the younger man, and

217

took it away with him. Then they left the hut, locking the door behind them.

In spite of his tiredness and anxiety, Markos laughed when he looked at Bernie.

'Thank God for sleeves. We all ought to wear shirts with sleeves.'

It was then that she noticed he'd torn out his own.

'What happened to yours?' she said, as they went down to the boat.

'It's a long story. But first we must get back to Nick and Petra. God knows what happened to them. I even stole his car.'

Her legs were trembling with weakness by the time they reached the shore. Markos lifted her into the boat, and started the engine. Just as the sun began to sink behind Skiathos, he brought Bernie home.

Chapter 21

Nick, after one look at Markos to see if he was all right, set off down the tunnel after Takis. Petra, like the shade of Euridice, followed closely behind. At the junction to the main shaft, he paused. Which way? Had Takis gone up into the crypt, or chosen the sea route through the cave of Cyclops. But after he'd shone his torch down into the black depths of the main shaft and had heard nothing – not even the sound of falling stones, or the grating of shoes on a ladder – he decided he must have gone up into the church.

Once in the crypt, he waited for Petra. He was about to tell her to wait for him in the church, but one look at her face told him that she fully intended to go with him. So, with Nick holding her hand, they dashed out into the afternoon sun.

Outside, he paused. Takis could have gone back to Steni Vala by the road. Or he might have taken to the hills to wait for night fall. Then, suddenly, they heard the noise of an engine starting up. They rushed round to the eastern end of the church, and saw the grey van just about to move off over the rough ground. There was no time to think. Nick pulled out the gun which Markos had given him and fired at the back wheel. It was an easy shot as the van hadn't yet gained momentum, but even so he was surprised to see it lurch across the path and come to a stop at right angles to the wall. The door of the driver's seat fell open, and Takis jumped out.

He fired again but Takis was too quick. He ran off through the garden like a streak of lightning, leaving Nick and Petra running towards the van. They watched him clear the stone wall, which marked the boundary of the monastery, and then he disappeared.

'Which way?' shouted Nick, blinded by the sunlight.

'Up there,' she said, looking towards the ridge of hills that ran along the centre of the island. 'There's a path along the top. It's really only suitable for goats, but he could get to Steni Vala along it. He probably thinks he'll be safe up there, as cars can't go along it.'

They ran across the monastery garden where once the monks had tended their vegetables and vines. Now it was completely overgrown, a tangle of weeds and roots. The vines were heavy with grapes, like rows of cows waiting to be milked. Everywhere, figs had fallen to the ground, bursting open and providing a feast for hordes of insects. There was a smell of ripeness and fermentation, mingled with herbs. They slipped on the rotting fruit, and it was with relief that they reached the boundary wall.

Then they were out on the open hill-side. The sun beat down relentlessly on the exposed rocks and parched grass. The tamarisks drooped lethargically in the heat. Already Nick's shirt was soaked in sweat, and clung to him like a wet towel. The sun was shining straight into his eyes and he could see nothing except the outlines of the cypresses and the white shining rocks. There was no sign of Takis.

Petra seemed unconcerned by the heat. She was staring at the ridge of hills in front of them. To Nick, they looked miles away, across a bare plain of rock and stunted bushes.

'There he goes,' she said. 'He's making for the ridge. We'll have to get him before he reaches the top otherwise he'll have a straight run to the village. Someone will hide him there.'

He nodded, already out of breath. Nick was a reasonably fit man, probably fitter than most academics, but he wasn't used to running and climbing over rocks in a temperature of over ninety degrees. He was amazed at Petra's stamina. Even though her face was streaked with sweat and dirt, her breathing was even and steady.

'Just take it steady,' she said. 'It's uphill, remember. It will be easier on the way down.'

As they got nearer the ridge, the ground levelled out. The goats had been there before them. The hill-side was crisscrossed with their tracks. Halfway there, they came across a herd of the strange black beasts, picking their way daintily from one favourite bush to another. They stopped their grazing to stare at Nick and Petra with great yellow eyes. Melancholy creatures, they had been there since the beginning of time. Before the Greeks invaded the islands from the mainland, they were there. The Turks hunted them for food. They were as old as Pan, as old as the Devil.

'I'd give anything to have a set of hooves like theirs at this moment,' gasped Nick. 'Look at that lot up there. Don't they know about gravity?'

A couple of goats had strayed away from the rest of the herd and were climbing up towards a shelf of rock which jutted out from the hillside. Some clumps of grass had found a place to grow, and looked temptingly green and luxuriant in that barren place. Possibly, thought Nick, there was a spring there, and the grass seeds had been lodged there by accident, borne on the wind. Now, straight up the side of the rock, the goats marched like flies on a wall. Even in that position, they were able to turn their heads and gaze reproachfully at Nick and Petra.

'Don't talk,' said Petra, 'but save your energy. You'll need it for the last bit.'

They were almost there. In front of them loomed the jagged ridge of limestone that marked the centre of the island. They stopped to listen. Only the goats' bells, and the continuous chatter of the cicadas. There was no sign of any other human being. Already the bright light of the day-time sunshine was deepening into the golden glow of late afternoon. They would have to catch him soon or else, as soon as night fell, he would be lost forever and off the island by dawn.

Then they saw him. He was climbing towards a gap in the ridge of rock, towards the path. Nick aimed his gun and fired, but Takis was too far away. The shot rang out across the clear air, setting the goats into a frenzy of terror. The two on the ledge slithered down to join the others, and started a landslide of stones and earth. Takis continued to climb. They watched as he dropped down over the top. Then all was quiet once again.

'Has he got to the road?' asked Nick.

221

Petra shook her head. 'Not yet. He's in a sort of valley between two sides of the ridge. It's like a fortification. The path is just over the second ridge. We could get there if we hurry.'

She set off up the ridge like an expert mountaineer. Nick, his heart pounding, his mouth parched with thirst, set off after her.

Blinded by the sunlight, his hands scorched by the rockface, clawing desperately for footholds, he slipped and slithered up to the top of the escarpment. Once there he threw himself down by the side of Petra, who was stretched out face down on the grass. They lay there for a few seconds, in the shade of a laurel tree, not speaking. Nick waited until the pounding of his heart subsided. Then he sat up and looked around.

It was a beautiful place – a fertile basin between two ramparts of rock, like the inner and outer fortifications of Maiden Castle. The grass was greener here than on the dry hill-side, and the place was covered with goats' droppings. In the middle of the open space stood two walls. They were all that was left of some chapel or farmhouse. The roof had long since fallen in, and there was no door and no partitions betwen the walls. So it had once been a single-roomed, single-storied building. The walls were of the usual type in those islands, small blocks of stone placed one on top of each other.

He turned to Petra, who was sitting up and wiping her face on the sleeve of her blouse.

'What a magical place. Is that a church there? Or a cottage? What happened to it?'

'The earthquake,' said Petra. 'It used to be a small chapel – possibly a retreat for the monks from down below. It's built on the foundations of a much older temple. This was a special place in ancient times. It's much greener here, as you can see, so there's probably a well here, or a spring of fresh water. There was a shrine to Apollo. Some say there was an oracle here. It always has a holy feeling about it.'

Nick looked at her. She was soaked with sweat, her eyes ringed with shadows of exhaustion. Yet she could sit on a hill-side and talk about Apollo, whilst somewhere on the other side of a patch of grass a murderer was waiting for them. He leant over and kissed her.

222

Then they heard it; the trickle of falling pebbles, like the sound of water. It came from only a few yards away.

Nick got slowly to his feet. He slid down the rocky bank on to the grass. He drew his gun, and began to make his way towards the other side.

'Stay back, Petra,' he said. But he might just as well have saved his breath. She followed him, a few feet behind.

Stopping every second to listen, his eyes fixed on a rock in front of him, Nick crossed the glade, past the ruined chapel. Then Takis moved. He had no gun, but he was expert with a knife. He had been hiding behind the far wall of the chapel and now he stepped out, throwing his knife, and caught Nick on the right shoulder blade. The knife ricochetted off the bone and landed on the grass. For a second no-one moved. Then Nick dropped his gun and fell on to his knees, clutching his arm.

Takis came for him, a jagged piece of rock in his hand. He lifted the stone above his head with both hands, ready to crush Nick's head. But he'd reckoned without Petra.

Quick as a flash, she leapt forward and picked up the gun. Then, aiming with both hands, she pulled the trigger. She couldn't fail to hit him. He took the bullet in his chest, on the left side. She saw the look of astonishment on his face as he dropped the stone and sank down on his knees. Then he fell forward on to his face.

She ran to Nick. There was a patch of blood on his shoulder, spreading rapidly down his arm. His face was grey with pain.

'Can you stand up?' she said, her voice strained and unnatural.

'In a moment. Just give me a few seconds. But you, my darling? Where did you learn to fire a gun?'

'Markos taught me. Sometimes I go with him when they go off to shoot goats – the old and sick ones that have to be put down. Wait here. I think I know where there's water.'

Not looking at the body of Takis, she ran across to the other side of the glade, taking off her blouse as she ran. A pool of water had collected in a natural basin below some rocks on the other ridge. The grass around it had been trampled by hundreds of feet. It was the watering place for the goats. It came from a spring high up in the rock, and was pure and clean. She tore a piece off her blouse, and dipped it in the freezing water. Then she ran back to Nick, and squeezed some of the liquid into his mouth then washed the wound with the damp cloth. It was deep, as the knife had reached the bone, but it was clean. She went back to fetch more water, then tied the cloth as tightly as she could around his shoulder. Afterwards she helped him to his feet, and together they staggered back to the laurel bush. The effort exhausted him, and he lay back against the tree with his eyes closed.

'You shot him,' he whispered. 'Is he dead?'

'I think so. I had to shoot him. He was going to kill you.'

She had to go back to Takis. She couldn't leave him there, in the middle of that grassy place, still alive. She left Nick and went over to the black figure lying face downwards by the chapel.

It took all her strength to push him over but one look at the staring eyes told her all she needed to know. The bullet had entered his chest near the heart, and he must have died almost instantly. She tried to pull him nearer the wall of the chapel, where there was some shade, but after a few inches she gave up. He would have to stay there until they got help.

She walked slowly back to Nick, and sat down beside him.

'Yes, he's dead,' she said. 'There's no doubt. I can't get him into the shade, but it will soon be dark.' She spoke automatically, her voice dull and lifeless. Then the reaction set in. She put her head between her knees, and sobbed uncontrollably for a few minutes. Nick knelt beside her and held her with his sound arm. He understood.

'My darling, don't worry. You had to kill him. You are the bravest of women. Remember Spiros, and Yannis. He probably killed both of them. He was a murderer, and he was going to kill me. You saved my life.'

Slowly the sobbing subsided. She grew calmer, and Nick wiped the tears away from her face with his bare hand. It was cooler now, the sun rapidly sinking in the west. It would soon be dark.

'Come,' he said. 'Let's get back to the road. It will be easier downhill. I shall need your help again,' he said, as he took her hand. 'I think I am always going to need your help.'

224

They stood up and made their way back to the monastery, using the goats' tracks and stopping every few yards for Nick to recover his breath. The crimson stain on his back was growing larger by the minute and his face was grey with pain. But they gradually covered the ground, Petra almost dragging him the last few yards.

It was almost dark by the time they reached the monastery. Nick sat down against a fig tree, smiled at Petra, and fainted. She stood looking at him, trying to decide what was the best thing to do. Finally she left him there, and went off to get help. He would never be able to drive back to Steni Vala. The pain, the loss of blood, the exertion, had taken its toll. She picked a bunch of grapes, and a handful of figs, and put them where he could reach them when he came round. Then she went down to the road and the place where they'd left the car.

It wasn't there, of course. For a moment she stared at the place under the tree where Nick had left it that afternoon. Then she set off along the road, on foot. It was now dark. There was a cool breeze blowing off the sea; the moon was rising over the island of Peristera. Still numb with the shock of killing a man, and exhausted by the climb, she despaired of ever reaching the village. But then she saw the headlights of a car coming towards her. She waved frantically for it to stop, hoping the driver could see her in the dark. The car stopped, and someone jumped out. It was Markos in Nick's Volkswagen. He put his arms around her, and looked at her tired face.

'Petra, my dear, are you all right? Where's Nick?'

'He's hurt' Come quickly, he needs help. Where's Bernie? Is she safe?'

'Yes, she's fine. Back at the house. She's had a bad time, but now she's being looked after. But where's the other man? Takis?'

'Up there. In the hills, He's dead.'

Markos said nothing, but helped her into the car and drove back to the monastery. Nick was just coming round when they got to him. Exhausted with pain and loss of blood, he still managed a grin when he saw Markos.

'Hallo,' he said, his voice coming from a long way away. 'Where have you sprung from?'

'Don't speak now. Save your strength. We'll get you home.'

With Petra's help, they got him to the car. Gently they laid him on the back seat.

'Petra killed him,' he managed to say.

'Who?' asked Markos, as he started the engine.

'Takis, of course.'

Markos turned to look at his sister. 'Women shouldn't fire guns,' he said disapprovingly.

'I do. But then I'm a Greek woman,' she said quietly.

Chapter 22

Akileas Terzopoulos had been a police sergeant in Patiteri for twenty years. He had long ago given up any ambition of being anything else. Now fifty-six, and grossly overweight, he was content to sit for most of the day in the main square of the tiny fishing port with his friends and drink *ouzo*. Nothing much of police business ever came his way. Sometimes a tourist ran amok in the streets, crazed from a mixture of *ouzo* and cannabis. Sometimes a husband murdered his wife, but that didn't happen very often. There were not many suicides, and very little theft. Rape was unheard of amongst the islanders. When it happened amongst the tourists, they kept quiet about it.

The life suited him. He could tell a good story, and he was popular. He lived in a small flat over the police station, just two rooms and a bathroom. He lived on his own. Rumour had it that there had once been a wife, and possibly a child. But all that had happened a long time ago. Now he was looked after by Maria – an old lady with grey hair, and whiskers on her chin. She always wore the same black dress, lace-up boots, and black stockings. With a figure like a water melon, she puffed and wheezed her way round the flat, shaking her broom into the main square and cooking Akileas' midday meal.

Sometimes she pushed her way over to the table where he sat with his cronies and spoke to him with a voice like a soldier's. He never looked at her, just put his hand into his pocket to give her money. He never bought her a drink or wished her a good night.

Everyone in Alonnisos knew Akileas. They also knew where to find him. And that was not in the police station. The door was locked for most of the day. Sometimes, in the evenings, before the drinking started, Akileas would go into the tiny office, light a cigarette, and fill in a form. Usually, he would make up the day's activities. Then he would watch the boats come into the tiny harbour and tie up along the quay. He knew all the boats, and who they belonged to. Mentally, he checked them into their berths. Later, he would stub out the cigarette on the table top, and throw it on to the floor with the thousands of others. No-one ever cleaned his office. No-one except himself ever went into it. If he was needed, then people came to him in the taverna. His superiors ignored him. Athens and Volos might have been in different countries; different worlds even. When all the boats had come home, he would heave his great bulk out of the chair – his one prized possession – lock the door, and join his friends once more until it was time for bed. It was a peaceful life and he wanted nothing more.

Then, that Saturday night, the last one in August, it happened. He would never forget that night. Memories of it haunted him for the rest of his life. Certainly no-one talked about anything else for years after.

He was in his usual place in the taverna, playing backgammon with his friends. He sat at the table nearest the quay as the electric lights worked best there. It was quiet for a Saturday. Tourists were leaving the island to go north. The hydrofoil was leaving the island full and returning empty. It was how he liked it. Tourists only made trouble. Greece was returning to the Greeks.

He saw the Volkswagen drive into the square and stop outside the police station. From the corner of his eye, he saw his friend Karakulas get out. His sister followed him. Akileas knew Karakulas very well. Most people expected him to be the next Mayor of the island. They had always been friends, so Akileas waved to him and pointed to the chair next to him.

'Come over and join in,' he called out. But Karakulas ignored the invitation, and only nodded perfunctorily to the group of friends.

'There's no time tonight, I'm afraid,' he said. 'There's work

228

to do. We shall need that telephone of yours. You'll have to open up the shop, I'm afraid. Something's happened. Serious things.'

But nothing could make Akileas hurry. 'Sit down. Sit down. There's plenty of time. Serious things can always wait. It's early yet.'

He handed Markos a glass, but he pushed it away impatiently then got hold of Akileas and almost dragged him to his feet.

'Come on, you great barrel of grease. We want your telephone now. Move yourself! If you don't, there will be hell to pay and you'll be thrown off this comfortable perch of yours.'

Grumbling and cursing, he nevertheless opened the door of the station for Markos. Then, because his friend looked as if he meant business, he sat down behind his desk. He wanted to take out a note-book but couldn't find one. Besides, he'd lost the pen.

'Now listen. I have a wounded man in the car. He'll need a doctor. There are two men tied up in Jakovas' hut on Peristera, and one inside the cellar in the monastery. One man is dead on the hillside above the monastery, and Spiros' body is in one of the caves. I'll tell you which one later. And that's not all.'

Akileas listened with mounting alarm. At first he thought his friend had been drinking, but one look at Markos' face told him that he was quite sober. Akileas hadn't been blessed with a lot of intelligence, but he knew what to do when action was needed. He picked up the telephone and called Volos. He was going to call Athens, but the men in Volos said they would see to it. He was to do nothing except clear the harbour of boats. The police would need all the space going for their own boats and equipment. The helicopters would land where they could.

Akileas was appalled. Clear the harbour! They didn't know what they were asking. Where were all the boats to go? And then there was the Englishman to see to. His friend, Theodorus would be able to stitch him up. It was only a knife wound. But Theodorus, as the only doctor on the island, also owned the biggest boat. And it was out there, tied to the quay with all the others. How to ask him to move it? And quickly?

The police would be here in four hours. It would take the helicopters a lot less. He wouldn't tell him to move his boat until he'd seen to the Englishman, otherwise the poor fellow would bleed to death. It was going to be a bad night, followed by an even worse day. Drugs, gold, murder. This wasn't Alonnisos. It was more like Athens.

The wounded men were taken away by police helicopters. No-one saw them go as they were taken off in the early hours of Sunday morning so the islanders missed the spectacle of Maria, wife of Sarantis, being hauled off kicking and screaming to the waiting helicopter. Inside, her husband, still bleeding from Markos' blow to his head, refused to go to jail without her.

Then, later on Sunday, they brought back Spiros' body to his distraught family. No-one knew why he had been murdered. Had he been a member of the gang? His wife doubted it. Had he been an informer? That seemed to be the most likely explanation. Recently, he had been exceptionally generous with money. Now Katerina would never get her annuity.

It was a sad day when they buried him. For once the two women stood side by side in the church, and they grieved together by the graveside. A cousin came over from Skiathos to keep the taverna going for the time being. Later, it was said, Spiros' wife would run the place on her own. She was certainly quite capable of doing it.

Later in the week, the Chief Inspector from Volos came to the house in Agios Demetrios. They were expecting him. For days now police launches had been going out to the sunken yacht. They had all seen the divers in heavy duty diving gear leaving Steni Vala in police boats. They even continued to work at night, and everyone on the island had seen the floodlights out at sea.

The Inspector was a charming man, already turning several female heads on the island. He terrified Akileas by his relentless efficiency, his constant demands for reports, and his immaculate appearance. He was everywhere. Not once since that Saturday had Akileas been allowed to sit with his

230

cronies in the square. Not once had the Inspector allowed his men to relax in a taverna. No-one had ever seen him drinking a glass of wine, or even coffee. He seemed super-human. An Immortal, with no vices.

But that morning, he'd taken off his hat and stood there in the sitting room in his spotless white shirt and grey tie. His gun gleamed in his waistband. Probably, thought Nick, he believed the thieves might still be lurking in the house. He fought back the temptation to tell him to take off his gun. Policemen, he knew, felt undressed without their guns.

But that morning the Inspector accepted a cup of coffee and sat down at the table. They waited for him to speak. It took him two cups of coffee to relax, lean back in his chair and turn to Nick.

'I hope you are feeling better, sir. Nasty things, knife wounds in the back.'

Nick, his arm still immobilised, smiled across at the man.

'Thanks, yes. It wasn't in the back – the wound, I mean, Fortunately he only got me in the shoulder blade. Otherwise I wouldn't be here now.'

'I'm glad. And Miss Fitzpatrick?'

'She'll be down in a minute. She's getting along fine. Funnily enough, those days in captivity took a heavy toll on her. Physical wounds seem to heal quicker than mental ones.'

'That I understand,' said the Inspector. 'Wounds to the body are nothing compared to wounds to the mind. Captivity, the uncertainty of not knowing what is going to happen to you from day to day, leaves scars. They will heal in time, though.'

At that moment Bernie, still in her dressing-gown, came in. She looked pale and tired but otherwise recovered. The Chief Inspector stood up, and bowed gracefully.

'It's good to see you looking so well, madam,' he said. Bernie, who'd met him before, smiled her thanks and sat next to Markos on the sofa.

'Thanks, I'm feeling fine. Still a bit tired but I suppose that's to be expected. But what is your news? Have you finished with the boat yet?'

'Almost. There's not much more we can do now. We can't raise it as we've established the identity of the owner, and its up to his heirs to salvage it if they want to.'

231

He looked at Bernie. 'It was Nelson Donelley's boat all right. We traced the serial number and the hull number. It took only a matter of minutes, after we found the name of the boat on the hull, to put a 'phone call across to the maker's office, and find out who bought the boat and when. They remembered the deal well. Mr. Donelly bought the boat in England, and then had it shipped over to Boston. He flew home by air. Then he insisted on sailing the boat back again to Europe single-handed. The boat owners thought he was mad. One man, not young, going to all that trouble. But it appeared he wanted the challenge.'

'Yes,' said Bernie quietly, 'he was like that. He liked challenges. Especially as he grew older. But the man in Alexandria? Did they murder him too?'

'Yes, we checked with the Egyptian police. Apparently a body was found in a canal about that time. He was the local dealer in antiquities, and one or two other things. We also asked whether a large amount of money had been paid into his bank account, and that was confirmed. Mr. Donelly paid a lot of money for that statue and necklace.'

'Yes, I know. It was to be a present for me. But as it happened I received another necklace. Just as beautiful, and just as valuable to me.'

She fingered the amber beads round her neck. Markos put an arm round her shoulder.

The Inspector stood up. He had only come to tell Miss Fitzpatrick the news about the boat. He was glad she was taking it so well. Probably she had guessed the truth a long time ago, but here was proof positive.

'The rest of the news is good. I'm sure you've seen the papers this morning. We found a lot more stuff in Piraeus. In your crates, Mr. Harding, mixed up with the jars. Some had already left, but, more to the point, we got the chap who's been letting the stuff through. He's made a hell of a lot of money out of this affair. Not that it'll be much use to him. He'll spend most of his active life in jail.

'At least we stopped the treasure from leaving the country, and most of the gold bars. They kept them back till last. I suppose until they got the other stuff out of the way. It was going to the States, by the way, but the treasure was booked on a ship leaving for Rio. The man in Athens has done a lot of harm, but his run of luck is over now.'

Bernie thought momentarily of the pale young man she'd met in the café at the start of her search for Nelson. He hadn't seemed to be the type one would expect to be in the pay of an international gang of thieves and drug runners. But then people did anything for money.

'The gang,' she said, as the Inspector went towards the door leading out on to the terrace. 'Did you catch them?'

He shook his head. 'You never catch those people, you know. They always get away. We tried to get Papadopoulos to tell us, but the poor bastard didn't really know. Even if he did, he'd never tell us. They never do. It's more than their life's worth. If they do tell, then wherever they go, in prison or outside, now or twenty years later, they'll get him. It's the risk they all run. Thanks for the coffee. I suppose you'll be off home now, sir?' he said to Nick.

'Soon. But I'll be back again.'

'Good. It's safer in England I understand.'

'Not these days, it isn't,' said Nick.

The Inspector strode off briskly on to the terrace, out into the garden and up the path to the waiting car.

'There goes efficiency and energy,' said Nick. 'Still he's got this lot cleared up. I wonder what they'll do with the rest of the amphorae? I'm glad most of them are still in Greece. That's where they belong. And after I've seen this chap from Cairo on Thursday, Selket and the Eye of the Sun-God will be back where they belong.'

He stood up and walked stiffly over to the window. For a minute, he looked out over the bay. One or two police launches were still out by the wreck. He turned to Bernie.

'How about you?' he said. 'Now that you know the yacht's Nelson's, what's the next step?'

'New York. On Friday, if there's a flight to Athens. But like you, I shall be back.'

The yacht *Monte Christo*, a fifty-five foot ketch made in the ship-yards of Hamburg, was ready to leave at a moment's notice. The crew of five were waiting for final instructions. Most of the provisions were on board but until they knew the final destination it was impossible to cover all contingencies. But the champagne was on ice; the refrigerator packed with prime cuts of meat. The special delivery of Angus steaks had been flown in from Harrod's Food Halls yesterday.

The bowl of chocolate truffles, especially ordered from one of the most famous patisserie houses in Paris, was in place on the table. Magnus had a passion for truffles. They seemed to relieve a certain inner tension. For instance, when they set sail from his home port of Marseilles, Magnus would watch the crew set about their work, a bowl of truffles by his elbow. Not naturally a sailor, he liked to consider himself a navigator. So his place, as they sailed west, was by the compass. There he would set down the bowl and eat his chocolates, one after another. He never asked for them to be there but the crew knew they would all be sacked if that bowl was not in place when Magnus came aboard.

At that moment in early September he was standing at the window of his apartment, looking down on to the Bay and noting with satisfaction the crew's activities. There was no doubt but that his boat was by far the biggest, and most luxurious in the Bay of Marseilles.

He turned to the little man standing by the Louis XVI table. A dapper Frenchman dressed in a grey pin-striped suit, a perfect example of English tailoring. He could have been an ambassador, or a Fine Arts dealer; the sort of man who never set foot in his own shop. Certainly a distinguished man. Neat, silver-grey hair, polished shoes, a credit to any gentleman's club in Europe.

'Help yourself,' said Magnus, indicating the bottle of cognac. The man shook his head.

'No thanks. You know it doesn't agree with me. One glass, and two days on Perrier water. A fine day tomorrow, I think. Just right for your crossing.'

'Yes. The weather forecast was perfect. Let's hope the hurricanes are late this year. I don't want to be caught in the Windward Islands in their centre. Damn those Greeks, and their bloody incompetence! I hoped to be away a fortnight ago.'

'But the Greek affair took a bit longer to finish off than you expected, I hear.'

'Yes. I won't deal with Greeks again. They're too bloody jumpy, and trigger happy. But all the same, not a bad deal. Enough to live on comfortably next year, I think. For both of us, that is.'

'I should hope so. Certainly you can keep your yacht another year, and pay for my next trip out East. Pity about Papadopoulos, though. He was useful. It's not easy to find accommodating Customs officials. They're usually a pretty awkward breed. I suppose, now that Piraeus is out of bounds, we might have to go back to those illegal land-falls as you so aptly describe that part of our operations.'

'Maybe. But there are always plenty of people around like Papadopoulos – little men with big ambitions. It's just a question of getting my team started again. It takes a while to spot a likely candidate for recruitment but there's always one in financial trouble, usually with a pushing wife behind him. Thank God for human nature, and greed.'

'You're quite the philosopher, Magnus,' said his friend sardonically. 'But whatever you call yourself, thank God for you. A good holiday – and fair winds.'

235

Chapter 23

Twenty minutes after taking off from Salonika, the BAC I eleven from London, Gatwick, began its descent to Skiathos. Bernie looked out of the window at the toy ships scattered over the Aegean, each one with a white ribbon of foam in tow. She felt Olympian. She need only stretch out a hand to move the tiny pieces round the board. She need only take a deep breath and blow to raise a great wind and sink the whole lot. Here was power indeed.

Then they were skimming low over the sea, and like a giant seabird swooping down on to the short runway that was only just long enough to take jets. With a nerve-shattering bump, and a sickening screech of rubber on concrete, they were down. In front of her was the shed which served as passport control, and the single storey building which was the departure lounge. But outside, waiting by the car, was Markos.

He looked at her uncertainly, suddenly shy of this new Bernie. She looked intimidatingly smart in her blue dress with white polka dots, white handbag and high heeled shoes. She even wore stockings. Her hair had been professionally cut in London and her luggage looked almost aggressively affluent. But she was still Bernie. Leaving her two bags on the tarmac, she ran over to Markos who took her in his arms. They stood there, lost to the world.

'Just like the films,' said a sentimental tourist. Finally they forced themselves apart, and he looked at her.

'You look fine,' he said. 'Everything all right?'

'You look good yourself,' she replied. 'Yes, all is well. There's a lot to tell you.'

'Then it's lucky I've brought some food. The boat's waiting. It's early yet, so we can make the island.'

'Which island?'

He looked at her in astonishment. 'Our island, of course.'

The sea was as calm as a millpond. The air fresh, with a hint of autumn. It was still hot, though. Hot enough for Bernie to wish she'd worn shorts, and for Markos to take off his jacket. They landed at the little bay on the island of Peristera, where they'd come before on her birthday. They made their way up to the church overlooking the bay, and to the wild place where they had first discovered each other. But now, after three weeks' separation, they were both shy and uncertain. Markos threw his jacket under the fig tree, and put the basket of food on the ground beside it. Then they looked at each other and burst out laughing. Everything would be all right. The old magic was still there.

'Food,' he said, and opened the basket.

He'd brought a proper meal – cheese and ham, sausage and peaches, and a bottle of retsina. She'd forgotten how hungry she was, and how good food tasted eaten in the open air. Three weeks of eating in London and New York had made her forget the taste of real food.

She kicked off her shoes and sat beside him on the bed of soft pine needles.

'We'll swim later,' she said, as she took the bread and ham. 'It's still warm, even for the first of October.'

'Do you really want to? You aren't exactly dressed for climbing over rocks. But the water's certainly still warm.' They talked as if they were strangers, but they knew it was only a matter of time before the barriers would be removed.

'I took my dress off once before, and I can take it off again. Forget my clothes. I had to see a lawyer in London before I caught the 'plane, and there wasn't time to change. I could have gone back to the hotel and put on jeans, but then I would have missed the 'plane and I wouldn't have been here until Thursday.'

They ate together in silence. Finally, she took the glass of wine he offered her, and leaned back against the tree.

'I am his daughter, you know. His real daughter. He never married my mother.'

237

Markos was waiting for this. He had suspected it all along. 'How did you find out?'

'Through his solicitor. They were friends, you see. They had always been friends. He'd seen Nelson with Alison Fairfax. She was my mother. Nelson had met her in London when she was an actress there. A bad actress, I gather. The play only lasted two nights. But Nelson fell in love with her, and brought her back to New York. She was very striking looking. Tall like me. She ought to have been a dancer.'

They sat there in the afternoon sunlight. Markos said nothing. He waited for her to continue.

'She was left a lot on her own in New York. Nelson was always away. He was building up his empire of restaurants at that time. He was only thirty-three or so. It was inevitable that Alison should meet someone else. He was the manager of one of Nelson's hotels, a Gerald Fitzpatrick. They married, and five months later I was born. Nelson was heart-broken but realised that it has been unrealistic to leave Alison alone in New York. So he became my godfather and later, when they were both killed in that 'plane crash, he looked after me. My grandparents brought me up but he provided the money for university and so on. We were very close. I should have guessed. I can hardly remember my parents.

'The solicitor knew all this but had decided never to mention it. Now Nelson's dead, it all came out. I'm his heir, by the way. He left me everything. That's why I had to go to London, to see the solicitor there who handled the London end of things. He owned several restaurants in London, in Soho, all of them with an American-Irish flavour. They are still popular with tourists. I'll sell them, of course.'

'And you'll live in London?'

'I'm staying here with you.'

'Here?'

'Exactly here. On this island. We'll build a house on this spot. On the other side of the straits we are going to build villas, and a hotel and a restaurant. Tourists will come here to get away from it all. It's what Nelson would have wanted, and what he would have set out to do if he had been a younger man.'

Markos was staring at her in amazement. 'And who is going to build all these villas and hotels?'

238

'You, of course. You'll be my investment. And I'll be around to supervise.'

'A hotel, you say? Not one of those sky-scraper things. This is Greece, remember. Not New York. We do have the occasional earthquake.'

'Nothing more than two storeys high. Not a tree to be cut down. Everything just as it should be for a hotel in a wonderful natural setting.'

Markos got to his feet, and walked to the edge of the garden where he could look across the straits to Steni Vala.

'It can be done. A hotel, places for people to live in all the year round, and a marina.' Then he had another thought. 'Nelson's yacht? What are you going to do about that?'

She didn't answer, and when he looked round she'd taken off her dress. She stood there, tall and slender, her body firm and bronzed. She was wearing the amber beads.

'Forget the yacht. We'll salvage it. What about that swim?'

'Forget the swim,' he said, as he went to her and took her in his arms. Then he lifted her up and carried her over to where he had laid his jacket under the tree.

'*Nereus* will be our yacht,' she said.

'But I already have a boat,' he said, laughing.

'Not one with sails. You'll have to sail again, you know, with me around.'

Markos said nothing. He took off his shirt, and lay down beside her. It was much later in the evening before they went down to the beach and dived off the rocks at the entrance to the bay.

October 24th. The autumn gale whipped the sea to a frenzy of spume-capped, snarling waves. The wind lashed the windows of Nick's room with a mounting ferocity. Outside on the promenade, two Lowry figures, bent double against the wind, walked towards Brighton. Over towards the Isle of Wight the sun, an angry ball of crimson, sank behind the ragged black clouds of the depression.

It was cold even though the central heating was on. The draught from under the badly fitting door met up with the current of cold air coming through the sash windows. The two streams centered on Nick's feet.

239

But he liked the room. He'd rented it from the university when he came back to England for the beginning of term. It was a front room in one of Brighton's Regency houses, part of a crescent overlooking the Marina. He'd been lucky to get it. Once students had lived there, but now the university reserved it for visiting professors or teaching staff looking for temporary accommodation. The room had a high ceiling, making it impossible to heat properly. The cornice, embossed with cupids entwined in vine leaves, gave the room a faded elegance – a relic of earlier days. Then someone in Victorian times had added a cluster of plaster Tudor roses to each corner, and there was a giant circlet of nymphs and satyrs around the central light.

The wallpaper showed signs of wear, and the carpet relied on the strategic placing of the furniture to hide the threadbare patches. But Nick was happy there, as happy as he could be away from the Sporades. There was a bed in one corner, which had to serve as a sofa in the daytime, and a small cooker and refrigerator in the other. A yucca and a rather forlorn rubber plant stood on the table near the door. Someone, a long time ago, had tied a Christmas star to the rubber plant and no-one had bothered to take it off. It would stay there until the next Christmas.

The rest of the furniture was strictly utilitarian. A stained wooden coffee table, a worn out armchair, and the table in the window which served as a place to eat from and a place to work. His typewriter and a pile of books had been pushed aside so that he could write his letter.

A particularly violent gust of wind made him look up from his writing. A small coastal cargo boat was bucking and rolling its way to Shoreham harbour. Nick felt sorry for the crew. Then he picked up his pen, and finished the letter.

'It requires a great stretch of the imagination to think of you in Greece today, my love. There's a mighty gale blowing outside, and the sea is the colour of gun metal. Two brave souls are trying to battle their way along to Brighton. But I have the photographs, and I only have to shut my eyes to conjure up your face. I miss you more than I thought possible, and I will the days away until I can be with you in Athens. Not long now.

240

Term finishes on December 11th, and I shall catch the first 'plane after that. There's been no trouble about leaving here at Christmas. The university is already making plans for me to come back from time to time to give the odd lecture. We'll try and come over in the spring, when England's at its best.

'I got official confirmation from Athens yesterday about the job. I shall work in the Department of Antiquities, and they want me to teach. That's why I battle away at Greek in the evenings. Also I shall be in charge of the Iura Roman galley. They are even providing me with a team to put Bernie's amphorae to rights. The publicity over the Eye of the Sun-God affair did wonders for my career. Some compensation for all the other traumas.

'I am delighted about Bernie and Markos. A pity I couldn't come over for the wedding but maybe we can repeat the celebrations in May when you will become Mrs. Harding. How unromantic that sounds! But really, there's nothing romantic about me. I'm just a typical pedantic academic who had the incredible good fortune to meet the most beautiful Greek girl since Helen of Troy, and who still can't get over the fact that she has agreed to marry him. I pray every night that you won't regret your decision.

'Marion and I will be free of one another in November. The new people have moved into the old house in Rottingdean, and Marion has moved in with Simon in their cottage in Lewes. He's fifteen years younger than she is but they seem very happy. She certainly seems a lot brighter.

'Another piece of news. I'm meeting Ibrahim Aziz next week in the British Museum. He's over here organising an exhibition of Egyptian treasures to be shown in the Museum next spring. Selket and the Eye of the Sun-God will both be on display here. Let's hope the electronic warning systems here work properly. It would be too bad if the Eye disappeared yet again! Takis might be dead, but there are a lot more like him around.

'Keep well, my love. I'm glad you are happy in Athens and enjoying the teaching. I shall be with you very soon.

'And know that you have always, all my love,
Nick.'

He folded the letter, and put it in the envelope. Then he

looked out to sea again. Two yachts, both with bare masts and storm jibs, fought their way westward.

'All sailors,' thought Nick, 'are maniacs. And English sailors are masochists.'